Change of Heart

Also by T. J. Kline

Healing Harts Novels
Heart's Desire
Taking Heart
Close to Heart
Wild at Heart
Change of Heart

Rodeo Novels
Rodeo Queen
The Cowboy and the Angel
Learning the Ropes
Runaway Cowboy

Change of Heart

T. J. KLINE

AVON IMPULSE
An Imprint of HarperCollins*Publishers*

Excerpt from *You're Still the One* copyright © 2016 by Darcy Burke.
Excerpt from *The Debutante Is Mine* copyright © 2016 by Vivienne Lorret.
Excerpt from *One Dangerous Desire* copyright © 2016 by Christy Carlyle.

Avon, Avon Impulse, and the Avon Impulse logo are trademarks of HarperCollins Publishers.

EPub Edition MAY 2016 ISBN: 9780062456304
Print Edition ISBN: 9780062456311

AM 10 9 8 7 6 5 4 3 2 1

*For my boys, who constantly inspire me
to create new heroes who remind me of the men
you are growing up to become far too quickly for
your mother's liking. You're my two favorite boys!*

Chapter One

"JESSIE, COME ON, you know I'm good for the money."
Gage leaned his elbow over the railing of the corral but
moved it quickly when Jessie's horse started lipping at his
shirt sleeve.

Gage Granger couldn't believe he'd been reduced to
begging. But if Jessie, his sister-in-law by marriage, didn't
have room for him on the ranch, he was going to have
head into San Francisco, which was exactly what his
partners would expect of him. After all, he was officially
here to oversee the opening of Iconics' new office. However, at the moment, he wasn't exactly ready to face them.

"You know that's not the issue. I'd let you stay in one
of the guest cabins for free. I just can't spare the room.
We've got camps lined up all summer, and the new therapist is finally arriving today." The black horse Jessie had a
hold of shook his head impatiently, and she ran a calming
hand over his neck. "I would if I could."

Gage ran a frustrated hand over his jaw and looked around the horse ranch, wondering where else he might stay while he was hiding out after his colossal screw up. He didn't know of any open B&Bs in town, and his business partners would be expecting him at the ritzy hotels between Sacramento and San Francisco. At least here on Jessie's ranch, he could lay low until he had an answer for them. Jessie's place offered the best of everything—a place to hide away while still being close enough to the only family he had left—his brother, Dylan, and his wife, Julia, as well as Gage's month-old niece, Emily. Then, once he'd made some sort of decision about his future at Iconics, he would contact his partners.

Gage ran his hand over his head, feeling the rasp of the short hair against his palm, and sighed. "Don't worry about it, Jessie. I'll figure something out." Her horse shoved his nose into Gage's stomach, and he reached forward, rubbing the center of the animal's face. "Needy bugger, aren't you?"

Jessie laughed. "Jet's pretty demanding when he likes someone." She looked back toward the barn where five cabins and a new modular home currently sat empty, waiting for the arrival of the at-risk youth she would finally be serving at her camp this summer. Biting her lip, she gave him a pensive look. "How long do you think you'll need to stay?"

She was going to give in. He could hear it in her voice.

"A month, tops. Just until I get a few things shuffled around and can look into buying a place in town."

She raised her brows in surprise. "You're moving here permanently? I thought this was just a temporary thing."

"Long-term temporary right now."

She didn't press for more information, and Gage was glad. He wasn't sure he had it in him to rehash his mistake that might destroy the company he and George had built. It was his name on the dotted line approving the faulty computer security system. His name that was going to forever be linked with the hundreds of thousands of dollars lost by corporations who'd entrusted Iconics to protect their investments. Worst of all was that his system had been hacked by teenagers. They might have been genius teenagers, but still. He couldn't help but wonder if he would ever live it down once the media was able to dig deep enough to see who was to blame. Some creative publicity and an amazing team of lawyers had convinced the companies affected that settling out of court was the best option, but the final damage count was still coming in, and it was possible the entire company might still crash and burn. All because of a backdoor coding error. An error he'd missed.

Hell, he had a distinct hunch at least one of the partners wanted to figure out a way to get rid of him without facing legal repercussions, which was part of the reason for his sudden departure. Gage knew how much trouble he'd gotten himself into, but he also didn't need everyone else in his family to know it just yet. He just needed a little time to get everything straightened out. In the meantime, let them think he was just here for work.

"I've got a big camp coming in the middle of July. That's almost eight weeks. Until then, I'll double everyone up in the other cabins. But I can't do more than that."

Gage jerked her into his arms, giving her a bear hug. "Thanks, Jessie."

"All right, all right." She pushed him back as Jet jerked at the lead line. "For big, tough guys, you and your brother are sure touchy-feely."

"We get it from Mom."

Gage wanted to kick himself when he saw Jessie's eyes mist over slightly. He'd had years to come to terms with his mother's death. In fact, it had almost been a relief for both him and his older brother, Dylan, after watching cancer ravage her body, but it had been less than two years since Jessie had lost both her parents in a car wreck only to find they'd actually been murdered.

"Ah, man, I'm sorry, Jessie."

She waved a hand at him. "It's fine. I just really miss them sometimes." She looked at the cabins again. "Makes me wonder what they would have thought about what I've done with the place."

According to her brother, Justin, Heart Fire Ranch had been a premier dude ranch until their parents were killed and Jessie fought to turn it into an abused horse rescue and camp for at-risk youth. "You know they'd have been proud of you. From what Justin said, your parents were always proud of you, especially your dad."

A sad smile tipped the corner of her mouth up on one side and she sniffed. "Go, get your things while I put this guy back in his stall. Take the cabin just before you get to the modular. I can't promise it will be quiet or peaceful, though."

"Honestly, I couldn't care less. I'm just looking for a place that's off the grid."

When you were running away, being picky was the last thing to worry about.

LEAH MCCARRAN COULDN'T believe her luck as she popped the hood of her classic GTO and glanced behind her, down the deserted stretch of highway in the Northern California foothills. Steam poured from her radiator, and there wasn't a single car in sight.

She blew back a strand of her caramel-colored hair as the curl fell into her eye and caught on her mascaraed eyelashes. Even those felt like they were melting into solid clumps on her eyes. It was sweltering for mid-May, and, of course, her car decided to take a dump on the side of the highway today. She fanned herself with one hand as she looked down at the overheated engine. It probably wouldn't have been nearly this big a deal if her cell phone hadn't just taken a crap, too. To top off her miserable day, she'd spilled her iced coffee all over the damn thing getting out of the car and likely destroyed it once and for all.

This wasn't the way she'd hoped to start her new job or her new life at Heart Fire Ranch.

Walking back to the driver's side of the car, Leah had no clue what to do now. Luckily, her boss wasn't expecting her until this evening, and she'd had the foresight, knowing her penchant for bad luck, to leave early. But until some Good Samaritan decided to drive by *and* stop for her, she was S.O.L. She kicked the tire as she walked by. As if trying to deny her even that small measure of satisfaction, the sole of her worn combat boot caught in the tread, nearly making her fall over.

"Son of a—"

Leah caught herself against the side of the car, willing the tears of frustration to subside, back into the vault where they belonged. That was one thing she'd learned as a child: tears meant weakness.

And showing weakness was asking for more pain.

She bent over into the car, looking for something to mop up the sticky mess the coffee was making on the restored leather interior of her car. She reached for the denim shirt she'd been wearing over her tank top before she'd left Chowchilla this morning, before the air had turned from chilled to hell-on-earth-hot.

"Shit," she muttered. Trying to sop up coffee with denim was like trying to mop a floor with a broom: it did absolutely no good.

"Hot damn! That is the most incredible thing I've seen all day."

The crunch of tires pulling off the asphalt of the highway was a welcome sound, but the awe she heard in the husky voice was enough to send a chill down her spine. Leah threw the shirt down onto the coffee-soaked floorboard. Standing up, she spun on the heel of her boot, her fists clenching at her sides as she tried to control the instinct to punch a man in the mouth.

"Excuse me? Do you really have so little class?"

"Oh, shit! No, that's not…" She watched as the man unfolded himself from a late model Challenger and shut the door, jogging across the empty two-lane highway to her side. "I'm sorry, I meant the car."

Leah crossed her arms under her breasts and arched a single, disbelieving brow. "Sure, you did."

A blush flooded his dark caramel skin. "I swear I meant the car. Not that you're not...I mean...crap." He cursed again. "Let me try this again. Do you need some help?"

Leah nearly laughed as he tried to backpedal, embarrassed by his hastily spoken comment. Instead, she just lifted the brow higher on her forehead, leaning her hip against the driver's side of her broken down vehicle as she looked him over. The man looked like he'd just stepped out of a magazine ad with his designer jeans and T-shirt.

Who the hell wore designer T-shirts, for crying out loud?

But she couldn't fault the way he filled those clothes out. He had definitely been gifted in the looks department. After what she'd just heard, she couldn't help but assume that his physical gifts were the only ones he had, since brains didn't appear to be high on his list of attributes.

"No offense, but you don't look like you get your hands dirty too often. Although, if you don't mind letting me borrow your cell to call for a tow, I'd really appreciate it."

He shot her a playboy smile that she was sure had charmed plenty of women out of their panties. "Just because you say 'no offense' doesn't mean it's not offensive, you know."

His voice was deep and rich with a slight rasp that was sexy as hell. Too bad he acted like he knew it.

"Says the man who just commented on my ass."

The smile instantly disappeared. "I meant the car. I wasn't even looking at you."

So much for my ego, she thought.

Leah wasn't about to admit any sort of disappointment, not even to herself. Narrowing her gaze, she watched as he slid one hand over the curves along the frame of her car, making his way to the front and peering down at the engine.

"Radiator?" He leaned to the side and looked around the top of the open hood at her.

"Yeah." She knew it was the radiator; it had been giving her trouble before she left, but she'd been hoping it might last until her first paycheck. But he didn't look like the kind of guy who'd have any clue about the inner workings of a car engine. "So, can I use your cell?"

Looking back under the hood, he slipped his hand into the front pocket of his jeans, pulled out the cell phone, and held it to the side. Leah reached out to take it when he pulled it back.

"Do you even know who to call?"

She realized she didn't have a clue, since she'd turned down the roadside coverage on her car insurance to save a few bucks. She supposed she could call Heart Fire Ranch and ask her new boss. If she did that, she could also let them know the situation and kill two birds with one stone.

She plucked the phone from his fingers. "Yes, I have someone I can call."

Leah pulled the folded paper with the address and phone number for the ranch from her back pocket where she'd shoved it the last time she'd looked up directions nearly an hour ago. She ignored the man watching her from the front of her car and wandered toward the trunk for some privacy as the call went through.

"Hey, Gage, what's up? Did you forget something?"

"Hi...um, this is Leah McCarran, I'm your—"

"Leah?" The woman on the end of the phone sounded confused. "Are you with Gage?"

So that's his name?

"I'm actually just a few minutes away, but my car broke down, and this guy stopped to let me use his phone. Is there a local tow company I could call?"

"Where are you?"

"On one ninety-three, almost to your place."

"I'll call Dave and send him to find you. I trust him. Is Gage going to wait with you?"

Leah glanced at the man standing at the front of her car, watching her like she was some sort of oddity from outer space. She was fine with waiting by herself; she'd been taking care of herself for a long time, too long. "I'll be fine."

"Have him bring you back to Heart Fire. He's staying here for a few weeks. The two of you are neighbors."

Leah's gaze shot back to the wannabe fitness model, reclining against the side of her car, now staring down the highway as he pretended not to be listening. Leah shook her head, wondering what in the world she had done that deserved this kind of bad luck.

GAGE FOUND HIMSELF watching the woman as she talked on the phone. He'd already put his foot into it when he pulled up, so he could understand her being a bit prickly, but she made a cactus look cuddly. Which was surprising because, looking at her, she was hotter than the sweat-inducing sun beating down on them and the muscle car she drove put together. She might be a tiny thing, but she was sharp dips and rounded curves in all the right places. With her shorts showing off plenty of leg, and her rock band tank top showing off toned arms, he didn't have to look too hard to see those curves. Now if only those golden brown, whiskey-colored eyes would stop glaring at him, he could appreciate the rest of her.

He couldn't hear much of the conversation but, judging from her stiff posture and the frown causing a wrinkle between her brows, he could tell she didn't like the news. She pressed the button to disconnect the call and handed his phone back to him.

"I take it you're Gage?"

His brows shot up in surprise. "Yeah, how—"

"I'm your new neighbor, apparently."

She didn't sound overly thrilled about it. Gage crossed his arms over his chest, waiting for her to elaborate.

"I'm the new therapist at Heart Fire Ranch. Jessie is calling a tow truck out but wanted me to ask you if you'd mind driving me back out to the ranch after Dave leaves with my car."

A measure of satisfaction spread through him as she muttered her request. Little Miss Independent wasn't nearly as smug now that she needed him for more than his phone. A self-righteous grin tugged at the corner of his lips as he saw a way to break through her icy exterior. He could be charismatic when he wanted to be, and this seemed like as good a time to turn on the charm as any other.

"I think I could do that." Her shoulders relaxed slightly as she took a step toward him with her hand held out, preparing to introduce herself. "If you say you believe me that I was talking about the car."

She dropped her hand and gave him an unconvinced scowl. "Really?"

"It's up to you." Gage was a gentleman, through and through, and there was no way he was leaving her on the side of the road. He knew that, but she didn't. He wasn't about to cave just because she bristled and let out a sigh of frustration as she looked back at the highway, taking in nothing but empty space in either direction. He tucked his fingertips into his pockets and moved away from the car. "I guess I'll just be heading the way I was going."

"All right, fine." She huffed out a breath. "We'll agree that I've got an incredible *car.*"

Gage shook his head at her stubbornness but wasn't going to waste energy arguing with her, especially when it looked like they might be waiting for a while. "So, the new therapist, huh?"

She rolled her eyes in his direction, appearing disinterested in conversation while they waited, and walked back toward the driver's seat, bending into the car again.

"Bet you can't guess what I'm thinking."

She stood slowly and turned to look at him, tossing a denim cloth onto the seat and crossing her arms again. "Are you going to tell me that innuendo was about the car, too?"

"What?"

Aw, crap.

He hadn't even thought about how sexual that might sound to her, especially since she didn't seem inclined to trust him in the first place. He took a deep breath and took a step closer, realizing he towered over her by at least a foot. And damn, she smelled so good. Like sunshine and woman and fresh rain. But then she turned those derisive golden brown eyes on him, and he could read the disdain in them. Gage didn't usually have to work this hard to convince a woman that he had honorable intentions in mind.

"Look, lady, let me make one thing clear before you get yourself all worked up again. You're pretty, but you're just not my type. I like women who won't bite my head off every time I open my mouth."

"Well, it's a good thing we're on the same page then, because I like my men to have brains." She let her mocking gaze slide over his chest and back up to his face. "Not just brawn."

Gage arched a brow back at her, daring her to say more, but he refrained from defending himself. They stood, toe to toe, neither willing to take even a slight step backward and admit defeat to the other.

He had a feeling it was going to be a long, *long* month living next to this woman. Sacramento was suddenly looking like a better option.

Chapter Two

LEAH WAS TRYING desperately to ignore the man leaning on the back of her car. He'd already loaded her embarrassingly meager belongings into the back of his rented Challenger, while trying to make conversation about their shared interest in muscle cars. She didn't want to talk to him. She didn't want to talk to anyone right now.

What she needed to do was figure out how she was going to pay to fix her car, and that would require some careful planning, and quiet. Just because she was a therapist didn't mean she was on duty all the time, ready to listen to every thought that might run through his head. He just talked so much.

"Look," she said, finally holding up her hands and standing in front of him. "I'm a *child* psychologist. That means I work with kids."

"And?"

"And maybe we could just sit here quietly for a few minutes while I try to figure a few things out. Dave should be here soon to tow my car. Until then…"

"Are you suggesting we play the 'quiet game?'" he asked, shaking his head and crossing his arms over a broad chest. "I just thought that since we're going to be neighbors, we should probably get to know one another. But, hey, no worries. I have a hundred things that I should be doing instead of sitting here trying to make conversation with you. I'll just head over here and get some of my work done until Dave arrives."

He walked across the highway toward his car and jerked open the door. "Don't worry. You haven't already inconvenienced my plans for today at all," he added, letting the sarcasm drip from his husky voice.

She watched him as he folded himself into the driver's seat and pulled out his phone, tapping away at the buttons. Guilt rose up from her stomach, making her feel slightly ill. Or maybe that was the iced espresso on an empty stomach she'd had before spilling it on her phone. Either way, it wasn't his fault that her life sucked, or that, even when she tried to make it better, it just seemed to go from bad to worse.

She crossed the street and leaned inside his car window. "Look, I'm sorry I'm being such an ingrate. You've been more than patient, waiting here with me, and I've been rude."

He simply looked at her expectantly, and she noticed he didn't contradict her assessment.

"I mean, it's not your fault I'm having such a bad day," she continued. "So, again, I'm sorry."

She waited as the silence between them stretched out awkwardly. She'd learned a long time ago that remaining silent usually brought deep comments to the surface, but this man simply stared at her.

She prompted him. "So…"

He tossed his phone onto the console before turning back toward her and opening the door. Leah took a step back as he exited the car.

"Aren't you going to say anything?" she asked.

"Like what?" Gage crossed his arms. She was sure he was trying to intimidate her, but she dealt with far more difficult men than this guy.

"I don't know. Maybe apologize?"

"For what? Saying you have a nice car? Waiting here with you for the tow truck to arrive?"

"For insinuating your sexual fantasies in regards to my ass?"

Gage shook his head. "I already told you, I was talking about the car. For a therapist, you sure don't listen very well."

She heard the roar of an engine climbing the hill and prayed it was the tow truck. As soon as it rounded the curve, she spotted the lights flashing on top of the truck and sent up a prayer of thanks. It would save her the effort of coming up with a scathing retort for this infuriating man.

"Sorry for the delay. I got here as quickly as I could. I'm Dave." A young man who barely looked twenty hopped down from the driver's seat of the tow truck. "Wow," he said, turning toward Leah's baby. "That car is a beaut!"

"Thanks. It's the radiator. She's going to need a new one."

Dave rubbed at the dark blond whiskers that graced his square jaw and hesitated. "That's not going to be a cheap fix, and I'm going to have to order the part unless I can find one in Sacramento."

"That's what I was worried about." Leah cringed, wondering if fate would continue to conspire against her.

Dave filled out the paperwork and passed it in her direction. "I'm going to need a credit card to order the part, too."

Shit.

Her card was already at its limit, and there wasn't much left in her checking account. The savings had been depleted a long time ago. Leah didn't want either man to suspect her predicament, so she reached into her purse, trying to stall the driver while she figured out how to convince him to hold off a couple of days. She heard Gage clear his throat.

"Here," he said as he passed a credit card to the tow truck driver. "Just put it on my card so we can get this show on the road."

Her gaze met Gage's, and she instantly understood that he wasn't doing this because he was in a hurry. He'd seen right through her ploy and knew she didn't have the money.

No matter how hard she tried, she'd never shake that poor kid stigma. It clung to her, lingering like the stench of cigarette smoke from the bars she'd worked in to put herself through school. Leah narrowed her gaze, wishing she had the luxury to throw his credit card back in his direction. She didn't want charity in general, and not his specifically, but she didn't have any other options. Unless she wanted to try to con them both—and that was something she'd stopped doing at sixteen, once she chose the straight and narrow path in order to become the woman Nicole had thought she could.

Saying nothing, she signed her name to the bottom of the tow slip, passing it to Gage, who scratched his signature at the bottom of the receipt while she handed Dave her keys. She would find a way to repay him. She wasn't going to remain indebted to this cocky, arrogant, self-righteous—

"I'll take good care of her and will call you in a couple of days when I find the part." He handed Leah the receipt and a business card. "Feel free to call if you need anything or have questions before then. I'm guessing it'll be around a grand by the time we add in parts and labor."

Leah tried to contain her despair. That was almost half of her first paycheck from the ranch. She glanced at Gage, who didn't even flinch, and then watched as Dave jumped back into his truck, driving away with the baby she'd practically lived in at one time.

What sort of man had that kind of money to toss around willy-nilly?

She felt the old Leah, the con artist who'd survived years in a nightmare childhood, press her face against the cage the new Leah had confined her to and whisper,

"Men like him don't even notice when money goes missing. There's plenty more where that came from, and you know exactly how to get it."

GAGE WASN'T SURE what he'd expected from the short ride back to the ranch, but her complete silence surprised him. He ran a hand over the back of his head and down to his neck, massaging the muscles he could feel tensing up already. When his phone rang, the woman in the car glanced at him but turned back to the window almost immediately. He looked at the caller ID and saw George's name. Sliding a finger over the screen, he sent the call to voice mail.

It wasn't usually his style to hide, or run away, but it also wasn't usually his style to screw up so royally.

Gage gripped the steering wheel, twisting his hands against the leather, his knuckles turning white as he tried to control the frustrated rage beginning to build in his gut. It simmered and rolled, like a slow boil, threatening to spill over. He knew he needed to tell someone about it, to release this pent-up frustration, and while his brother was the logical choice, he couldn't bring himself to confess his failure to the one person who believed in him. Dylan had practically raised him after their father took off during a drunken binge. He'd sacrificed his own happiness and dreams to make sure Gage had his, even to the point of almost losing his life. Gage wasn't about to repay him by telling him that it had all been for nothing.

He could almost hear his mother's voice, reassuring him the way she always used to. *It was a mistake. Everyone makes them.*

Gage knew it was true, but that didn't change the fact that *he* didn't make them. Not to this degree. It was something he prided himself on—his talent, his work ethic, and his near flawless performance. To have that all come crashing down around him destroyed every bit of his self-confidence, rocking the foundation of belief in every area.

If he could destroy something he was good at so easily, what hope was there for the other aspects of his life, the ones where he didn't excel?

Turning off the main highway and onto the dirt road that lead to Heart Fire Ranch, he heard a sharp intake of breath from the seat beside him and glanced her way. She chewed at the corner of her lip nervously before jamming her thumbnail between her teeth. It struck an empathetic chord somewhere deep within him and he slowed the car.

"You okay?"

Like closing shutters over a window, the nervousness disappeared, replaced by the fierce self-assurance she'd displayed even while stranded on the side of the highway.

"I'm fine."

Gage didn't buy it for a second. He knew the ploy because he used it himself on many occasions.

Fake it 'til you make it.

"Because you look a little…uptight."

She glared in his general direction but wouldn't meet his eye. "You've known me all of an hour."

Gage rolled his eyes back toward the road and clenched his jaw. He'd been nothing but nice to this woman. Hell, he'd just dropped who knew how much to fix her car. The least she could have done was offer a simple "thank you."

"It's enough to tell when you're being bitchy," he muttered.

"Excuse me?" Her voice rose at least two octaves. "Did you just call me a bitch?"

Gage tried to hold back the grin tugging at the corner of his mouth. "No, I said you were being *bitchy*, there's a difference." He slowed the car as he approached the main house. "I'm guessing you need to see Jessie, so if you want to head inside, I'll take your things over to your house."

"My house?" She sounded surprised, and Gage pointed in the direction of the modular home.

"Yeah, your house. Jessie said that's where you'll be staying and having sessions." He pointed at a small cabin past the house. "And that's where I'll be. I'm assuming the other four cabins are for the campers and counselors Jessie said were coming in."

Gage parked the car and turned toward the woman in the passenger seat. "You know, you've been trying so hard to avoid any and all conversation that I don't even know your name."

Her gaze slid over him slowly, taking in every inch of his face, as if she was trying to read his intent. Gage slid one arm to the back of the seat, waiting her out.

"Leah." She bit her lip again, but seemed to catch herself giving in to the brief moment of weakness and let it go. The tip of her tongue snuck out and wet the soft flesh, and he felt a kick of attraction settle south of his belt, surprising him.

Down boy. You already have enough trouble to take care of.

"Leah McCarran." She held her hand out to him.

It didn't suit her. Her name was a soft breath of sound, rolling off the tongue gently, soothing. The woman in front of him was hard. Her entire demeanor was as abrasive as sandpaper, and he couldn't help wondering what had made her that way.

"Gage Granger."

He grasped her hand and felt the callouses on her palm. This woman knew what it meant to work hard, physically. But there was a warmth there that he hadn't seen in her demeanor. Maybe he was reading far too much into a simple handshake.

His hand enveloped hers, his thumb dropping over the pulse at her wrist, and he was surprised to find it racing. Just as he suspected, her confidence was a sham.

"Don't worry, you'll fit right in. Jess and Bailey are going to love you."

Another speaks-her-mind, takes-no-prisoners woman on the ranch. God help them all.

LEAH HADN'T BEEN sure what Gage meant, until she met Jessie. The woman was a fireball and Leah immediately liked her. Especially when she slid the contract across the desk to Leah. As she read it over, she realized Jessie was giving her full freedom to develop a program that suited her needs rather than some cookie-cutter service that she couldn't tailor fit to the teens they would be seeing.

"We're not exactly like most organizations. I want to keep this place fluid, changing and adapting as we need to. The same training doesn't work for every horse, and

I'm assuming it's the same with the kids we'll be working with."

Leah's gaze lifted from the terms of the contract long enough to meet Jessie's deep blue eyes. "I don't know anything about horses, but you do realize that a lot of these kids aren't going to *want* to be here. If it ends up being a court-mandated facility, they are going to throw attitude from the moment they arrive."

Jessie chuckled and the German shepherd at her feet lifted his head, gazing up at her adoringly. She rubbed behind the dog's ear and he settled again. "Leah, I'm accustomed to plenty of attitude. Most of the horses I work with have come here after leaving abusive situations. They're fearful, angry, and fifteen hundred pounds of attitude. It takes patience, understanding, and in some situations, discipline, to reach them. I'm not afraid of attitude."

She was surprised by Jessie's almost blasé reaction. Most people didn't want to deal with the trouble at-risk teens offered. Jessie seemed to welcome it. "What sort of precautions are you taking to ensure safety?"

"First, and foremost, we aren't yet a court-mandated facility, so coming here is still a choice. It's just one of many options available, so, as of right now, most of the kids don't see it as a punishment. We're working closely with several foster parents who continue to bring their kids here, even after they've completed the initial camp."

"So it's a reward instead of a punishment."

"Exactly," Jessie said, folding her hands. "That doesn't mean we aren't careful. Nathan, my husband, has several men on staff he trusts to maintain the perimeters of the ranch for the safety of everyone involved. No one comes in or goes out without our knowledge and approval. We also work closely with the local sheriff's department."

Leah paused with the pen held aloft over the document. "This isn't what we agreed on." The salary listed was significantly higher than they'd discussed. "And I was supposed to be staying in one of the cabins."

Jessie smiled brightly as she shrugged. "Nathan found another donor, and we were able to raise the salary to something more in line with what we felt matched the value of what you're offering on the ranch. As far as the house, the cabins would have been too cramped to provide room for living quarters and sessions. This gives you far more room and a dedicated office space."

Leah pressed her lips together, trying to force back the tears of relief burning the back of her eyes. Until this moment, she'd never felt wanted or appreciated, and she'd certainly never felt needed. A lump lodged itself in her throat, threatening to choke her with foreign emotions and she cleared her throat.

"I…thank you. I can't wait to help make Heart Fire an amazing place that helps a lot of kids like m—Kids at risk."

Jessie tipped her head to one side but didn't comment on what she'd almost revealed. Leah worried that she'd slipped up, letting on to the fact that she'd once been in the same position as these kids. But there hadn't been a ranch for her to find herself, no one to lead her back to the straight and narrow.

She scribbled her signature at the bottom of the contract, committing herself and the next five years of her life to Heart Fire Ranch in exchange for a home. Or, at least the closest thing she'd ever known.

"Welcome to the family, Leah. I have a feeling you're going to love it here."

Chapter Three

GAGE WIPED HIS face against the shoulder of his T-shirt, leaving a sweat mark on the dark cotton. Movement across the driveway caught his eyes, as Leah and Jessie headed toward the main barn.

"This is where we keep all the horses that the kids will be working with. Over the next few days, I'll help you gain confidence around them so that you can understand exactly what the kids will be doing with them." She raised a hand toward Gage and Moose, her dog, ran over, yipping happily for attention. "Hey, Gage, you're going to be here for dinner tonight right? I thought we'd have everyone over for an impromptu welcome party for Leah."

His eyes flicked to Leah's face, and he could easily read the open challenge. The last thing he wanted to do was spend time in the presence of the prickly shrew again, even if it meant getting to spend some time with his brother and niece. He'd see them plenty over the coming weeks.

"I don't think so. I have a lot of work to catch up on."

Jessie shrugged. "No problem. I'll have someone bring you over some leftovers." She continued into the barn. "Over here are the girls…"

Leah hung back for a minute, watching him as he finished unloading the last of her boxes on the porch of the house. Gage crossed his arms over his chest, waiting for some sort of gesture of gratitude. Instead, she looked away and hurried after Jessie into the barn.

Figures.

Gage hadn't really expected anything different from her after the way she'd acted on the highway and the ride to the ranch. Except, as much as he wanted to believe she was as self-involved as what she appeared to be, he didn't. His bullshit meter was working overtime every time she came near, and he wondered what she was trying to hide. Because he was sure she was hiding something.

He wasn't even sure why it mattered to him. He was hiding plenty of his own secrets. He certainly wasn't about to push someone else to tell theirs.

Gage made his way to the cabin he'd be staying in and opened the cupboard. He let out a quick sigh. Of course, there was no food; his trip to the store had been derailed this morning. He headed back to his car.

Driving past the barn, his eyes slid to the doorway where he saw Leah grooming one of the horses while Jessie instructed her. He tried to tell himself it was because he was just being cautious, making sure no one came out in front of the car. It absolutely was not because he wanted to see her again. Jessie raised a hand, waving as he drove past, but Leah simply followed him with her eyes. Gage clenched his teeth, willing himself to turn away. He didn't care that she didn't seem to like him.

At least that's what he was going to keep telling himself. Eventually, he might believe it. Because it *did* bother him, a lot.

LEAH FLOPPED ONTO the couch in the living room of the three bedroom house Jessie and Nathan had provided for her. After a lifetime of nothing but hard times, she was finding it difficult to believe that something this good was actually happening to her. A job that had been a great opportunity this morning was, with each passing moment, becoming a dream come true.

She looked around the room at the boxes stacked on the kitchen counter and the island. There weren't too many, considering her entire life was packed into them. Then again, when most of childhood was something you'd rather forget, there wasn't much time to collect too many objects. She pressed her hands against her knees, forcing herself off the couch, and carried the first box into the master bedroom.

Jessie must have been the one to decorate this house. Everything seemed like her style, maintaining the western ranch theme with dark woods, neutral browns, and tans, and plenty of leather. Instead of feeling imposing, Leah found it comforting. A picture of a silhouetted cabin hung on the wall over the bed, catching Leah's attention. It took a moment for her to realize it was the main house, with the sun a bright ball of fire in the background, whose oranges, pinks, and reds lent the only spot of color to the room. It was gorgeous, and she couldn't help but feel a gaping sense of yearning. She wondered what it must have felt like growing up here, with parents and siblings, a home.

Leah ran a hand over the foot board of the bed, her fingers trailing over the smooth log furniture. She opened the box and pulled her clothes out, folding them and placing them into the dresser. As she finished, she ran her hand over the top of the dresser, void of any knickknacks to personalize it.

She had never kept pictures of her family. She'd never known most of them, and the ones she knew, she wished she didn't. Growing up, Leah pretended she had a family somewhere who would someday come and rescue her. When that didn't happen, she convinced herself that if she loved her mother enough, it would change things.

Tucking a loose strand of her hair back into the knot at the back of her head, she took a deep breath and went to the window, pulling back the sheer curtains. From her bedroom window, she could see the cabin where Gage would be staying. Jessie had offered his background freely, making Leah feel harsh and judgmental for assuming he was nothing more than a good-looking meathead. The man ran an IT company specializing in security software. He was a prodigy and a genius, if she was to believe Jessie, who sounded like a proud mother telling her about Gage's accomplishments. It was easy to see her boss held him in pretty high regard.

And you insulted him as soon as you met him.

It wasn't her finest moment, to be sure, but it was hardly the worst thing she'd ever done. However, that didn't excuse her actions. Leah could see his car parked in front of the cabin again, assuming he'd returned at some point while she'd been riding with Jessie. She battled with the urge to go over and apologize to him, yet again.

When he'd left earlier, she'd seen him watching her in the barn, and she hadn't missed the look of disgust on his face when he turned away. Leah wasn't stupid. She knew it was because he didn't want to be around her. When Jessie had invited him to dinner, he hadn't even hesitated before refusing. But she couldn't exactly blame him. She'd been pretty awful today.

She glanced at the old watch on her wrist. Other than her car, it was the only memento she'd kept from Nicole, the foster mother who'd turned her life around. She felt a twinge of melancholy each time she saw it, missing the vibrant woman she'd shared too little time with. But this wasn't the time to get sentimental. She needed to head over to the main house. Jessie was expecting her in less than thirty minutes, and she hadn't even changed yet, not that she had anything but jeans to change into.

She pulled open several boxes still in the kitchen until she found the box with her black jeans. Tugging them from below two other pair, she located a black button-up shirt that didn't look too wrinkled from being packed and her knee-high black boots. Hurrying to the guest bathroom, Leah tugged the hair tie from her head, trying

to finger-comb her caramel waves back into some semblance of a style before giving up and pulling it back with
a barrette. It was a far cry from the professional doctor
image she'd wanted to project, but it was going to have
to do. Her sweaty tank top and broken-down car had
already destroyed that facade.

Trotting down the steps, Leah hurried to the back gate
and let herself into Jessie's yard. A handsome dark-haired
man, who was standing at the barbecue on the patio by
the pool, looked back over his shoulder at her.

"You must be Leah. I'm Nathan. Jessie should be out in
just a minute, and I'm sure the rest of the clan is already
on their way." His gaze, sparkling with impish humor,
shot to the back door of the house conspiratorially. "Did
she warn you yet?"

Leah felt oddly at ease with Jessie's husband. She
tended to keep her distance with men, but his open, genuine smile made her feel more at home. "About what?"

"The rest of the family." He closed the barbecue, letting it heat up while he flipped off the pool skimmer,
tugged the machine from the water, and set it aside.
"You'll like them, everyone does, but they can be a lot
to handle if you're not expecting the wild, rambunctious
crowd that will be here."

Great, this sounds like a blast, she thought, barely
keeping herself from rolling her eyes.

"Justin's the oldest. His wife, Alyssa, used to be a
pretty big deal in Hollywood. They have a little boy,
Sam, who's about six months old. Then there's Julia and
Dylan, Gage's brother. She trains service dogs and he's a

paramedic in town. They have a little girl, Emily, who's only about a month old now. I think Bailey's coming with Chase, too, unless he has to work tonight. She helps Justin at the clinic, and he's a deputy sheriff in town."

"Jessie mentioned him earlier."

"Yeah, he refers a lot of kids here. Matter of fact, I think he's sending over a few this week."

"Already?" Leah felt her stomach clench. It wasn't a shock—this was her job, after all—but she'd been hoping for a little more time to prepare and make some plans.

He shrugged, a grin spreading over his face. "Jess isn't big on taking things slow."

"Are you talking about our wedding again?" Jessie came out onto the patio with a bowl of salad big enough to feed a small army, which, from Nathan's description, was exactly how many people might be showing up.

"No." Nathan chuckled as she moved closer, slipping his arm around her waist and pressing a kiss to her cheek. "But I'd be happy to if you want me to tell Leah the story."

Jessie rolled her eyes but smiled broadly at Leah. "He took advantage of me, ran away, and came back ten years later to beg me to marry him. There, that's it in a nutshell, right?"

Nathan shook his head. "Not exactly the way *I* remember it."

"Trust me," she whispered loudly to Leah with a laugh. "That's exactly the way it happened."

"We finally made it!" A woman's voice announced her arrival, just before the largest dog Leah had ever seen ran through the gate and straight for her.

"Tango, sit!" Immediately, the dog skidded to a halt and sat. A petite blonde scowled at him, and the dog hung his massive head apologetically. "Sorry about that, he's been cooped up with me and the baby for the last week. He wants to play, badly. I'm Julia."

"Leah."

"And that's my husband, Dylan, and his dog, Roscoe." She held her hand out as a golden retriever ran into the backyard, followed closely by a man who looked uncannily like an older version of Gage. Not exactly, he was even bigger, which she hadn't realized was possible since Gage was already built like a Mack truck. This must be the brother Nathan mentioned. As he met her gaze and shook her hand, she recognized the grave solemnity in his eyes even as he smiled in welcome. This man had been through hell and back. She'd seen the same look in several of the clients at the medical clinic she'd worked at over the past two years.

Who was she kidding?

She saw the same look in her reflection every morning.

GAGE SAT ON the front porch of the cabin, trying to ignore the laughter coming from Jessie's backyard. Three dogs barked and yipped happily as voices rose and a cheer went up just before he heard a loud splash. He couldn't make out the conversations, but it wasn't hard to tell everyone was having a good time. He tipped back the bottle of beer in his hand as a loud rumble sounded from an engine coming up the driveway.

Bailey didn't bother to park at the front of Jessie's house like everyone else had. She drove her motorcycle right to the front of his cabin and parked. Sliding her helmet off, she shook her hair loose and swung her leg over the seat before climbing the porch steps.

"Just the guy I wanted to see." She smiled brightly at Gage. "What the hell are you doing over here when the party is over there?" She jerked her thumb at the house.

"I'm not exactly in a celebration kind of mood," he said with a shrug. He doubted that she'd believe it, since she'd gotten to know him pretty well over the last year, but it was the first and easiest excuse that came to mind.

She arched a dubious brow and tipped her chin down. "Sure you're not. You're *always* in a party mood. What gives?" Bailey waved off the chilled bottle he offered her.

Gage had met Bailey when he'd stayed at Julia's for a short time while his brother was paired with a therapy dog. They'd immediately hit it off, but as much as they'd enjoyed one another's company, after one date, they'd both realized they didn't have a spark. They did, however, share an easy friendship, and she'd quickly become the little sister he'd never had.

"I've had my head bit off enough times for one day."

"By Jessie?"

He shook his head and took another sip. "Nope, her new therapist."

"Leah? Jessie said she's great. She loves her already." She dropped into one of the chairs Jessie had commissioned to grace the front of each cabin and kicked her feet up onto the table, clasping her hands over her flat stomach.

"That's exactly how she *should* feel, since she's hiring her. I, however, am not her biggest fan."

"What's wrong, Gage? Is she ugly?" Bailey mockingly stuck out her lower lip in a sad face.

Gage clenched his jaw and scowled at Bailey. Usually he would have just told her what happened, but he wondered if he shouldn't just bullshit his way through this conversation. If Bailey was concerned with his love life, she wouldn't pry into the real reason for his visit this time around. If she started asking questions, he knew her suspicions would only get stronger. Then again, he wasn't sure he wanted any of the Hart women trying to play matchmaker for him, the way they were all prone to do, and Bailey would likely read far more into his distaste for Leah than she should.

"I'm not that shallow. Besides, you know I only have eyes for you," he teased, hoping she'd drop the subject altogether.

"Ah-ah-ah!" she scolded playfully, holding up her hand and wiggling the diamond engagement ring his friend Chase had only recently placed there. "I'm off the market. You missed your chance."

"Darn it." Gage winked at her. "Just when I was going to make my move, too."

"So, what has this terrible woman done to offend your delicate sensibilities? You get along with everyone."

Gage took a deep breath, but instead of answering, he simply shrugged. Now that he thought about how he'd explain his reasons why, they sounded petty and ridiculous. The circumstances of their meeting hadn't exactly been primed for pleasantries. And, while it was a misunderstanding, he could see where his comment could be misconstrued. He was basing his opinion on what would have been a pretty bad day for anyone. Maybe he was being too harsh in his estimation of her. If nothing else, he should at least apologize for calling her bitchy in the midst of a rough day.

Bailey grinned at him and stood up, slapping her hands on her thighs. "Good, then you can walk over to the main house with me. Chase has to work late tonight, and that means I'm flying solo." She held her hand out to him. "Come on, stud muffin, I'll protect you from the big, bad therapist."

Gage rolled his eyes but couldn't help but smile at Bailey's antics. He tossed back the last sip of beer in his bottle and stood up. "Lead the way, hot stuff."

When they reached the house, Bailey opened the back gate, dragging him through it into the party already in full swing. "Look who I found!"

Seven sets of eyes turned toward them, every pair welcoming except one. Leah's gaze fell on him, and it didn't take a genius to read the only emotion in her face: irritation.

Gage realized too late that he hadn't misjudged anything.

THE PARTY WAS loud, far louder than Leah imagined nine people and two infants could ever be. But with three big dogs added to the mix, it was barely controlled chaos, and although everyone was having a good time, she needed a breather. She eyed the back gate and wondered if she could sneak out for just a moment of silence. With everyone concentrating on getting the fire going in the pit in the center of the lawn or moving chairs closer, Leah edged closer to the exit, sneaking out without being noticed.

She took a deep breath and tucked her hands into the pockets of her jeans, the gravel of the path between the main house and hers crunching quietly under her boots. Turning right, she made her way past the other cabins toward the corral where two horses munched on hay. The sun had dipped below the horizon and pinks and oranges streaked through the sky before deepening into dark blues, looking much like the picture hanging on her wall. The first stars were just beginning to twinkle high in the sky, and Leah marveled at the sharp turn her life had taken.

She'd never been anywhere like this before. Her fingers wound around the railing of the corral and one of the horses glanced up at her before turning back to its dinner. Growing up in the central valley of California, she'd seen plenty of farms along the outskirts of town, but it had always seemed like a different world. When you grew up in the slums of the inner city, even the outskirts seemed foreign. Her world more closely resembled the war zones she saw on television, with everyone struggling and fighting for every scrap they managed to hold onto. Between the rival gangs, drug deals, and poverty, peace was something she'd never experienced as a child, let alone hoped to have on a consistent basis.

Hope.

It was a futile emotion in her world, only leading to pain and disappointment. She'd learned that lesson the hard way. Yet, here she was, living in a place she couldn't have even dreamed about, working with kids she might actually be able to help, with people who shared her vision. For someone with nothing but bad luck, good luck had seemed to finally smile down on her.

Until it all comes crashing down.

Leah wanted to ignore the needling pessimism, but based on her past history, she couldn't help but feel like she was waiting for the other shoe to drop or to find out this was all some sick joke. There had to be some sort of down side. Good things like this didn't happen to her.

"Are you trying to escape, too?"

She jumped at the sound of Gage's husky voice, her heart pounding painfully against her ribs. She wasn't sure what it was about him that immediately set her on edge, making her pulse race and her stomach churn at the same time.

There's the down side.

She kept her gaze focused on the pair of horses in front of her, even as they continued to ignore her presence completely. "I just needed to catch my breath for a second."

"I see." He didn't sound convinced, and Leah swung her eyes toward him, waiting for him to say more. She wasn't in the mood for his sarcasm. "It's been a pretty hectic day for you all the way around today, hasn't it?"

It wasn't what she expected him to say, and it took her by surprise. "I guess so."

She turned, leaning an elbow over the corral railing, and eyed him. For someone who was supposed to be able to read people well, she was having a difficult time with him. She could see the sympathy in his expression, but she could also read distrust there. His tone was friendly, but it also held a note of cynicism. The man was so many contradictions wrapped up in one package.

Although, it was a mighty fine package. Even she had to admit it, but she knew better than most how overrated lust was.

"Thanks for—"

"Look, I wanted to—" Gage paused as they spoke simultaneously and let a small grin lift the corner of his mouth. "Go ahead."

"I was just going to thank you for your help with the car today. I shouldn't have been so grouchy. Well, I guess after everything it might be understandable, but I shouldn't have taken it out on you."

"I appreciate that." His shoulders relaxed slightly. "Guess the heat got to both of us today. I'm sorry for the things I said, too. You were under a lot of stress, and I didn't give you much of a chance to adjust before I started shooting off my mouth."

She turned back toward the horses as one of them started walking toward them. If they were going to live in close proximity, maybe they could at least get to a point where they could tolerate one another.

"We should start over." Gage held out a hand. "I'm Gage Granger, your neighbor. It's nice to meet you."

Leah bit the corner of her lip as the horse nudged her hand. "Don't do that," she said quietly. She rubbed her hand over the animal's face the way Jessie had told her they liked. "We're both old enough that we don't need to pretend we get do-overs in life."

"Ah, another cynic." He reached out and patted the horse's neck. The second horse seemed to take notice and ambled slowly in their direction.

"A realist," she corrected. "Another?"

"Like my brother, or at least, he used to be one." Gage shrugged but looked back at her, curiosity clear in his dark eyes. "So, you don't think you can forgive and forget? There's no starting over?"

"Not really. You can forgive, but it's a conscious choice. Forgetting something ever happened? That's impossible. It's like saying there's such a thing as love at first sight."

"Next you're going to tell me you don't believe in happily ever after either." He clucked his tongue and shook his head with a grin tugging at the corners of his full lips. "What kind of therapist are you?"

She didn't return his smile. "A good one. One who knows what I'm talking about and uses hard facts to get through to people who've see far too much reality in their daily lives to believe in fairy tales."

She leaned one elbow on the railing and faced him. "The people I work with don't need illusions. They need coping skills because life isn't some kind of fantasy. Most people you meet aren't good, and they don't want to help you."

Gage narrowed his eyes, trying to see more than what she would allow anyone to see. Leah wondered for a moment if she should have just kept her mouth shut. There was something about this man that made her usual calm, reserved demeanor take a vacation and made her tongue run away without her brain. If she wasn't careful, she'd end up telling him her life story, and no one deserved to bear the weight of that nightmare.

He shook his head and gave her a look filled with such empathy that it nearly brought tears to her eyes. She steeled herself. Leah didn't want his sympathy. She'd gotten enough of that when she was a kid, from teachers, therapists, and social workers as she bounced from one foster home to another. She was an adult now.

"Don't do that either. Don't act like you understand where I'm coming from. You don't know me."

Reaching a hand out to pet the horse at the fence, Gage sighed. "You're right, I don't, and I get the feeling there aren't many people who really do. But you should probably drop the eat-shit-and-die attitude or you'll never understand where other people are coming from. No one wants to open up to someone they're sure is a hard-ass."

Gage walked away before she could even formulate a response. In truth, she wasn't even sure how to respond.

She wanted to rail at him, to throw the reality of her past into his face and embarrass him for his audacity in thinking he could make assumptions about her. In his worst nightmares, he couldn't imagine even half of what she'd been through. Staring at his broad back, walking away from her toward the cabin he was staying in, she took in the confident swagger.

"Arrogant ass," she muttered. "If you think *this* is an attitude, you're in for a treat."

[faded text from previous page visible at top of page]

Chapter Four

THE KNOCK ON the back patio door jerked Leah upright in bed, struggling to remember where she was. She rubbed at her eyes as the pounding came again.

I'm at Heart Fire Ranch. New job, new life.

The mantra she'd been reciting to herself since she'd received the call offering her the position did nothing to shake the nightmares that had plagued her into the early morning hours, keeping her tangled in the sheets, crying out and waking herself, wanting to hide under her bed, the way she'd done when she was little. Leah brushed her curls back from her face and took a deep breath as she swung her feet over the side of the bed.

"Coming," she called as she shuffled to the door and swung it open. Seeing Gage standing in the doorway, she groaned. "You again?"

"I see a good night's sleep hasn't done anything to improve your mood."

She glared at him but he only chuckled. It was too early in the morning to deal with his misguided attempt at humor. She glanced at the clock on her stove as she made her way back into the room.

"You do realize it's only…oh."

"Indeed, Sunshine. It's almost ten a.m., and I'd think you'd be far more grateful for my presence when you see what gifts I bring." He held up two cups of iced coffee. "I knew you liked iced after I saw it spilled in your car yesterday, but I wasn't sure what kind you liked best so I guessed. I figured a guy can't go wrong with caramel and vanilla. I'll give you your choice."

She reached out, snagging the cup with caramel syrup drizzled along the inside. "Mmm." She closed her eyes to enjoy the drink. "I might have to rethink killing you for waking me up."

"I appreciate the effort."

He set the other cup onto the kitchen counter and made his way back to her small porch, retrieving several paper bags and bringing them inside.

"What are those?"

Gage lifted his arms, his lips curving into a slight smile. "Groceries. I figured with your car in the shop and you arriving early, Jessie hadn't stocked your cabinets, and since I was already heading into town this morning…" He shrugged as if the resulting bags were self-explanatory.

Leah felt guilt slam into her chest. She'd been rude to him yesterday—okay, maybe even worse than rude—yet he'd still been thoughtful enough to pick up groceries for her, to do one more thing she couldn't do for herself. Leah's ability to remain aloof slipped as regret for her actions needled her. She'd been on her own, answering to no one, for so long she didn't know how to react to the foreign feeling and the remorse irritated her. She clenched her jaw against the smart-aleck comment that tried to slip past her lips. She took a deep breath and buried the irritation.

"Why are you doing all of this?"

Gage took a drink of the coffee before setting the cup aside and leaning a hip against the counter. "All of what, Leah?"

"The car, unloading my things, the groceries?" She frowned, trying to figure him out the way she would one of her patients.

"I'm just being nice. Is there something wrong with that?" Gage didn't miss anything and his grin widened. "Instead of complaining, I think this is where you say 'thank you,'" he said.

"Thank you," she muttered.

"See?" he said with a laugh. "That didn't hurt, did it?"

Leah rolled her eyes and reached into one of the bags, finding two boxes of cereal, pancake mix, syrup, lunch meat, bread, a head of lettuce, and tomatoes. She held up the box of Cinnamon Toast Crunch. "Do I look like a ten-year-old boy?"

He plucked the box from her hands with a grin and slid it into an empty cupboard. "You don't have to be ten to enjoy these. Plus," he pointed out, "you're probably going to have hungry boys showing up. You should have a few things they might like."

It wasn't a bad idea, but she wasn't about to admit it to him. Gage reached for the loaf of bread.

"And I was thinking the two of us could get to know one another over lunch."

Leah crossed her arms and leaned against the edge of the counter, keeping the width of the kitchen between them, fixing him with a pointed look. "Get to know one another?" She took another sip of the coffee, stalling. "That's the best line you could think of?"

She couldn't deny that he had the boyish charm down to an art form, but she wasn't buying it.

Gage's eyes flashed with mischief as he opened the mayonnaise he'd bought for her and spread it on the bread he'd laid out on two paper plates. "What makes you think it's a line?"

"Gee, I wonder. Maybe it's the ease with which it falls off of your tongue. Or the confident way you take over my kitchen."

He glanced at her. "And that makes you think I'm trying to seduce you with sandwiches?"

"Maybe." Leah shrugged. "Although you didn't hesitate to point out yesterday that I wasn't your type," she reminded him, tipping her cup in his direction.

He set the butter knife aside and closed the distance between them, forcing her to move backward, pressing herself into the counter in an effort to create some breathing room between them. Gage already filled the small space, making it feel minuscule, but when he approached, he erased the rest of the room. Her vision was engulfed by him—his broad shoulders, the expanse of well-muscled chest, his chiseled jaw that was shaved smooth this morning, his deep, penetrating brown eyes. Gage raised a hand, and she could feel the electricity jump between them. He didn't even touch her as he laid a hand against the cupboard behind her, but she felt the current between them all the same.

"Trust me, Leah." His voice was a husky sound that made her stomach do a flip and a spin. It reminded her of the only roller coaster she'd been on during a senior trip in high school. "If I was going to seduce you, it wouldn't be over sandwiches. I can think of far better ways."

She found herself wanting to lean into him, to let his fingers brush over her skin, to see if his hands were as warm as she guessed they would be. Leah cursed her own fantasies. She'd just told him last night that she didn't believe in that sort of nonsense, and here she was letting herself get swept away by a little sexual attraction. Her gaze fell on his mouth, lips that made her wonder what it might feel like to kiss him, to be kissed *by* him, to feel them over her skin. Okay, so maybe this was more than a *little* sexual attraction. It felt like a live thing, growing and spreading through her with each passing second.

Snap out of it!

Leah looked up and met his eyes, forcing her lips to spread in a disdainful smirk. "So, this is what usually works for you?"

She saw the doubt flash in his eyes. It was brief, but she was sure that was what she saw before he quickly masked it with his impish humor.

The corners of his mouth tugged upward. "Usually, but I should have known you wouldn't be like other woman, Leah. You've been in a league all your own from the first moment I saw you."

She peered up at him, bristling slightly and arching a questioning brow while she waited for him to elaborate on his statement.

"Not many women would drive a car like yours," he explained. "And, even if they did, they wouldn't know what a radiator was, let alone if it needed replacing. You're definitely one of a kind."

"This is your version of a compliment?"

She kept her voice dispassionate, but inside she celebrated the fact that he noticed the differences. After their short conversation at the corral last night, he hadn't bothered to return to the barbecue, which must have been a cue to everyone else in attendance to act as if it was their family duty to extol the amazing attributes of Gage Granger, including his brilliance and the way people fawned over him like a celebrity. Just because other people treated him like a god didn't make him one, and she wasn't about to become one of his overly large harem of Granger-groupies.

"And the cynicism returns." Gage moved back to the bread and slapped some deli meat onto it before reaching into the bag again. "Cheese?"

She shook her head. "Nothing for me. I'm not a breakfast person."

"This is brunch."

"Sorry, I'm not a *brunch* person. And since when do you have sandwiches for brunch? That, sir, is lunch."

His gaze slid over her, taking in every inch, from the top of her mussed waves, over the tank top and yoga pants she'd slept in, all the way down to her stocking feet. "Not at ten a.m. it's not. Besides, you need to eat. You could use a little meat on your bones."

Leah fought back the urge to wrap her arms around her waist self-consciously. She was thin, had always been built that way, and it had earned her plenty of jabs from kids in school growing up. But when you didn't have food in the house to eat, it was tough to gain weight.

"I'm sure you'll try to convince me that innuendo was about my car, too?" Sarcasm dripped from her voice.

She snatched the paper plate with the sandwich he'd made and took it around the counter to sit on the other side of the island, leaving him to make another for himself.

Gage watched her for a moment before he laughed, shaking his head, and turned back to the food, making himself another sandwich. "No, *that* one was about your ass." She spun to look at him, her mouth falling open in surprise at his audacity. "You're not as hard to figure out as you'd like to think you are."

She picked at the corner crust of the bread. "I thought I was the therapist."

He shrugged as he slapped the meat onto his sandwich. "You may think you're a tough nut to crack, but you're more like an M&M."

Leah nearly choked on the bite of food in her mouth. "What?" she asked through a cough. "I'm a what?"

"M&Ms, the candy. You know, sweet center with a hard outer shell."

"I know what they are." She hoped he heard every bit of the bitterness she was feeling toward him right now and made sure it was clear in her tone.

Gage turned to look at her, calling her bluff. He slid his plate over the top of the bar and came around to sit next to her, making her wonder if he had a death wish or was just that oblivious to her irritation. "The funny thing about M&Ms is that the outer shell isn't really all that hard or durable. It's an illusion."

That was the last thing she wanted anyone to think. "Then I guess that's where your metaphor falls apart."

"I doubt it." He bit into the sandwich, ignoring her ire, which only served to annoy her more. She was fairly certain that was his intent.

"You shouldn't." She tossed the sandwich back onto her plate and stood up. Whatever appetite she might have had was long gone. "Tougher men than you have tried to break through. Trust me, this 'shell' is impenetrable."

Gage sighed and set his food back onto his plate. "I'm not trying to piss you off, Leah."

"Yeah? Well, consider yourself successful without even trying. From what everyone said last night, that's sort of how you manage to do everything." His jaw clenched, and she knew she'd struck a nerve. "Trust me, there wasn't one person there last night who didn't want to tell me all about how wonderful you were. I get it. You're an all-around nice guy with the Midas touch. Well, guess what? You don't know a thing about me or my 'shell,' and if you had me even close to figured out, you'd know that a flirtatious playboy is the last person I'd open up to."

She stalked through the kitchen to the back door and jerked it open. "So, thank you for the groceries, but be assured, I'll add them to what I pay you back for my car. If you don't mind?"

Gage cocked his head to one side and stared at her for a moment before grabbing the plate and heading for the door, pausing as he reached her. Mere inches separated them, and she could feel the heat radiating from his body as he looked down at her. She'd expected his anger, but the disappointment filling his dark eyes surprised her.

"It must be pretty lonely being you, Leah. I'm just trying to be nice to you, but you sure make it difficult."

She'd wanted to sound strong, adamant in her refusal, but instead, her voice came out sounding breathy and desperate. "I didn't ask you to."

Something deep in his eyes flickered to life, like a candle lighting in the darkness, but she couldn't quite put a name to it. A slow smile broke over his lips. "I'll see you later."

Leah narrowed her eyes as he brushed past her and headed back toward his cabin. She didn't trust him or his expressive eyes.

Hope.

That's what she'd seen in them a moment ago. She'd felt it herself last night, remembered it from her youth. The only thing hope had ever managed to accomplish was to disappoint her. Gage and his hope needed to both stay far away from her.

THAT WOMAN WAS the most confusing, infuriating, hot mess Gage had ever had the misfortune to meet. He'd dealt with plenty of difficult people in his career, but she definitely took the prize as *the* most difficult. She couldn't seem to let anything go. Even last night at the barbecue she was on edge. Each time he saw her, she seemed more like she was giving a performance, playing a part for the world to believe, but then he would gain brief glimpses of genuineness, especially when she talked about her past, and he could see remorse break through.

There were little comments that caused Leah's eyes to shutter, her face to become shadowed and bleak, like a dark cloud passed overhead, but at least it was a real emotion. It wasn't difficult to tell that something had happened to her, something that had shaped her as much as his own bleak past had shaped him and the choices he'd made, as well as the mistakes.

Gage had seen far more in her expression than she'd want to believe she revealed, and maybe it was only because of his own past that he could see it. After growing up with a father who was in a drunken stupor more than he was sober, then watching his mother waste away as cancer ravaged her body, he recognized her ability to hide the trials and to try to minimize what had forced her to become the cynical person he'd met. He also didn't miss the pain that flickered in her whiskey-colored eyes when she'd mentioned others trying to break through to her.

She might deny the possibility, but he saw the brokenness inside. He'd seen it in his brother after he'd survived his last tour, the one that had returned him home from Afghanistan with physical and emotional wounds, some of which were still healing.

He saw the same haunted pain in Leah's eyes. She had fought a war of her own and was trying to hide it. It explained so many of her reactions, and overreactions. Gage slumped into the leather couch in the center of the cabin living space and rubbed a hand over his eyes. Or he was reading far too much into things and she was just a bitch.

But he didn't think so.

His cell phone rang from the kitchen counter where he'd left it, and Gage rose with a sigh. Glancing at the screen, he saw his partner's number, dragging him back to his own problems and his own dire circumstances. He thought about declining the call again, but ignoring the issue wasn't making it any better. It was simply making his partners more adamant about reaching him. He couldn't continue to avoid them forever.

Before he could change his mind, Gage swiped his finger across the screen. "Hey, Georgie."

"Gage, where the hell are you?"

"I told you I was coming to visit my brother and his family for a while."

"You screwed up and then left us to deal with the media frenzy that followed, not to mention the lawsuits coming in right and left. You're the face of this company, you should be the one doing these news conferences."

The pulse in his temple pounded, and Gage felt the tension build in his shoulders. George wasn't wrong. The two of them had built this company from scratch, starting with a few small software programs in college and expanding until they'd practically formed a security software empire. Until last year.

"George, we both know you're not doing the news conferences either, so don't try to bullshit me. That's why we hired good lawyers." He sighed. "And now that two of the companies have settled out of court, they're all going to follow suit."

"And what's that going to cost us? Masters and Cooper are going nuts right now. They want your head, Gage, and I can only hold them off for so long. You can't just skip out on this. This isn't like you." His voice sounded desperate, pleading.

They'd known each other long enough for George to tell there was far more to this than just Gage running away. He was hiding like a coward, afraid to admit to this mistake, let alone confess it to the world. As long as he remained out of sight, Gage could let someone else remedy the situation, and once the worst blew over, he could return to face the reality, or not.

"I'm sure they do, but they're going to have to wait until I get back."

"And when will that be?"

"A few weeks."

"Weeks?" George cleared his throat. "I'm sorry, it sounded like you said a few weeks. I know that can't be right."

"I'm visiting my brother and his family. You remember? My new niece. You guys are just going to have to handle things until I get back."

Gage hoped George only heard the calm determination in his voice. He didn't want him to hear the shame ringing in it, nor did he want him to point out the disgrace Gage had brought upon them both.

Silence echoed through the receiver. Gage wondered, briefly, if the call had been disconnected when he heard George take a deep breath.

"Maybe Masters and Cooper aren't too far off the mark, Gage. If you don't care enough to be here to resolve this in person, maybe it's time for us to go our separate ways."

Chapter Five

AFTER TWO DAYS of an equestrian crash course with Jessie, Leah could barely walk the short distance from the barn to her house without limping. What she needed was a long soak in a warm bath. Leah brushed her bangs back from her eyes, wrinkling her nose at the sweat she could feel on her cheeks and the back of her neck. No, what she really wanted was to relax in Jessie's pool. She'd made the offer the night of Leah's welcome party, insisting it was there for anyone and that they considered Leah part of the family, but Leah hadn't dared take her up on the offer.

Family.

Leah scoffed at the thought. She'd never had any family to speak of. For most of her childhood, it had only been her and her mother. After what that woman had done to her, if that was what it meant to be part of a *family,* she'd rather do without.

At the same time, the idea of belonging, of being wanted, tugged at her core, making her heart ache with loneliness. She'd always wanted those things, wanted someone to see her as valuable and worthy of love. She'd thought she'd found it when Child Protective Services had finally removed her from her mother's machinations and put her into her first foster home, but she realized quickly that she was only a means to an end there as well.

Her first foster mother was a nice woman with high ideals, but she hadn't been prepared to cope with the emotional trauma of a ten-year-old girl who'd endured the kind of abuse Leah had. The homes she'd bounced in and out of afterward hadn't even cared enough to try. Most of them had either been content to collect their monthly checks and drop her off at therapy or just ignore her altogether.

It wasn't until her high school counselor, Nicole Campbell, had pulled her into her office after Leah had broken into her algebra teacher's car and had sex with a boy in the parking lot, that she'd finally felt like someone cared about her or her future. It had taken Nicole only ten minutes of really listening to Leah to hear the cry for help below the surface of her tough words. Within just a few weeks of constant pursuit, Nicole finally broke through. When she offered a room in her home, Leah jumped at the opportunity. It wasn't exactly a chance to start over, but with strict boundaries enforced, Nicole had turned Leah's life around and had given direction to a sixteen-year-old kid hell-bent on destroying her life. Losing Nicole to breast cancer just before her high school graduation had been the most painful experience of Leah's life—more than the abuse, the rejection, or the loss of her childhood. It had also been the day she decided to close herself off from caring about anyone that much again. Caring meant getting hurt.

"Hey, where are you running off to?"

Leah spun at the sound of Jessie's voice. As kind and welcoming as Jessie had been, she was still Leah's boss, and it wasn't a fact Leah was likely to ignore anytime soon, regardless of how often Jessie insisted she should.

"I was going to shower, but if you need me for something, I can stay."

"No, it's fine, but don't you want to go for a swim?" Leah shrugged and Jessie shook her head. "I just wanted to make sure to tell you we have a group of boys coming this weekend."

Leah's eyes widened instinctively as she realized this was the first opportunity she'd have to prove her value to the ranch. She needed this to go well, or Jessie might decide to buy her out of her contract.

"Don't look so worried. It's only four boys, and they're only staying through the weekend. All you'll need to do is a couple of team-building exercises for them, highlighting the benefits of working together, cooperation, not killing one another, that sort of thing." Jessie's eyes glimmered with humor, but Leah wasn't sure she was joking. "These are all boys Chase has been working with. They're in the system but not considered high-risk."

"Oh, okay." She bit the corner of her lower lip, wondering which exercises might work best for the group. "I guess I could plan a morning session where we—"

Jessie laughed and grasped her by the shoulders. "Don't stress yourself out over this, Leah. Nathan will be there to help with them in the morning when they do chores, and we'll take a ride to The Ridge. We'll manage lunch after. I'm betting you and I can come up with something fun for them to do. We'll reserve some time after dinner to get them to open up and talk as a group, once you get to know them. It won't be anything too formal this time around."

Leah nearly breathed a sigh of relief, her shoulders drooping as she released the tension that had been building. Most programs she'd applied to wanted a structured program that would adhere to rigid guidelines, but from the way Jessie was describing things, she wanted something organic. It would require more skill and finesse on Leah's part, an ability to read the boys and their needs in the moment, but would give the participants a far greater sense of being heard and understood. It surprised her again to find such a forward-thinking facility.

"You really just want me to let them talk?" Leah shook her head in disbelief. "Are you sure you don't want me doing something a bit more...clinical? You're paying me an awful lot to just listen."

"Not when you think about everything you're giving up. You're committing to this ranch for five years, Leah. We've worked our way through a lot of applications to find just the right person that we thought would fit our program. It means the world to me and Nathan that you believe in what we're doing here enough to put your life on hold."

Leah lifted a shoulder. She wasn't about to tell Jessie she hadn't really had a life before accepting this job. Everything up until this point had been just stepping stones to land a position even half as promising as this one was. She wasn't sure why others hadn't jumped at the chance.

"I appreciate you both giving me the opportunity."

She couldn't help the doubts that crept into her mind. What if she couldn't connect with these kids? What if she could and everyone figured out why? No one knew about her past. Her mother was in jail and would be for the next fifteen years, at least, and no one else cared enough to look for her. This was the new start she'd always prayed for, the second chance to find a life free from the shackles of her past.

Jessie smiled at her, cocking her head to one side, her long, dark ponytail flipping over her shoulder. "We're happy you see it as an opportunity. I know it's a lot of work, more than just sitting in an office at a desk seeing patients, but we hope you'll find it worth the effort."

A soft, muffled mew sounded from their left and Jessie paused, listening.

"What's that?" Leah walked toward the sound.

"One of the barn cats must have kittens nearby."

Jessie crossed her arms and waited for Leah at the porch steps. Leah had expected her to follow and try to find the source of the sound—it was her ranch and kittens, after all—but Jessie didn't seem fazed and let Leah search for the kittens alone. Making her way around to the side of the patio, she continued to hear the soft mew but couldn't locate the source.

"Here, kitty," she called, squatting down in hopes the animal might come to her. With several shrubs around the edge of the house, it was likely it was a litter behind the plants.

"Don't worry, Leah," Jessie called from around the corner. "The mom won't go far. She probably went hunting and left her babies under your porch where they'd be safe."

Leah tried to move the bush aside, peering through the branches to find the kitten, but she couldn't see anything in the dark recesses of the shrubbery. As much as she wanted to continue trying to find the poor thing, Leah figured Jessie knew better than she did. The only time she'd ever been around cats were the strays in the alley near where she grew up. She rose and made her way back to the front of the house.

"I leave food and water for them in the barns, so they'll be fine," Jessie said.

Leah glanced back over her shoulder at the side of the house and thought she saw a small pair of eyes peering out at her, but they were gone too quickly for her to be sure.

"What do you say we go to my office and look over the files for the boys before they arrive, so we can coordinate our efforts between the sessions with me and the horses and their evening sessions with you?"

Leah could feel herself slipping into her doctor mode, ready to read the background on each teen, so she'd know exactly what sort of issues she'd be facing when she met with each boy. This was her comfort zone, where she excelled. While she wasn't about to let anyone know *why* she was so good at her job, she was eager for them to see just how good at it she could be. She would help these kids realize how much control and power they had over their lives, even facing desperate and hopeless circumstances, the same way her mentor had with her.

"Lead the way."

GAGE FELT LIKE he was drowning in recriminations. He'd finally contacted his team of attorneys today, only to be told that his mistake was going to cost the company nearly twenty million in settlements. They hadn't been prepared to take a hit like this. It was going to set them back by almost ten years in research and technological advances, unless they cut costs somewhere else in the budget.

A quick call to George had made one thing clear: Masters and Cooper were adamant that the cuts come from staff layoffs. George, on the other hand, wanted to figure out another way and needed Gage, as CEO, to back him against the other two.

Now, not only was he faced with a twenty-million-dollar mistake on his head, Gage could be the reason nearly four hundred of their employees were laid off. Logically, it was a simple decision that would solve every issue they faced. If he sided with Masters and Cooper, they could put the entire mess behind them.

But the decision wasn't as simple as it sounded. These were good people, with families, people who had worked with him for years, helping to build this company into what it was today. These were people who had taken a chance on the new start-up, entrusting their livelihood to two graduate students. The risk had been accepted years ago and should have passed by now. These families should be celebrating security now; some of them were nearly retirement age. It was wrong to let them go simply because he'd made an error. It was *Gage's* mistake, not theirs, and now, the company would recover but those four hundred employees might not. He didn't want to punish their loyalty and betray them so that he didn't lose money. But, if he didn't, there might not be an Iconics if he couldn't figure out a way to recover.

Gage couldn't live with himself if he backed Cooper and Masters, even if it meant saving his own reputation. He had to figure out another way.

A quiet knock at the door jerked him back to his present, where he was busy wallowing in self-pity on the queen-sized bed in the cabin. Closing down his email and setting his laptop to the side, he headed for the door wearing nothing but his sweatpants.

He opened it to see Leah leaving. "Did you knock?"

"Um, yeah." She hesitated as her gaze slid over him, looking like she'd just been caught with her hand in the cookie jar.

He stepped out onto the small porch when she retreated like she was about to leave. "Did you need something?"

Leah took another step down the stairs, away from him, her gaze cutting back toward her place. "I...no, never mind." She'd barely made it a few more steps to her house when she turned around, suddenly far more confident than she had been just a moment ago. "Milk. Do you have any?"

"I should. Come in while I look." She followed him but paused at the doorway, her eyes wary. "It's okay to come inside, Leah. I won't bite." She leaned against his doorway, trying to appear nonchalant, but he could read the trepidation in the depths of her eyes. "Suit yourself."

He had enough concerns weighing heavily on him without worrying about what this woman thought of him, too. Frustration made him clench his jaw. He didn't *need* to care about her opinion, but he did. She'd completely avoided him over the past few days, since he'd brought her groceries, making sure they were never in the same vicinity, and when they were, she barely maintained civility in spite of his attempts at friendliness.

Gage reached for the milk in his refrigerator and turned his back to her to open the cupboard. "You need a little or a lot?"

When she didn't answer, he faced her, grinning when he saw the blush creep over her cheeks as he caught her staring at his him, her eyes darker than usual. If he hadn't known better, he'd have thought she found him attractive.

Leah quickly looked away and took a deep breath. "I'm…I'm not sure. It's not for me."

He slid the plastic jug onto the counter and crossed his arms over his chest. "Okay, now I'm curious."

She pushed herself from the doorjamb. "I think I have some kittens under my house. They keep meowing, but

I can't find them. Jessie said the mother was probably nearby, but they haven't stopped crying all afternoon." Gage slid the milk jug back into the shelf on the door of the refrigerator. "What are you doing?"

"It's an old wives' tale. Milk isn't good for cats."

He walked into his room, plucked the T-shirt from the end of the bed, and slid his feet into sneakers. Pulling the shirt over his head, he walked past her out the front door. He really didn't need to get involved. He doubted she'd even appreciate this, but Gage tried to convince himself that he wasn't trying to impress an unimpressible woman. He was simply trying to save the kittens. Too bad even he wasn't buying it.

THE MAN NEARLY took her breath away. Watching Gage move through his kitchen with no shirt practically made her mouth water. The muscles of his back and chest looked chiseled from granite. When he'd turned and faced her, her heart dropped to her toes before bouncing back up to her stomach to roll and tumble, making her feel dizzy.

This wasn't who she was. She didn't swoon or get light-headed, and she didn't like the way her body reacted to being near him. She had no use for men, hadn't since she was a little girl and realized how easily manipulated they were. But Gage wasn't acting the way she was accustomed to, and she was having a difficult time fighting the way this man seemed to make every cell in her body spark to life. She wanted to run toward him and away from him simultaneously, the conflicting reactions making her confused and irrational. Which might explain the antagonism that seemed to overflow from her whenever they spoke. She'd spent too many years perfecting her jaded apathy to let this one man get under her skin.

"Where do you think you're going? I just asked if you had milk, not for your help. Contrary to what you might think, I have survived this long without you."

Gage stopped so quickly she nearly ran into the back of him and threw her hands up to stop herself. When they landed on the wall of muscle, somewhere deep inside her, she felt the desire to slide her hands down his back. The corded muscles under her hands no longer reminded her of stone. He was warm, living breathing masculine perfection. She jumped backward, unwilling to allow herself to acknowledge even a moment of desire.

Gage turned to face her slowly, his eyes so dark she could see herself in them. And she didn't like the fear she saw reflected. A slow, almost seductive smile spread over his lips, and Leah felt her breath catch in her throat.

"Are you telling me that you're planning on diving into the crawl space under the house?"

He was speaking but her brain was too focused on the movement of his full lips, the way they curved around each syllable, the sandpaper quality of his voice that stirred her. She couldn't string the sounds together to form a coherent sentence. Blinking stupidly, Leah tried to clear her addled brain.

"What?"

"Those kittens are probably under your house. So, unless you want to go sliding under there with the spiders and possibly a snake or two—"

"Snakes?"

"Sometimes." Gage easily read her trepidation and laughed, crossing his arms over his chest. "I'm sure you'll be fine. I doubt the rattlesnakes would mind you at all."

"You're lying. The mother cat wouldn't have gone under there if there were snakes." She sounded far more sure of her logic than she felt. A cat wouldn't have kittens where there were snakes, would it?

Gage shrugged a shoulder. "You could be right. Or they could have moved in after she had them. Either way, I'm sure you'll do fine." He brushed passed her, heading back to his cabin.

She knew this was a test of wills, and he was simply forcing her to admit she needed his help. It was the last thing she wanted to do. No, the *last* thing she wanted to do was to crawl under the house to come eye to eye with a snake. She ground her teeth together and forced the words from between her lips. Knowing she needed to say them didn't make them any easier to get out.

"Please, help me get them."

Gage turned back toward her, his eyes glinting brightly and a wide smile curving his lips. It made her heart skip a beat, and she cursed herself for her girlish response, reminding herself that he was nothing more than a rich playboy flirting to gain the upper hand, although she couldn't imagine what he hoped to gain.

"See, that didn't hurt, did it?"

For a brief moment, Leah wished she had something to throw at him.

Chapter Six

GAGE TRIED TO ignore the pea gravel scraping the hell out of his back, even through his T-shirt, as he scooted out from under the house, clutching the quietly mewling ball of fluff to his chest.

"Did you find them?" He could hear the concern in Leah's voice, but he doubted it had anything do to with his welfare.

Digging his heels into the mulch in the flower bed, he slid the rest of the way out until his head was clear from the house and he could sit up without risking injury. "Just this one little guy."

He held the kitten aloft, passing it into Leah's hands as she gasped and hurried forward to scoop the animal from his grasp. She surprised him when she held out a hand to help him up. He took it, but not because he needed help standing. It was more because he didn't want to reject the first friendly gesture she'd initiated.

He wasn't surprised by the heat that traveled up his arm when their hands connected. He'd been attracted to her from the start, but he hadn't expected it to come on so intensely, as if this longing for her had been smoldering since he'd first seen her stranded on the side of the road, as if the mere touch of her hand was enough to ignite it into a wildfire. She sucked in a breath sharply, and he wondered if she didn't feel it, too, which explained why she let go abruptly, nearly knocking him back into the side of the house.

"Um…"

Gage could see her discomfort and decided to extend an olive branch. They'd finally come to a semblance of coexistence, and there was no sense in letting awkwardness shred that thread. He reached over and ran a hand over the dust-covered, cream fur. "So, what are you going to name him?"

"Him?" She eyed the kitten as it stared up at her from cuddled between her breasts with innocent blue-gray eyes. "What makes you think it's a him?"

Gage looked down at the kitten, curled in her cleavage, as content as could be. *Lucky cat.*

He arched an eyebrow. "Just a guess." She shot him a scrutinizing look, but he didn't want to pursue the train of thought. He reached forward and plucked a cobweb stuck between the tips of the kitten's dark brown ears. "Why don't we take him inside and clean him up?"

"How do you clean up a cat?"

Gage frowned, realizing they were probably in the same boat when it came to taking care of animals. He'd never had any, and while Dylan had learned to care for dogs since marrying Julia, that wasn't going to help them.

Bailey.

He pulled out his phone and scrolled through his contacts, pulling up the number at Justin's vet clinic where she worked most days, ignoring the suspicion in Leah's eyes as he followed her into the house.

"Hey, Alyssa, is Bailey or Justin around?" He waited while she put the call through.

"Gage," Justin's voice came over the line. "Alyssa said you needed help. What the hell kind of trouble did you get yourself into now?"

"Not that it matters, since you owe me after that rodeo," Gage teased, reminding him of the Cowboy Poker event Justin had convinced him to do recently. The same one that had nearly gotten him put into the hospital the way Chase had been. "I've got a kitten over at Jessie's place and I don't see a mother nearby. I think he's stranded, and I'm not sure what to do with him."

"Just leave him, maybe set out some water. If the mom is around, she'll come back."

Gage eyed the kitten, purring loudly in Leah's arms. "Yeah, it's a little late for that."

"Any idea how old?"

"I have no clue," Gage admitted. "He was crying under Leah's place, so I got him out, but he's pretty dirty and, I'm guessing, hungry."

"Eyes open?"

"Yeah."

"Color?"

"He's very light brown with dark brown on his ears, nose and feet."

"I meant the color of his eyes." Gage could hear the smile in Justin's tone.

"Oh, bluish gray. He didn't try to run away or anything. He's friendly and came right up to me under the house."

"Okay, then he's walking around? Not dragging his body or crawling. Does he fit in one hand or two?"

"Two, but mostly because he's a big ball of fluff and I didn't want him to squirm too much."

"I'm guessing he's at least five weeks if he's moving around that well. Jessie feeds all of the feral cats around the barn kitten food, so just ask her for some and moisten it with warm water. No milk. I'll close up in a few hours and be out."

Gage disconnected the called and shifted his gaze toward Leah. "Well, there's good news and bad."

She dipped her chin and cocked her head to one side. "What?"

"Justin's guessing he's about five weeks, which means he *can* eat solid food if it's moistened but..." She glared at him when he paused. "You're going to need to go ask Jessie for some food."

He saw the relief flood her face, and her lips actually quirked into a genuine smile as she passed the kitten off to him. "Jerk. I already asked Jessie for food to try to coax him out earlier."

She reached for a plastic lunch bag in the cupboard and poured some of the food into a bowl.

"Justin said to use warm water."

She dribbled enough water into the bowl to make the food slightly soupy. "You think that's enough?"

"I have no clue." He shrugged with a quiet chuckle. "I'm as lost as you are."

She brought the food back, setting the bowl on the floor as he put the kitten in front of it. The poor thing must have been starving because he immediately hurried over, lapping at the water, halfway climbing into the bowl, attacking the food with relish.

"Look at that," he teased, leaning his hip against the kitchen counter. "You saved him."

Leah smiled broadly, her eyes lighting up with pleasure. She leaned over the small island, crossing her arms on the counter, and watched the kitten. Her ponytail flipped over her shoulder and as a few long strands fell forward into her face, she blew them back. For the first time since he'd met her on the side of the road, she looked happy and relaxed.

"I guess I did…well, *we* did." Her gaze lifted slowly to meet his. "Thanks for helping me."

It was the first concession she'd offered him, and he wanted to believe it was genuine, that maybe they could leave the territory of coexistence and arrive at a place of friendship.

"Wow, twice in one week. Careful, you might make it a habit." He gave her a quick wink.

She straightened and he could see the battle within her. At first she seemed confused, but he recognized the moment she realized she'd let her guard down. And she wasn't sure whether or not to put it back up. He liked this Leah, the woman beneath the smoke screen. Gage looked back at the kitten, not wanting her to feel pressured into putting her walls back up, and saw him move away from the half-empty bowl of food.

"Looks like he's done." The kitten opened his mouth in a wide yawn and stretched. "And needs a nap."

He chuckled and scooped him up from the floor, walking with him to her couch and settling himself into the corner.

"Won't you make yourself at home?" She crossed her arms over her chest and stared at him pointedly, her aggravation plain.

He shot her a sheepish, albeit slightly cocky, grin. "Don't mind if I do." As the kitten curled under his chin, against his chest, he reached a hand out and pat the couch beside him. Leah arched a dubious brow his direction and tipped her chin, scowling at him. He smiled broadly.

"I'm not going to bite, Leah. You're too purrfect. Get it? See what I did there? Ah?"

The irritation in her eyes was immediately replaced by amusement, even though she tried to hide it. The corners of her pursed lips twitched as she tried to keep from smiling. "That was terrible."

Gage laughed and saw her shoulders relax. "I have a million of them, each one better than the last."

She held up a hand. "Please, spare me. Bad puns are my downfall."

"I hope you know CPR, because you're taking my breath away." She groaned and he laughed again. "I think I'll keep going until you take a seat."

"Fine, just please stop." She dropped onto the couch but made sure there was an entire cushion between them. "You're quite the player, aren't you?"

Gage stuck out his lower lip, rubbing two fingers over the kitten kneading his shoulder. "Not really. I just like to have fun."

"And pickup lines are fun? Toying with women's emotions is *fun*?"

He was treading dangerous territory with her. He could see it in those whiskey-colored eyes and the way they seemed to be lit from an unseen flame within. She thought she had him pegged but she was wrong.

"I don't toy with people, ever. I'm not into teasing women, one-night stands, or meaningless relationships, but I do like to talk to people. I don't think there's anything wrong with making a woman feel good about herself and pickup lines are funny. If I can give someone a compliment, even if it's cheesy, why not?"

Leah leaned back in the couch, tipping her chin up and looking down her nose at him. It wasn't difficult to see she didn't believe him. "You're a pretty cynical person, Leah. Let's pretend we're at a bar. You're having your drink, and I walk up and say, 'Excuse me, are you a photographer? Because every time I look at you, I can't help but smile.' Is that really going to make you tear your clothes off and jump into bed with me, fighting off visions of marriage?"

She pinched her lips together, trying not to smile. "No, probably not."

"What if I said, 'Honey, I think they're going to ask you to leave soon. You're making all the other women look bad'?"

Leah snorted, then blushed. "Those are so bad."

He shrugged, dislodging the kitten and earning a soft mew of protest. A rumbling purr broke out against his neck as the kitten cuddled closer and closed his eyes. "It's all in the delivery."

"You put him to sleep." She reached across the couch and rubbed the soft fur on the kitten's head, her fingers brushing against Gage's jaw.

Even over the scent of dust coating the kitten curled at his neck, he could detect the clean scent of soap coupled with the slight muskiness of Leah's skin, and he felt a slow heat building in him, spiraling outward.

"I think he likes you." Her voice was slightly breathless, but sweet.

Hopefully he's not the only one.

"That just proves I'm a good guy."

"Does it, now?" One corner of her mouth lifted again. He'd seen her smile more this morning than over the past several days. "It could just mean he doesn't know the difference between good and not good. He *is* just a kitten."

"Nope," Gage assured her. "Animals know. Ask Julia or Jessie. They'll tell you that animals can sense things, better than people can."

As soon as the words slipped past his lips, he regretted them. The smile died on her lips and her eyes flared again as she pulled her hand back. "Then maybe you should take him. The two of you can be a couple of good guys together."

He wasn't sure exactly why she was angry but he knew it had everything to do with what he'd said. Somehow, he'd managed to insult her. The woman could change moods like a light switch. Instead of annoying him, he found her intriguing.

He kicked off his shoes and settled deeper into the corner of her couch, determined to make her realize that he wasn't a threat. "Nope, he picked your place and that's where he belongs."

"He likes you better."

Gage tipped his chin to one side, the kitten's fur tickling his cheek, and smiled at her confidently as an idea dawned on him. "Then I guess we'll be coparenting the little guy. You're going to just have to get used to having me around more often."

LEAH WOKE TO a paw tapping gently against her nose. She opened one eye and stared into the sweet face of the Siamese kitten she'd begun calling Puma after he spent most of the night trying to attack her feet.

"You are a pain in the butt," she informed him. He simply cocked his head to one side and put a paw over her mouth, effectively curtailing her playful insult.

His nap on Gage yesterday had only served to give him a burst of energy when Justin arrived last night and pronounced him a completely healthy seven-week-old kitten before giving him his first set of shots and a bath. At least now he smelled better. As if reading her mind, he head-butted her on the chin and let out a pitiful yowl of protest.

"Okay," she said, pulling him from her face. "Let's get you some breakfast before you starve."

As if he could understand her, Puma bounded from her bed and leapt to the floor, scuttling out the door ahead of her. He bounced over her feet as she walked down the hall to the kitchen and attacked her bare toes as she pulled the bag of food Justin had left for him from the cupboard.

"Will you stop, you little pill?" She reached down and picked him up, rubbing her nose against his as a rumbling purr sounded from his throat. She tucked him into the crook of her arm and reached for his bowl when a knock sounded at her door. "That better not be who I think it is because there is no reason for him to be here this early."

Setting Puma and his bowl on the floor in the entry, Leah opened the door. She rolled her eyes when she saw Gage standing on her porch, holding out a cup of steaming coffee and a smile. "Good morning, Sunshine."

"I think I might have to kill you."

"You hear that, little man?" Gage didn't wait for an invitation and walked into her entry, scooping the kitten from the floor and pressing the mug of coffee into her hand. "Your mom is threatening me again."

"I'm only letting you live because you brought me this." She took a long sip of the brew. "I need it after last night."

Gage eyed her, his gaze sliding over the loose T-shirt and yoga pants she'd slept in. "Long night with Junior?"

"Every time I fell asleep, he'd pounce on my feet. For such a sweet kitten, he's got some sharp claws."

Gage chuckled quietly. "Well, I'm sorry to come over so early but Dave called. He said the part came in yesterday and he'll have the car ready for you today. If you want, I can drive you into town so you can pick it up. I thought while we were there, we could pick up a few things for this little guy, too."

Anxiety burrowed deep into her chest, and she tried to hide it by taking another sip of coffee. She didn't have the money to pay for her car repairs yet, let alone to buy anything for Puma. Her solitary credit card had been maxed out before she arrived, and she only had a few hundred dollars to her name, which the auto shop would wipe out easily. Maybe she should ask Jessie for an advance. Not a lot but enough to pay for the car repairs. She cringed at the thought of approaching her boss of a mere few days and asking for money.

That will make you look like a real winner.

Gage eyed her speculatively. "Go, get ready. I'll take this little guy out to use the bathroom, and then I'll buy you breakfast."

"I don't think—"

"Not asking you to think about it," he interrupted, reaching for her shoulder to turn her around and press her toward the hallway. "Now, go before I change my mind and just take this little guy to breakfast instead."

"Puma," she said as she made her way back down the hall to her bedroom.

"Puma? They're sleek, and he's nothing but a cotton ball."

"Yeah, well, let him attack your feet all night and see if you don't change your tune."

Leah heard the front door shut as Gage took the kitten outside and grabbed a towel before turning on the shower, trying to figure out the best way to sneak off to find Jessie without Gage realizing what she was doing. She could only imagine what he already thought of her. He already thought she was bitchy; she didn't want to tell him she was broke, too.

Slipping under the warm spray, Leah tipped her head backward and lathered up her hair. She knew she shouldn't care what Gage thought. He was a visitor at the ranch and only for a short time. In reality, he was more of a nomad than she was, and she found herself wondering what his story was.

He didn't seem like the kind of guy who'd just hang out on a ranch for a month. He'd said he was here to visit his brother, and Jessie had mentioned that he was overseeing a new office opening in San Francisco, but so far, he hadn't left the ranch long enough to even drive to the Bay Area, let alone oversee anything. Not that it was any of her business where he went. Nor was she going to let him know that she was watching his comings and goings.

In truth, she *was* watching for him, and that detail had her more than irritated with herself. Gage had stayed at her house until Justin left last night, well after nine, but even as she escorted him to the door, she found herself wanting to ask him to stay longer. As much as she wanted to deny it, she was having a difficult time keeping her guard up when Gage was around.

He was endearing in a way she thought she'd never feel about another person, let alone someone who was practically a stranger. But she liked that he didn't press her to talk about her past when it came up. He seemed content to let her talk as much or as little as she chose to, which made her almost feel like she could open up to him without judgment—something she hadn't felt since Nicole.

And he made her laugh, a genuine laugh. That was something she hadn't done, hadn't even felt the urge to do, since she was a very little girl. Back when she was young and naive, before she'd recognized her mother's addiction and why the men were really coming around. Before they began to notice her.

"Leah, you might want to hurry up."

She jumped at the sound of Gage's voice from just outside her bedroom door. She'd locked it but it wasn't like that would stop him if he decided he wanted to barge in. She felt a fearful shiver run down her spine.

"Stay out!" she yelled.

"I am, but we have a little…complication."

Leah hurried to rinse and wrap herself in a towel. She knew she didn't have to, but she edged to the door to make sure it was still locked before pulling on her clothes. She brushed her teeth quickly before running a hairbrush through the tangled wet mess of hair before giving up and letting her natural waves take over.

As she headed back into the kitchen, she could hear Gage talking to Puma. "What's the problem now?"

"You don't have a litterbox, so I took him outside and…" Gage turned to face her, but it only took her a moment to realize that he wasn't talking to Puma as she first thought. Gage held two kittens, one in each arm, trying to keep them from batting at one another.

"Someone made a friend."

Leah felt her heart skip a beat. Never, in her life, had she ever seen anything as heart-wrenchingly seductive as this muscle-bound man playing referee for two tiny kittens.

"Oh!" She reached forward and took the newest addition, running her hand over the darker stripes in the cream-colored fur. This one was just as fluffy but had what appeared to be a reverse mustache on its face. The kitten instantly began to purr in her hands, rolling onto its back while she rubbed its chin.

"Meet Lynx. I'm guessing this must be a sibling. She crawled out from under the house while I was outside."

"She?"

"I don't know." He shrugged. "He, she…does it matter? Now you have *two* kittens."

"Two? I barely got any sleep with one."

"I'll tell you what. Let's lock these two in the bathroom so they can't cause any damage to the house, and we'll talk about what to do with them on the way into town." He scooped the second kitten into his large hand and carried them both to the hall bathroom while she got them food and water.

She narrowed her gaze at his back as they walked to his car. "Why do I get the feeling I'm about to be conned?"

"By who, me?" Gage chucked but the mischievous glint in his eyes did nothing to dispel her skepticism.

She'd seen first-hand the way he could lay it on thick when he wanted to. However, instead of the annoyance that usually rose in her chest, she found herself curious about his proposition. Leah bit the corner of her lip nervously, trying to force herself back to a place of annoyance with him. Any sort of warming to him was a dangerous change—one she'd need to nip in the bud.

Chapter Seven

LEAH STARED OUT the window, avoiding conversation, as Gage barreled down the two-lane stretch of highway into town. The roar of the engine as he gunned it drew the corner of her mouth up slightly in an amused grin. His Challenger was nice, but even he knew it didn't compare to power in her GTO. He felt a quick sense of camaraderie at their shared interest in muscle cars and almost asked how she'd developed such a keen sense of car taste when she spoke up.

"You're being awfully secretive about this plan for the kittens."

"I don't think it's a good idea to split the pair up again."

"Obviously, neither of us meant to the first time."

She sounded defensive and that wasn't his intention. She'd just begun to warm up to him last night, and he didn't want to go back to the blatant antagonism she'd had for him when he found her on the highway.

"Right, and we can't turn them back outside. I don't know if you heard them last night but there's a pack of coyotes nearby."

He saw her pale a bit when she realized what that would mean for two helpless kittens.

"But I can't keep them both unless I lock them out of the bedroom at night. One pouncing on me was bad enough. I can't imagine the trouble two might cause." She twisted her mouth to one side, thoughtfully. "And then there's the fact that I'm going to be working with kids soon for sessions in the office, so I can't exactly keep them in there."

"True."

"Maybe you should just take them both. It's not fair for me to keep them when they obviously like you better."

Gage didn't miss the note of sorrow in her voice as she made the suggestion. He'd seen the way she'd lit up when she played with Puma last night and again when Lynx curled against her. He wanted to see that look on her face more often and would do whatever he could to make it happen.

He laughed. "Leah, they're kittens. They like anyone who gives them attention. Lynx didn't stop purring until you put her down. My suggestion is that we keep them at your house with you during the day, and I'll take them at night. Then you can still sleep." He cleared his throat. "At least until I leave."

"What about you? You don't need to sleep?"

"For now, I have the freedom of sleeping whenever I want."

The unfortunate fact was that he was going to need to make a decision soon. If he continued to keep hiding the truth of his failure from his brother, he was bound to find out the truth and be even more disappointed in Gage. Dylan had already asked him about the security breach when he'd seen it reported on the news, but Gage had been able to put him off by changing the subject. But it was just a matter of time before Dylan figured out he was to blame.

"Are you trying to worm your way into my house by way of a pair of kittens? Is this just another one of your cheesy pickup methods?"

"You're not one to mince words, are you, Leah?" Gage smiled at her. "No. I'm not. We've already established that you're not my type, remember? I like my women to be less—"

"Intelligent? Confident, dignified?" she supplied with an arch of her brow, as if daring him to finish his sentence.

"Blunt," he answered with a laugh. "But you definitely fit the bill for all of those. Like I said, you're a different kind of woman, Leah."

"Different." Her tone made it sound more like an insult.

"I don't know how to explain it." He took the exit that would lead them into town. "I guess it's because you seem wise and naive at the same time. You're what people would call an old soul, but there's a guilelessness about you. You're kind of an enigma." He glanced away from the road and saw confusion in her eyes, as if she wasn't sure whether he was insulting her or giving her a compliment. "That's a good thing, Leah."

"Old soul, huh?" He saw a mask slip over her face as she tried to hide her irritation and turned toward the window. "You have no idea."

Gage looked at her. He recognized that tone. He'd heard it often enough after Dylan had returned from Afghanistan, when his brother had tried to give up, to give in to the nightmarish memories. There was pain in her voice, the agony of trauma held silent for too long. He knew everyone fought demons, but the thought that something in her past had wounded her so deeply made him physically ill.

"I might not be a therapist, but if you ever want someone to talk to, Leah, I'd be happy to listen."

She turned toward him slowly, her eyes filled with bitterness. "Talking about a wound doesn't always heal it."

"Odd thing for a therapist to say."

"Or maybe I just understand the limitations of my profession."

WHAT IN THE hell was wrong with her? Leah had never felt this burning urge to tell someone about her past—never. Not her own therapist, not any of her foster parents. Even Nicole had been forced to pry every detail from her, and she'd actually come as close to loving Nicole as a person could without coming out and saying the words.

Love.

What a pathetic waste of a breath. The idea was nothing more than a fantasy that kept weak people happily believing in fairy tales and hoping for someone who would actually give a shit about them when life got tough.

Love was a hopeless waste of energy. She'd rather spend her time caring.

Caring about someone was active. It required action and proof. It involved a decision on her part. She wasn't helpless, prone to some whim of fate to fall for some person, regardless of any choice she might make. She'd spent enough time unable to dictate the course of her life. She wasn't about to let some nonsense about *love* steal any more control from her.

Gage pulled the car to a stop in the parking lot of a small strip mall and turned to face her, twining his fingers with hers. Leah tried to ignore the wave of warmth that began at her fingertips and worked up her arms before flooding her veins. It spread slowly, heating as it traveled to her chest, relaxing her like a drug. And it scared her.

This wasn't the butterflies in her stomach or the sharp jolt of lust she'd heard so many women talk about. She'd never felt any sort of attraction to a man, had never been given that opportunity. But this wasn't the hunger she'd heard others describe when talking about a man.

There was something sweet and tender in Gage's touch, something gentle and filled with promise but in no way demanding. She'd never been touched by a man in a way that didn't lead to sex. But Gage's warm hand, covering hers, was supportive and comforting rather than insistent and domineering. She wasn't sure how to react, but she knew she was uncomfortable, nervous even, and she slid her hand from his grasp, wiping her palm on her pant leg in an effort to erase the slow burn of longing.

"Maybe you just need to practice what you preach?" he suggested, eyeing her hand against her thigh.

"Maybe you need to mind your own business."

The corner of his mouth lifted in a sad smile. "Probably."

He let the conversation drop, which surprised her. Most people would have pushed for more information. Gage turned toward the pet store in front of them.

"Breakfast first or cat supplies?"

She frowned across the car at him. "Look, Gage, I don't know what you're trying to do but..."

"I'm not trying to do anything, Leah." He let out a long sigh. "I guess I just assumed that you might need a helping hand. Between the car repair and moving somewhere new...I told you. I'm just trying to do something nice."

He slid out of the car and slammed the door shut, heading for the pet store without her.

"Wait a minute." She jumped out of the car and ran after him, reaching for his arm.

"What? Do you want to scold me for bringing you coffee this morning, too? No matter what I do, I can't win with you. I swear, you are the most disagreeable woman I've ever met."

Leah crossed her arms and narrowed her gaze at him. "Thanks."

"Just calling it like I see it."

"Right, because everyone offers to pay a thousand dollar repair bill on a stranger's car. Not to mention buy them groceries and take them to breakfast." She dipped her chin, not caring if he saw her skepticism. "Not with-out expecting *something* in return."

"I guess that says a lot about the people you're accus-tomed to, doesn't it?"

"What is it with you? Some overblown need to be a knight in shining armor?"

"For someone who listens for a living, you sure don't hear very well." He shook his head and shoved his way through the doors, leaving her standing on the sidewalk, watching his departing back.

Leah clenched her jaw. Maybe he *was* just being nice. Jessie said he was some bigwig IT CEO, so maybe he had money to throw around. Hell, for all she knew, he was planning to write it off as a charitable donation.

But the gnawing doubt in her gut said this was more, that he had some ulterior motive for helping her. The sim-ple fact was that she had little choice other than accepting his generosity. She hadn't been able bring herself to ask Jessie for a loan, and she certainly didn't have the cash to pay for her car repairs. Right now, Gage's offer was the only viable option she had, but she'd be damned if she was going to backtrack and start paying for anything with her body again.

GAGE IGNORED THE urge to turn around and see if Leah was following him inside. He was tired of fighting with her, of trying to convince her that he had pure intentions, when she was bound to continue assuming the worst about him. Being a nice guy, willing to help someone out, wasn't a bad thing, regardless of how she made it sound.

It didn't mean he had some need to be a hero. But there was a part of him that knew he was lying to himself. He did want to see her look at him with gratitude.

No, that wasn't exactly it either. There was something about Leah, something fragile beneath the shell, even if she denied it, but it was there and made him want to be protective, to take care of her, to be her rescuer. It didn't make sense since he barely knew her, but he'd seen that hollow emptiness in her eyes, and he wanted to show her that the void could be filled.

"Gage?"

Leah's voice was quiet from the end of the aisle, and he looked away from the litter pans to see her walking toward him. "I'm sorry. I guess I'm just projecting my past experiences on my current situation, and you got caught in the crossfire."

Her words sounded like something she would have asked a patient to recite, like the words had come from her mouth many times and held little, if any, emotion. It sounded rehearsed, like a role she was playing, and he wasn't buying it, but he also didn't want to antagonize her further. He wasn't sure how to respond.

"Did you hear me?"

"I did." He quickly decided that the best tactic would be to ignore her outburst. "Why don't you pick out some toys for the kids?" He walked back to the litter pans and dropped two into the cart, looking over the broad selection of litter. "How do I even know what kind to get?" he complained.

"Want me to ask someone for help?"

Gage rolled his eyes at her. "You're a therapist and I have an IQ of one-sixty. I think we can put our heads together and figure it out."

"So sorry, Einstein." She held up her hands dramatically. "I didn't realize I was coparenting with a genius."

Leah turned back toward the cat toys, pulling some sort of feathered wand off the wall. "Once you figure out the litter, how about a little help over here? I have no idea what they would like."

"Yeah," he muttered as he scanned the twenty different types of litter on the shelves. "I'm feeling a little overwhelmed over here, too. I don't know whether we need litter for multiple cats, or this one with scent-blocking. Maybe this natural one? Or natural pellets?" He held up the bag for her to judge.

"Natural cat litter? Face it, smarty-pants, we're both pretty much out of our league here."

He threw his hands into the air. "How would I know? I've never had a cat before."

Leah spotted a clerk walking past and reached for her arm. "Can you help us? I just found two kittens, and I have no clue what I'm doing or what we need to buy."

The clerk, a young girl who looked fresh out of high school, smiled. "Aw, I love kittens." She glanced down the aisle at Gage. "Are you two together?"

Maybe, if we could ever seem to see eye to eye.

Gage knew the clerk was asking if they were shopping for items together, but he couldn't help but relate the question to his relationship with Leah so far. He was trying so hard to find some sort of common ground with her, but she seemed to balk at every turn, pushing away every olive branch he extended in her direction. It was exhausting.

"Yes," Leah answered without waiting for him to respond. "We just aren't sure what we need for the pair of rascals."

The clerk smiled and bounced down the aisle. "Well, you've got litter boxes, but I'd suggest getting one of the automatic ones, unless you like cleaning it, a lot. With two kittens, you're going to need two, too."

Gage stepped back from the selection of cat litter. "Have at it. Whatever they need."

The clerk's smile brightened by several watts, and Gage wondered if she wasn't working on commission. She looked like a kid on Christmas morning when he'd practically told her money was no object. The girl lifted the litter box he'd selected from the cart and replaced it with two new automatically cleaning litter boxes. Then she proceeded to pluck several bags of litter from the shelf.

"You need this specific kind to go with this box," she explained. "And you'll need an extra filter for each. What kind of kittens are they?"

Leah looked at Gage as if she expected him to know.

"Our vet said they're part Siamese."

The girl giggled at him. "No, I mean, are they long-haired or short-haired?"

"Oh, they're both pretty fluffy," Leah answered.

"Okay, then you'll need a brush and nail clippers." She pulled a few more items from the shelf. "Why don't you pick out a few toys?"

"Um." Leah hesitated. "I'm not sure what to get."

"Oh, anything from there. I don't think there's anything on that wall kittens *won't* play with." She looked at Gage, her gaze skimming him quickly. "And you need to come with me so we can pick out some sort of scratching post for your two angels."

Gage looked back at Leah. That smile he'd hoped to see on her face again lit her eyes as she selected several toys for Puma and Lynx. He was hoping it was a sign that she was going to let her guard down today. In fact, she actually looked like she was having fun. Right now, she wasn't worried about the fact that it was his money. She was focused on the joy of buying something special for the kittens, and it made him swell with pride a little that he could be the one to coax that smile from her. Even if it was via two fluffy, rambunctious kittens.

Chapter Eight

"ARE YOU KIDDING me?" Leah gasped as she stared at the register when their cashier totaled the purchases.

Gage chuckled and handed over his card, bumping her with his hip. "Hush, it's for Puma and Lynx. Let me spoil them."

Leah bit the inside corner of her lip. Gage said "them," but the look he gave her said something different. His eyes were shimmering with delight, and a wide smile split his face. Everything about his body language said he was doing this for her, not the kittens, and she wasn't sure how it made her feel.

On one hand, it was exciting. She'd never had a man want to do anything for her. *To* her, but never *for* her, and she was surprised at the way it made her feel—protected, cared for, and like she mattered for a change. His eyes didn't look at her with lust but with a warmth that set her at ease. Being around Gage had the same effect on her as a glass of red wine and a warm bubble bath, and she found herself wanting to slip into the depths of the feeling, to find out what else might be different about Gage.

On the other hand, that feeling was exactly why he was dangerous. No other man had ever made her feel that way, and she wasn't about to let down her guard and chance drowning in the river of self-loathing that would follow giving in. Men like him were used to getting their way, using their money to make sure their demands were met. She'd seen it too often when she was younger. Hell, she'd used it to her own advantage before Nicole showed her a better way. She wasn't about to let this rich playboy con her, or drag her back to the dredges of who she'd once been. This was probably his MO—to set her at ease, buying her things and then demanding payment later—and she wasn't about to be a conquest for anyone ever again.

If he wanted to spend money on the kittens, she'd let him. But she wasn't going to be indebted to him any longer than she needed to be. She needed to pay him back for the car and the groceries as soon as she possibly could.

"You okay?" His question dragged her back to the present, and she looked up to see the concern in his deep chocolate eyes.

"Yeah, why?"

"I don't know. You got this faraway look in your eyes, like you were thinking about something. Like you're upset."

She plucked the bag of cat toys from his hands. "I'm fine. Let's just get finished and get to the auto shop."

He frowned for a moment then let a grin split his lips. "Well, you might not be hungry, but I'm ravenous, so I'm having breakfast first."

"Okay but if we hurry up at the grocery store and Dave's, we can get back to the ranch and just eat there."

You in your place and me in mine.

"Or we could just go eat and then get groceries. And since I drove, you're at my mercy." He gave her a playful wink.

That was exactly the problem, and since he was the one paying for her car, she really had no choice but to follow his lead. She didn't like being at anyone's mercy, especially this man who insisted on making her feel things she'd shut herself off from feeling after Nicole died.

Leah sighed loudly and pushed her way past him. "Fine, let's just get this over with, then."

He followed her out the door. "Leah, are you this friendly with everyone, or am I just one of the lucky ones?" She rolled her eyes at him and he chuckled. "So, the lucky *one*."

Gage pushed the cart out to his car and loaded their bags into the trunk. He paused, looking from the cat tree to the car and back again. The cat tree was at least a foot too wide to fit sideways in the trunk, and she waited to see what he was going to do.

"Didn't exactly plan that one out, did you, genius?"

"Ye of little faith," he said as he opened the passenger door and bent into the car. "There." He smiled at her broadly. "You think you have me all figured out, don't you, Leah? But I'm full of surprises."

"I'm sure you are."

She was trying to sound patronizing, but it was almost like he'd been reading her earlier thoughts. The fact was, just when she thought she had a handle on him, he would do something that would throw her for a loop. And she didn't like it, not one bit.

Leah watched his biceps strain against the seam of his shirt as he slid the heavy item into the car. She tried to ignore the flash of desire that was threatening to burst in her. Leah forced herself to tamp it down quickly. Lust was for the weak, and she wasn't pathetic.

"There." Gage shut the door, then the trunk, and locked the car. He ran a hand over his flat stomach. "I'm wasting away. Let's eat."

Leah shook her head at him and walked ahead to the diner. A bell tinkled over the door, announcing their entrance, and a waitress called from across the room for her to sit anywhere, informing Leah she'd be right there. Leah deliberately picked the only empty booth in the middle of the busiest section of the diner. She hoped it would be too loud for them to even try to hold a conversation. They could just hurry up and finish eating, so she could return to the safety of her little house on the ranch and send Gage home.

"Here?" Gage asked, sliding into the booth seat across from her.

"Does it matter?"

"I guess not." He watched her closely. "Relax, Leah. Are you always this tense?"

"Are you always this nosy?"

He laughed, a deep rich sound that vibrated through her, making her nerve endings sizzle. "This isn't me being nosy. I'm just afraid you might have an anxiety attack, and I want to be prepared to handle it."

She glared across the table at him. "I'm fine," she repeated for the umpteenth time since meeting him, grateful for the sudden appearance of their waitress.

"Hey Gage, about time you came back in." The woman had at least ten years on Gage, but he greeted her with a wide smile as she slid menus onto the table. "I heard rumors that you were back in town. Business or pleasure?"

The woman's voice was a seductive purr, and Leah didn't miss the wink she shot Gage. She wondered if this was the type of reaction he'd expected to receive from her. If so, he'd better settle in for a long wait.

"Visiting with Dylan and Julia, but I also have business in San Francisco, if I can ever motivate myself to leave town long enough to get there." His gaze fell on Leah as the waitress set two coffee cups in front of them. "This is Leah's first time into the Rusty Nail. She's going to be working out at Jessie's place."

Leah half-expected a catty glare from the waitress but was greeted with a warm laugh instead. "Are you the doctor Jessie's been bragging about? She was in yesterday to pick up some burgers and couldn't stop talking about you."

"I…well…" Leah wasn't sure how to respond. No one around here reacted the way she expected them to, making her wonder if she was the odd one.

"I'm Jillian, and my husband, Craig, works the grill. Since this is your first time here, don't even bother with menus. I'll have Craig whip you up his specialty—biscuits and gravy. Sound good?" She poured steaming coffee the color of tar into the mugs. The bitter scent of the brew wafted up to her, and she almost cringed.

"I'm up for it if Leah is." Gage lifted his eyebrows in question.

She caught a glimpse of Gage's grin, his eyes twinkling, and she saw the challenge in them. Anything smothered in gravy didn't sound too appetizing, but Jillian seemed so excited for her to try it, and Gage looked so sure she wouldn't that she wasn't about to give him the satisfaction by saying no.

"Sure. I'd love some biscuits and gravy." She met Gage's gaze with a daring one of her own. "I've never had it, so I can't wait."

As Jillian took their order to the kitchen, Gage leaned forward. "I hope you like pepper."

"It's okay, why?"

"Because Craig's biscuits and gravy have more pepper than any I've ever tasted. Delicious, but whoa."

"Now you tell me?" Gage shrugged innocently as she let out a heavy sigh. "You're exasperating. Do you realize that?"

"I do." He picked up his coffee and leaned against the back of the booth, giving her a quick wink. "But you love it."

"No, I don't," she argued. "You think that because other women fall victim to that charming smile and those stupid dimples, that they can't see right through this act of yours. You're just a spoiled little rich boy who thinks he can just take whatever he decides he wants. Well, I'm not going to be a part of your harem."

She hadn't planned to go off on him, but his comment had lit a fuse inside her and she hadn't been able to snuff it before her mouth ran away. Gage's smile immediately faded, his eyes clouding as he clenched his jaw and looked out the window. The hurt she could see in his eyes stopped her tirade cold. She might as well have thrown ice water into his face. Now that she'd blasted him with every negative thought she'd had about him today, her mouth didn't seem nearly as inclined to come up with an apology.

GAGE WAS DONE being Leah's punching bag, finished taking whatever crap she wanted to cast his direction. He'd done everything in his power to be nice to her, but this infuriating woman seemed inclined to only see what she wanted to. He took a deep breath, trying to control the feelings of hurt, disbelief, and anger that seemed to take turns rising to the surface. He would just seem to get one emotion under control when another would take over, and none were content to completely release the hold on him.

He shook his head. "I'm glad you aren't my therapist because you make some wild assumptions."

"Am I wrong?" She didn't sound worried in the slightest that she might be. In fact, she sounded downright cocky in her supposition.

"You couldn't be farther from the truth. My brother and I grew up broke as shit with a father who'd rather drink than be around us. When he was, we wished he wasn't. He'd just find a reason to beat one of us anyway, so we were better off with him gone. Even before he disappeared for good, it was up to Dylan and me to take care of Mom."

He saw the guilt flicker in her eyes as she looked into her coffee mug, unwilling to meet his gaze. She couldn't have possibly known about his childhood, but it pissed him off that she hadn't even tried to see past the man in front of her.

"Dylan joined the military and paid for anything I couldn't get financial aid to cover in college, so I made sure to use my degree to get us out of the mess we were in." He looked out the window again and took a sip of his coffee, surprised the brew tasted less bitter than his anger. "And you're going to sit there and fault me for rising beyond the crappy circumstances I had growing up because I made a good life afterward? Should I do the same to you?"

"I didn't know," she said, refusing to look at him.

"No, you didn't, and you didn't bother to ask. You're so busy judging me that you actually know absolutely nothing about me."

"I'm sorry."

"It doesn't even matter. I've been busting my ass to try to be a friend to you, but you don't want one. You want to be an island, be one." He tugged his wallet from his back pocket and dropped a twenty on the table. "I'll go pay for your car repairs and you can head back whenever you want."

He rose to leave but felt her fingers tremble against his forearm and he looked down. Heat radiated up his arms from her touch.

"I said, I'm sorry. I really am." She shook her head and brushed her bangs back from her face with one hand. "I don't know why I…I'm sorry," she finished with a whisper.

Gage slid back into the booth but leaned back and crossed his arms over his chest. "Is it something I did? Because I already apologized about the comment I made. It really was about the car."

"No." Leah ran a hand over her eyes, sweeping her hair back. "I just…I haven't had a lot of good experiences with men."

When she lifted her gaze to meet his, he could see the honesty in the amber depths. And fear. There seemed to be far more that she could tell him, but she was still holding back. Then the panic was gone, disappearing as she cleared her throat. "That's still no excuse to take it out on you. I shouldn't have said those things. I apologize."

Gage wasn't letting her off that easily. He leaned forward, his forearms pressing against the cool Formica tabletop as he reached for her still trembling hand. "I told you before, I might not be a therapist, but I'm a great listener if you ever want to talk."

She slid her hand from his grasp. "Gage, I'm here to do a job, that's all. I don't want you to—"

He laughed, cutting her off. "What? Get the wrong idea? Leah, you've made it perfectly clear, even if I was attracted to you, you have no interest. I'm not dense. Hello, one-sixty IQ, remember?" He smiled sadly as he leaned into the back cushion and reached for his coffee, tipping the cup her direction. "But you can have friends. That is a *thing* you know."

"Friends?" She didn't look convinced.

Gage raised a hand, trying to keep a straight face. "I, Gage Granger, solemnly swear, that I am only interested in being a friend to one Miss Leah McCarran."

Jillian chose that moment to return bearing two giant plates of biscuits and gravy in her arms. "Well, that's just a crying shame." She looked from one to the other and gave Gage a wink. "You're missing out then, Gage, because she's a beauty."

Gage didn't miss the way a blush crept over Leah's cheeks, staining them pink. Jillian wasn't wrong. Leah was beautiful. But something, or someone, had hurt her and the scars were deep. He wasn't even sure she realized the full depth of them. However, she'd made it abundantly clear, she didn't want help, not from him. Not with this or anything else.

But he couldn't help teasing her, either. "Don't blame me, Jillie. I have eyes. She's the one rejecting me." Gage waved a finger at Leah, across the table.

Jillian turned toward Leah then back to him with a broad grin, her eyes lighting up. "Yeah, darlin', I'm sure she's breaking your heart. Your regular pickup lines aren't going to work on her. That just means this one has a brain in her head and you need to work harder to impress her."

Leah laughed, out loud, for the first time since they'd met. It was a husky sound, relaxing and inviting, warming his insides, heating his blood, and Gage felt desire pool in him, curling slowly within him and spreading outward as he watched her eyes light with merriment.

Ah, hell. This is not *how you're supposed to feel about your friends, Granger.*

Chapter Nine

LEAH COULDN'T HELP but feel relieved as she slid behind the wheel of her car. Twisting the key, the engine roared to life, the deep rumble vibrating through the car like a purr. She loved this car and the freedom it had symbolized for her, but its sentimental value was something she couldn't put a price on. It was Nicole's final gift to her, from the hospital room where she took her last breath. Leah inhaled deeply, fighting back tears as she remembered the woman who'd changed her life.

If not for Nicole, she'd have eventually ended up traveling the same destructive path of addiction her mother had, a life filled with drugs and prostitution that fed the beast.

But Nicole had taken her away from all of it. Not the way other foster parents had, letting her bounce in and out of the system, always returning to her mother in spite of her pleas to never go back. Nicole had listened and made sure the judge listened. She'd also made sure Leah received everything from her estate, giving her a chance to make it through a good college. The inheritance she'd left for Leah had been enough to see her through when she fell short in spite of her two jobs and financial aid. Nicole had made her understand that hard work wasn't something to run from and her determination would be rewarded.

"I miss you, Nicole," she whispered, running her hand over the pebbled vinyl dash. "I hope you'd be proud of me, striking out, taking this job."

Leah knew she wouldn't approve of the way Leah had treated Gage. *Everyone deserves a fair wiggle*, she'd say. *You can't judge a book by your past.*

Leah smiled sadly, recalling how Nicole always seemed to quote every idiom incorrectly. It was just part of her charm and everyone loved her.

Just like everyone loves Gage.

Leah could practically hear Nicole's voice scolding her for her brash, judgmental attitude.

"Okay, okay. I'll make it up to him," she said, as if Nicole could hear her. "You're a bossy ghost, you know."

She backed the car out of the parking lot of the auto shop and followed Gage down the highway, heading back to the ranch. She knew Nicole was somewhere, watching her and, more often than not, proud of the changes she'd made in her life. But it wasn't like her to act this way, and she wasn't sure why Gage seemed to trigger it. He hadn't actually done anything to deserve it. Well, other than a misunderstood comment on the side of the road.

Just the thought of him conjured up images in her mind. The man was sculpted perfection. She didn't think she'd ever seen a better looking man in real life. While he and Dylan looked similar, Gage bore none of Dylan's physical scars, or the dark brooding she'd seen in Dylan's eyes. Gage had an aura about him that exuded quiet charisma, a confident charm that simply drew people to him. He was friendly and funny and handsome.

She rolled her eyes at the way her brain and body kept returning to that fact.

Who was she kidding? Gage wasn't just handsome, he was downright sexy. It wasn't just the way he looked either. It was the way he carried himself. She'd known plenty of men, most of them far too intimately, who believed the way they dressed made them sexy. Gage just seemed to have magnetism oozing from his pores without even trying. And then there was the way he looked at her, despite his reassurances that he only wanted friendship. That wasn't what his eyes said.

Leah saw desire there. She'd seen it from men since she was ten, the first time her mother traded her for drugs. Leah had used that desirability many times over the next few years to survive but, for the first time, she found that instead of disgusting her, Gage's desire intrigued her. He made her want to acknowledge the yearning she felt for him and relish the emotions swirling inside like a confusing tidal wave, threatening to capsize her.

Gage signaled for the highway exit, and she saw him glance into his mirror, making sure she was still behind him. His consideration never failed to surprise her. Even at the grocery store, he'd been adamant that he purchase enough food for her to fill her cupboards for the next two weeks. She'd been planning on grabbing nothing more than a few cans of instant soup when he stilled her hand and dragged her to the meat department, selecting choice cuts for her and himself. He'd even loaded her trunk for her.

"Dinner," she muttered to herself. "It's the least I can do to thank him. That's harmless enough."

When logic reminded her why she avoided most men, she steeled her resolve, focusing again on how Gage was different than men she'd been exposed to, ticking off the many times he'd helped her over the past few days. As they pulled down the long driveway, Gage stopped in front of her house, leaving his groceries in the car to help her unload hers.

"Don't worry about this. I can do it," she said, jumping out of her car. "Your freezer stuff will thaw."

"It's fine. I need to get the stuff out of my car for the kittens, too."

Leah reached for several bags at the same time he did and brushed her hand over his. The sizzle of electric heat traveled up her arm, shocking her and making goose bumps break out over her skin.

"Sorry," she said, pulling her hand back and letting him take the bags. "I'll just get the door."

Hurrying to the front door, Leah opened it just as the pair of kittens slid past the entry on their way across the tile floor, chasing one another.

"I thought the kittens were in the bathroom." She walked inside and surveyed her house. There was now a trail of toilet paper from the hallway, through the kitchen, to where it ended in a small, shredded pile on the living room floor.

"What in the world?" Gage stepped into the entry, careful to avoid the kitten who ran at his legs, trying to pounce on his feet. "I locked them in there. I—what the hell? Ow!"

Gage moved behind her but, apparently he hadn't noticed the kittens' rambunctious state. They were now climbing up his jeans, digging their claws through the denim into his knees.

Leah spun and squatted, plucking Lynx from his right leg as Puma continued to climb.

"Shit! Son of a—"

"Wait a second."

Gage didn't listen, hobbling past to drop the grocery bags on the kitchen sink and pulling the ball of fluff from near his hip pocket, lifting him to eye level. "Hey, Monster. You're probably making my leg bloody, you little pain in the butt."

The kitten meowed in answer and immediately began purring. "Here." Gage pressed the kitten toward Leah. "You hold them, and I'll get the rest of the things from the car. Then we'll clean up the mess they made."

She scanned the room. Several artificial plants were knocked over, with the decorative moss in tiny pieces spread across the living room floor. Somehow, they'd managed to drag the cord to the television from behind the entertainment center, and the magazines Jessie had left on the side table were strewn in shredded pieces through the living room and kitchen. Making her way down the hall, she found several *gifts* the pair had left her, and she was grateful it was on tile rather than carpet. She retrieved a new roll of toilet paper from the hall closet and cleaned up behind the kittens, locking them in her room temporarily.

"Since I don't know where you want things, why don't you come put the groceries away, and I'll finish cleaning up," Gage called.

Leah came back down the hall to see him already cleaning up the shredded paper with the broom and dustpan she'd stored beside the refrigerator. He looked up with a grimace. "I guess we should have gotten them a litter box sooner since they decided to make their own."

"Yeah, I already found a few presents myself." She moved to the sink to wash her hands as he dumped the paper into the trash. "Whose bright idea was it to bring in two kittens again?"

"That would be you, Dr. McCarran," he said with a laugh, as he moved into the living room and began stuffing moss back around the base of the plants. "You're just too kindhearted to leave the little devils outside to starve."

"Speaking of starving," Leah began, too embarrassed to turn around to see if he was looking at her. "I thought I'd make an early dinner. Something simple, like spaghetti, if you want to stay."

"Why Dr. McCarran, are you asking me out?"

"No, I—" Leah spun, her mouth falling open in protest, until she saw the wicked grin on Gage's face. "You're screwing with me."

"Yeah, I am. And you make it pretty easy." He carried the cat tree to the corner as she made her way down the hall to retrieve the kittens.

"Is that so?" She returned and plopped them into his hands. "Then you babysit while I cook."

THIS WAS WHAT he was reduced to? From running a multimillion dollar company to scooping litter boxes? The odd thing was that he didn't really mind.

Gage dropped one litter box in the utility room and carried the second one to the master bathroom as Leah had suggested. Both kittens followed him closely, pouncing on his feet the entire way. It made him feel awkward walking into her bedroom, even though he knew she'd just moved in, but it seemed too intimate considering this was the first time they'd actually gotten along since meeting. The scent of her hung in the air, sweet vanilla that marked the space as hers, and Gage couldn't help but take a deep breath. Longing kicked him in the groin, making him wish he hadn't inhaled at all.

He set the litter box down and Puma tried to leap in. "At least you know what you're doing with it," he muttered to the cat, walking back into the bedroom.

His eyes immediately strayed to the massive bed that engulfed the room. The head and foot board were knotted pine logs with intricately detailed wrought iron woven between. Strong yet delicate, like the woman who slept there.

"You taking a nap in there?"

Leah's voice carried from the kitchen, sounding surprisingly cheerful, and he wondered at the sudden change in her. He didn't want to jinx it by asking her about it, so he resigned himself to enjoy it while it lasted. That, however, didn't make him any less curious.

"Yeah, Puma's just testing things out." He wandered back down the hall, pausing at the bedroom that would double as her office once Jessie's campers started arriving. He walked inside and stopped in front of the degrees she'd hung on the wall.

"What are you doing?"

He turned to see her standing in the doorway, a dishtowel in her hands, and shrugged. "Fresno State, huh? Good school."

She pushed herself from the doorway and moved to straighten the frame, even though it didn't look crooked to him. "I guess. It was a friend's alma mater, and she was able to put in a good word for me."

"Where'd you do your residency?"

"UCSF, Fresno. I didn't really have the means to go anywhere else, and it offered what I needed." She slung the towel over her shoulder. "I couldn't afford the cost of living in the bigger cities and was already settled there so I stayed."

Gage eyed her. "Practical." He looked back at the wall, searching for pictures or mementos, something that might give him more insight into who this woman really was beneath the mask she slipped on and off. "No family pictures?"

He saw her jaw clench briefly before she moved to the bookshelf along the back wall and plucked a small frame from the middle. "I have this one."

Gage looked down at a young Leah wearing her cap and gown. "Your mother looks so young." He handed the picture back to her.

"Because that's not my mother. She was a good friend." She ran a hand over the glass before setting the picture back onto the shelf. "A great one. She's the reason I'm here today. Come on. Dinner will be finished as soon as the noodles are done." She turned quickly on her heel, heading into the hall.

Leah closed the discussion far too soon. She'd barely whet his appetite with that bit of information, just giving him a glimpse of the woman beneath the surface, and Gage wanted to know more. He was just going to have to become more creative with his methods of interrogation.

"I'LL DO THE dishes," Gage offered.

Leah pressed her hand on his shoulder. "Sit. It's my house and you're a guest. I'll do them."

She was trying to ignore the way her fingers tingled as they landed on his T-shirt and trying not to notice the firm muscles beneath the cotton. It was like the time she'd been shocked unplugging a toaster in her first apartment. The electricity traveled up her hand painlessly but surprised her. This little jolt was pleasantly unnerving and made her want to sigh, even though she wanted to curse her own stupidity as she carried the plates to the sink and rinsed them.

Gage was a damn fine specimen of the human male. Good looking, smart, and kind, and she was finding it difficult to remember what she'd learned the hard way over the years about men. How conniving and manipulative they could be, how overbearing and demanding. Gage was, in far too short a time, chipping away at the stereotype she'd constructed to label all men unsafe. He was a contradiction to the image she'd shaped, been forced to create in order to survive, and it was difficult to rationalize with the man seated at her table. It was easier, instead, to attempt a friendship and maintain a relationship within those boundaries. That she could do.

Now, if only her body would cooperate.

She could feel his eyes on her, watching her, unnerving her. Leah felt heat travel down her spine and across her shoulders, as if Gage was running a hand over her skin. It coiled, dark and twisted and wanton, low in her belly, heating parts of her she'd never wanted awakened, making her feel dirty again, used again, victimized again. The plate she was holding toppled from her hands and clattered against the bottom of the sink.

"You okay?" Gage asked, jumping up and coming to stand beside her.

Leah backed away from him, instinctively raising her hands to ward him off. "Stop."

She froze, knowing she was overreacting but unable to convince her mind that she wasn't being threatened. Instinct overruled her logic, and her body simply responded.

Gage took a step back. "Leah, you're fine. You're in your own house." He slowly tucked his hands into the front pockets of his jeans, where she could see them. "Look in my eyes. Take a deep breath with me."

Leah's heart was racing, her breath coming in shallow pants, as if she had just run miles. Meeting Gage's gaze, she could see his quiet composure, even in the face of her panic. She tried to do as he instructed.

"Good, now another."

He inhaled slowly, deeply, but never moved any closer toward her. His voice was soothing, easing the tension building in her chest, suffocating her. He took several breaths with her, and she was relieved when her heart rate slowed and the fear began to subside.

"Better?"

She nodded, not trusting herself to speak. Emotion choked her. It had been years since she'd suffered from an anxiety attack, years since she'd felt the trauma of her childhood overtake her.

"Go, sit down. I'll finish these."

Leah wanted to argue, wanted to remind him it was her house and he couldn't order her around, but she had no fight left. The panic attack had left her feeling weak and vulnerable. Her best option was to hide, unless she wanted to answer the questions she could see behind the empathy in his eyes.

Chapter Ten

GAGE LOADED THE dishwasher mechanically, listening for any sounds in the living room where he really wanted to be. Nothing but silence echoed through the house, and that worried him more than her fear. But as much as he knew she needed her privacy, it had taken every bit of his self-control not to try to reach for Leah when he'd seen the terror in her eyes. She hadn't even seen him.

He knew that look. He'd seen it often enough in his brother's eyes after returning from Afghanistan, when his PTSD had still controlled every facet his life. Leah had been in the middle of a flashback, and he'd done the only thing he could, the same thing that had helped his brother come out of his. He'd tried to talk her out of it, to make her focus on the present. But, Dylan hadn't ever been afraid of him the way Leah had.

Even when her focus had returned, even when she remembered where she was and the reality of her current situation, her gaze still held a guarded wariness.

He wiped at the table one last time before tossing the towel onto the counter. He gripped the counter's edge, fighting the urge to go into the living room to try to get her to open up to him, to convince her to tell him what had happened in her past. But he knew he couldn't push her. He'd learned that from Dylan as well. When she was ready, if she was ever ready, she'd tell her story, but until then he had to give her security, a person she could be with who didn't pressure her. She needed to know that, regardless of her past, she could trust him not to hurt her.

Dylan walked into the living room to find Leah on the couch with both kittens curled in her lap. Her eyes were closed as her hands moved slowly over Puma, stroking his fluffy body rhythmically, and he took the moment to watch her. She'd pulled her hair free from its usual low ponytail, and it hung in soft, caramel waves down the back of the couch. She inhaled slowly, deeply, trying to relax the tension he could still see etched in her brow.

As if sensing his presence, she frowned and turned in his direction. She stiffened and retreated further into the corner of the couch. Settling Puma on the arm of the sofa, she pulled her knees to her chest.

"Don't look at me like that."

Gage could see the embarrassment etched on her brow. With anyone else, he would have moved closer to her, reached out and held her in an effort to let her know he understood, but her body language was warning him to keep his distance.

"Like what?" He took a step toward the couch and paused, waiting for her reaction.

"Like I'm some sort of freak who has no business being a therapist for anyone else when I can't even keep my own shit together."

"That's not even remotely close to what I'm thinking," he said softly. "Mind if I sit?"

"Why? I had an anxiety attack because I'm tired. It's no big deal. I don't want to talk about it."

"Okay." Gage wasn't going to argue with her, but they both knew was a big deal. It was obvious to him that she'd responded to something he'd done, and he was afraid he was going to cause another one. "We won't talk about it."

She didn't look convinced as he moved around the other end of the couch and sank into one of the leather cushions. It was the seat farthest from her, but he saw the trepidation flicker in her eyes again and wondered if this might even be too close for her comfort.

She shook her head and gave him a sad smile. "You don't have it in you to give up that easily, so what's your plan?" she asked.

Gage stretched his legs out in front of him and crossed his ankles. "I don't usually, but I will if you want me to. No plan, Leah. I promise that I won't bring it up again."

Leah cocked her head to one side, her skepticism clear. "Why not?"

"You don't want me to, so I won't." Gage rubbed his palms against his thighs. Seeing the haunted look in

Leah's eyes, the way she was still trying to hide in the corner of the couch, he prayed he wasn't making a mistake. "I'm not heartless, Leah."

"I didn't think you were." She looked down at the kitten bumping her hand with his head, searching for attention. "For the record, it wasn't you."

"No?" Lynx jumped down from the couch cushion beside Leah and began climbing Gage's leg. "Son of a bitch this hurts. Did you teach them this?"

Leah responded the way he'd hoped she would, with a slight smile, and she uncurled herself slightly from the corner, dropping her knees to one side.

"No, but I'm thinking kittens can't be too different from kids. If you don't want her to do it, don't pick her up and reward her actions by petting her."

Gage plucked Lynx from his knee and lifted her in front of his face. "You hear that, little girl? Your mom says I'm spoiling you." He tucked the kitten under his chin, against his chest and she began to purr loudly.

"You're a nice man, Gage."

His head snapped up. The compliment had come out of the blue. Until today she'd never said anything remotely benevolent, and he wondered what had prompted the sudden change. He knew he couldn't ask her outright, but he didn't want to ignore the praise either.

He shot her a playful grin. "I've been trying to tell you that, but you wouldn't believe me."

Her smile faded, and she quickly looked down at the sleeping kitten again, avoiding his gaze.

"Leah?"

She took a deep breath. "It hasn't happened in a long time."

"You have PTSD."

She nodded slowly, keeping her focus on anything but his eyes. "How'd you know?"

"My brother." Gage prayed Dylan wouldn't fault him for telling her. "When he was in Afghanistan his entire unit was killed. He was the only one to survive. It messed him up pretty bad."

"Roscoe's his service dog."

Gage nodded. "We tried for over a year to find something to help. Medication didn't touch it. A therapy dog was his last hope."

"He's the reason you knew about the breathing technique."

"I learned pretty early not to touch him when he was having a flashback, but if I could get his attention, get him to focus on my voice, I could use it to help force his mind back into the present. It didn't always work, but it kept either of us from getting hurt."

"Thank you." Her voice was strained, frail, and vulnerable. When she raised her hand to pet the kitten, he could see it was unsteady.

"I didn't mean to trigger it, Leah. If you tell me what I did, I'll avoid doing it again."

"It wasn't you," she repeated, but he could easily read the lie in her eyes.

He set Lynx onto the couch and moved to sit on the table across from her. "We're friends, right? At least, as much as two strangers bound by kittens can be." She gave him the faintest hint of a smile and nodded. "Friends don't lie to one another, Leah."

Gage curled his fingers around his knees to keep from reaching for her hand. He could see the war waging within her—to purge the poison that was festering or to continue to try to hide it. She ducked her head so that he couldn't see her face, or read the emotion in her eyes.

"It's not anything you *did*. It's who you are," she confessed.

Damn.

Her words hurt more than he thought they would. Gage knew she didn't mean to hurt him, but it didn't stop the way his chest constricted. Deep down he'd been hoping she'd say something else had triggered her flashback, but hearing her admit it was him made the weight of the past few weeks crowd around him again, dragging him back into the pit of guilt he was trying to crawl out of.

He'd hurt yet another person, without trying. Even on the Heart Fire Ranch, where he thought he'd hole up, away from the trouble he'd caused his partners and employees, he just found someone else's life to ruin.

THROUGH HER LASHES, Leah saw Gage flinch at her words. Her breath caught in her throat at the agony she could see in his eyes. It wasn't fair to let him shoulder the blame that shouldn't be his to bear. As much as she didn't want to talk about her past, she wanted to hurt him less.

He pressed his hands against his knees and started to rise and she reached out a hand to still him. Now that she'd made the decision to tell him, she didn't want him to go until he understood.

"Wait, don't go."

He stared down at her fingers around his wrist. "Leah, I don't want to put you through this. I didn't mean to…I'm sorry."

"It's just because you're a man, Gage," she whispered.

Leah wanted to be strong, to deny that her past could still hurt her, but she couldn't stop the wavering in her voice, or the way her skin felt hot and raw, or the difficulty she was having just trying to remember how to breathe.

"I was eight the first time I saw her with her dealer. It was also the first time a man hit me. But I could handle that. That was something I could avoid by hiding. At least until the day it wasn't her they came for. I was only ten the first time a man…hurt me. I'd already seen them with her for years, so I knew not to cry, but it didn't stop them. Afterward, I wanted to die."

Gage slid back down to the coffee table, as if his legs couldn't hold him up. He didn't say anything—not that she expected him to—and she could see the empathy in his eyes for the life she'd led. Her brain warned her to stop talking, but she didn't really want to.

Now that she'd begun, she wanted to get it all out, to purge the poison festering in her. She was surprised at her voice. It wasn't angry or strained or wavering any longer. Instead, it sounded disembodied, like it belonged to someone reciting a story, like it had happened to someone else.

"After that, I stayed away from the house as much as I could. But she always found me, and she needed the money..."

"Leah," Gage began. She could hear the emotion choking him, his voice thick. She realized she was no longer holding his wrist, but his hand was closed around hers, her palm gently cradled in his. "Who?"

She looked up at Gage, her gaze crashing into his. His eyes were wet with unshed tears, tears for the child she'd once been, for the nightmare she'd lived. This man who barely knew her, this stranger who had offered more of himself than anyone in her childhood, was going to cry for her lost innocence. He had no idea how much worse it got.

"My mother."

Gage pinched his lips together and wiped the hand not holding hers over his eyes, rubbing at them roughly. "Fuck me." He slid his hand over his jaw, covering his mouth.

Leah felt suddenly guilty for laying the burden of her past on Gage's shoulders. She shouldn't have told him, should've kept the secret hidden in the vault of her nightmares. But after the kindness he'd shown her, she'd owed him some explanation for the way she'd reacted to him. She couldn't let him think he was to blame.

"It wasn't you. I just..." Sanity seemed to return in time for her to censor her admission. She couldn't tell him it was her attraction to him that had triggered her anxiety attack. "I just haven't been alone with men much since Nicole took me in as a foster kid."

It's not a lie. It just isn't exactly the entire truth.

Leah took a deep, cleansing breath and let it out slowly, waiting for Gage to say something—anything. His thumb brushed over the top of her hand, igniting a spark of affection in her that pooled in her chest, warming her. She was sure he had a million questions running through his mind, but to his credit, he didn't ask any of them.

"I'm sorry." Gage shook his head, still in shock at what she'd told him. "I had no idea, and I pushed you to go to town with me." Self-recrimination settled on him, and he ran a hand over his head.

"Gage, you didn't know. No one does."

She reached for his other hand. It seemed oddly comforting for her to be reassuring him instead of the other way around. It helped for her to analyze the situation clinically, void of emotion, as if it happened to someone else. She also didn't have to scrutinize how much she was still affected by her past. Or how her mother had betrayed her, the rage that fought to be released. But she'd battled all of those emotions, and more, when she'd let Nicole help her. She'd learned to keep them contained.

His gaze snapped up, his dark eyes worried.

"Gage, please, don't tell anyone. People don't want a therapist who has issues."

"We all have issues, Leah." He looked at his hand around hers then back to her eyes. She could tell he was searching for answers to the questions he was too afraid to ask. "It explains a lot."

"You mean, why I'm a bitch?"

"I didn't say that."

"Actually, you did. But don't worry, I won't hold it against you. It's not the first time I've ever been called a bitch, and I'm sure it won't be the last."

He studied her. "How are you just…okay with this?"

"I'm not *okay* with it. But it's over, and I don't want to rehash it."

Leah sighed. She didn't want to talk about the details any more than she already had. If she avoided the discussion, she could avoid reliving them. He didn't need to know how many nights she'd gone to bed hungry or praying her mother might overdose so the nightmare could be over. He didn't need to hear about how she'd been beaten at fourteen by a john who'd used her and refused to pay her mother afterward or about the favors she'd traded in high school just to be able to keep their electricity on. He didn't really want to know about the foster parents who'd failed her, making her live in a closet while they collected their monthly checks until she was sent back to her mother and wished for the closet again.

No one needed to know those things. It was bad enough that she'd lived through them.

She turned her back on Gage and walked into the kitchen, the way she had turned her back on everyone who'd tried to get close. It was her protection. Keep her guard up and no one could touch her heart; then she wouldn't get hurt. Except Nicole hadn't allowed her to put up a wall. She'd forced her way through the barrier, and now Gage was gradually making his way through with his gentle kindness.

Leah wasn't surprised when he didn't follow her into the kitchen, nor was she surprised when she heard the front door close with a soft click. She couldn't blame him. If she were someone like him, she'd run away from her, too. She was walking, talking baggage and issues.

She didn't want him to stay anyway. At least that was what she'd keep telling herself. But the ache in her chest felt an awful lot like rejection.

Or regret.

Chapter Eleven

GAGE NEEDED TO get out. He needed a breath of fresh air, something to give him a moment of perspective on what Leah had just revealed to him. He could see the emotions roiling in her, slowly boiling her alive, could feel her anger seething below the surface, almost palpable, and he wondered how she continued to control it. Or why she was trying to pretend it didn't exist.

Maybe he could see it because he'd seen his brother try to hide his own rage for so long. Maybe it was because he'd been abused in his own childhood, although from what he could ascertain from what she had shared, his experience had been a comparative walk in the park. Gage ran a hand over his shaved head, letting the rasp draw him back to the current predicament. Leah was hurting and angry, as lost as those kittens were, and as much as he needed to focus on his own troubles, he couldn't turn his back on her. It just wasn't who he was.

Walking to the cabin, he picked up the plastic case from on top of the DVD player and headed back to Leah's. He opened the door without knocking.

He could see Leah from the doorway, curled in the same corner of the couch she'd been earlier, and he felt the empathy slam into his chest, painfully digging into his heart. He caught his breath again. How could someone have looked at that face as a child, with her slightly upturned nose and her pink cheeks, and hurt her? His eyes skimmed over her thin limbs and her petite frame. How could someone have deliberately injured her?

Her head jerked up as the door clicked shut behind him, and he could see the shock register in her eyes. "Movie?" he asked, holding up the plastic case.

"You came back?" The words slipped from her lips quietly, and he could see by her wide eyes, she hadn't meant to say them aloud.

He walked to the television and slid the movie into the DVD player, grabbing the remote from the table as he walked past and settling himself in the corner of the couch opposite of her. He'd have loved to sit closer, to pull her into his arms and let her release the anguish he knew she was holding inside, but he could see she wasn't ready for that yet. She might have trusted him enough to tell him some of her past but not enough to dig at that festering wound. Until she was ready, if that ever happened, he'd be her friend. She needed one more than anyone he'd ever known.

"You're going to have to do more than break a few dishes to get rid of me." He kicked his shoes off and crossed his ankles in front of him, lifting the remote. "I hope you're in the mood for a comedy because it's pretty slim pickings in the cabin."

She stared at him for a moment before she arched a brow. "Depends on which one. I'm more in the mood for an action movie."

"*21 Jump Street*. I think that should cover your desires." Gage cursed his poor choice in words.

"Mmm, Channing Tatum? I think I can manage." She sighed, ignoring his slip or, he hoped, not even noticing it. She reached for the afghan folded on the back of the couch and tucked her knees to one side before covering herself, struggling to get it over her feet.

Gage reached for the end of the blanket and pulled it over her toes, tucking it under. "There. Bet Channing Tatum wouldn't do *that* for you."

She smiled sweetly at him. "I bet he would."

Gage chuckled quietly as the movie began. He was glad to see she had returned to their earlier friendly rapport, but it worried him that she could so quickly slip from one emotion to the next, disguising her pain so quickly. It made him suspicious what else she was hiding behind those whiskey-colored eyes.

LEAH FELT THE rumble against her cheek before she heard the quiet snore. She rubbed one hand against her face, wiping it over her eyes and trying to discern where she was. The disorientation alone should have been enough to send her into a panic attack, and she tried to figure out why it wasn't. She blinked, trying to clear the fog from her barely conscious mind, and moved to push herself into a seated position when her hand landed on a wall of solid muscle. It gave way but only slightly, and she couldn't move with the pair of massive biceps protectively curled around her.

Gage.

How had she ended up asleep in Gage's arms? The last thing she remembered was them laughing at a particularly funny scene then leaning her head against the back of the couch so that she could rub her cheek against Puma's soft fur. She must have fallen asleep facing him.

Gage sighed in his sleep, his breath fanning over the top of her hair where her head was tucked under his chin. She was practically curled in his lap with her arms wrapped around him. This wasn't like her. She didn't need to be touched, didn't crave the intimacy of a caress. Just the thought usually sent her backpedaling. To some, it made her seem cold or callous, but it made her a good clinician.

Move away, now, her mind warned.

She tried to obey, even splayed her hand over his stomach to slip out of his arms, but her body wouldn't cooperate. This felt good. Instead of panic, she felt completely at peace, secure and content. She felt safe with Gage, and she didn't want to move for fear that the feeling would dissipate like morning fog.

Longing slid through her veins slowly, like a drug, leaving warmth in its wake, pooling in her stomach. Leah had avoided men whenever possible. Logically, after all of her years in psychological medicine, she knew what happened to her wasn't her fault, but it had tainted her view of sex and men. She scorned the needful weakness and loss of control that lust encouraged.

But, right now, in Gage's arms, she felt like she'd been missing some vital piece of a puzzle. She wasn't feeling weak as desire moved in her, heating her blood. She let it dance through her veins, twirling and twisting, relegating the voices in her head telling her she was a dirty whore to the furthest recesses of her mind.

She wanted to be like other women, to know what it felt like to love and be loved. She wanted to feel passion, to touch and be touched, but more than anything else, she needed to feel safe. Gage made her feel that way.

Unlike the others in her life, he hadn't rejected her. Even when she thought he'd walked away, Gage came back, and for that, she couldn't begin to express her gratitude. That meant more to her than paying for her car repairs or rescuing her on the side of the road. Just the simple act of returning last night had indebted her to him in ways she could never repay.

Leah felt the strong, steady beat of Gage's heart under her ear, and her fingers curled slightly into the muscles at his waist before sliding up his ribs. He sighed softly in his sleep and curiosity overpowered her fear. She felt his hands move over her back and lifted her eyes to his face. His jaw was dusted with stubble, and her fingers itched to touch it, to feel the rasp over her palm. His full lips were slightly parted, and she wondered how a man so solidly muscular and with such chiseled features could have lips that looked so soft.

Gage dipped his face down farther and, through her lashes she could see him looking down at her, his eyes almost black.

"Leah?" he whispered, his voice still husky with sleep.

She wanted to kiss him. She'd never wanted to actually kiss a man before. She had always been forced to tolerate their touch, but this time, she wanted to see what it would be like when she wanted it. But she wasn't sure he would welcome the kiss. Gage brushed a strand of her hair behind her ear with his finger, letting it trail over the outer shell and sending butterfly wings of longing to flutter in her belly. It was enough to jolt her from her indecision.

Leah slid her hand up, curling around the back of Gage's neck and pulled him toward her. Relief flooded her when he came willingly. As his lips met hers, she gasped at the sheer pleasure of the touch, inhaling his breath as her own. His hands froze, one at her shoulder and the other at her waist, as if he was afraid any movement from him might scare her away. She brushed her lips over his slowly, and Gage seemed content to let her set the tone. He let her take as much as she wanted from him, allowing her to explore and decide where her boundaries were.

Leah realized she'd been right about two things: his lips were as soft as they looked, and Gage was safe.

Instead of making her feel good, that only made her more afraid. Safe meant she would be more likely to let down her guard. Safe meant he could break down the walls she'd built. Safe meant, for the first time, her heart was in danger.

BEING KISSED BY Leah was like entering heaven when he knew he didn't belong, but Gage wasn't foolish enough to try to stop it. He couldn't deny the attraction he'd felt from the moment he'd seen her stranded on the side of the road, in spite of what he might have told her. When her lips met his, she sucked in a soft, sweet intake of breath and stole his will to resist her. He'd been able to endure when she'd fallen asleep on his shoulder in the middle of the movie, in spite of the heady scent of her perfume that surrounded him. When she curled against his chest, he'd been content to hold her, knowing he would never cross a line she'd drawn. But waking to find her watching him, with those amber eyes practically glowing with yearning, he didn't have the strength to deny himself a taste of those lips.

Leah had somehow reached inside him and grasped hold of the honorable man he'd once believed himself to be, a man who would protect innocents and do the right thing. A man who would right wrongs, including his own. When he was with her, he could forget that he was fallible, capable of making million dollar mistakes because he'd been too concerned with investor pressure instead of his scruples. The more he got to know her, the more attracted he was, but after what she'd confessed last night, a kiss was the last thing he'd imagined happening between them, the last thing she needed. Leah made him feel like a super-hero, and he wanted to be *that* man. That meant thinking about her needs, even over his own burning desires. A kiss was something he couldn't allow to continue.

Gage drew back, running his hand over the back of her hair and pressing a chaste kiss to her forehead. His heart throbbed painfully against his chest at the denial, and he ignored the other body parts aching for release. He wouldn't be another man who hurt her and betrayed her trust.

"Leah," he whispered, laying his cheek at the top of her head and inhaling the honeyed scent of her, letting it flow through him. Her hand slid down to rest against his chest, and he tried to ignore his body's needful yearning. "I should probably go home."

He felt her stiffen in his arms and wondered if it was from the kiss or his suggestion.

"Why?"

Gage closed his eyes. He didn't dare hope that she'd want him to stay. He wanted nothing more than to remain on her couch with her in his arms all day. Lynx moved along the back of the couch, bumping his arm with her head, and he lifted his wrist to look at his watch.

"It's nearly six a.m. Doesn't Jessie have a group coming this morning?"

She sighed and nodded against his chest. He hoped that sigh encompassed the same disappointment he felt. Just when they'd started to make some progress, the real world would be butting in. Now he wouldn't have her undivided attention. He couldn't just stop by, unannounced, to steal her away. She would have sessions and cases. Plus, she had her car again, so she had little need for him at all. Other than helping with the kittens. He ran his hand over Lynx, who attempted to climb onto Leah's shoulder and curl up.

Gage knew he should apologize to Leah, but try as he might, the words wouldn't come. He wasn't sorry he kissed her. He would only be sorry if it drove a wedge between them.

"What time are they coming?" he asked when she made no attempt to move away from him.

Her breath fanned over his chest, heating more than his skin. He ached with need, and he prayed she wouldn't notice the distinctive bulge in his jeans as he tried to convince his body to behave.

"Chase is supposed to bring them around nine."

Gage traced the line of her cheekbone with his thumb, not wanting to let her go but knowing it was inevitable. Leah tipped her head up, looking him in the face, her eyes questioning but not filled with the regret he expected to see. Even with her hair mussed, her makeup slightly smeared under her eyes, and her cheeks flushed, there was a vulnerability in her face he'd never seen before. She'd never looked more beautiful to him.

Her lips parted slightly just before she bit the corner of her lower lip, and Gage couldn't help himself. He slid his hand through her hair, cupping the back of her head and drawing her closer so he could brush his lips over hers again. Her hand moved up his neck, sending his senses reeling and his hunger into hyperdrive as she pressed herself into his embrace. He swept his tongue against hers, teasing.

If their first kiss had been like heaven, this was pure ecstasy. Leah tasted like honey, a delicate sweetness he hadn't expected from someone as indifferent as she'd tried to act, and he wanted to hold onto everything she would offer.

But he wouldn't let himself accept it, not yet. Not until she was ready to let go of all her secrets, not until he'd told her his own.

Gage heard his cell phone vibrate on the side table where he'd left it during the movie. Reality reared its head as he realized there were only three people who would call him this early—any of his three partners demanding he make a decision about his share of the company he was single-handedly dragging through the mud. Gage ended the kiss slowly, wanting it to last as long as possible but knowing it couldn't. Leah gave a slight whimper as he pulled away, her fingers curling against the back of his neck in protest.

He pressed his forehead against hers. "I have to take this," he said against her lips. "I'll be right back."

Gage knew he could ignore the call, like he'd been doing most of the week, but if he didn't put some space between him and Leah now, he was going to forget his commitment to be her friend and move too close to being her lover. He was drowning in enough regrets without hurting her.

Chapter Twelve

GAGE HURRIED OUT the front door, answering the phone as he looked up to see Jessie watching him curiously from the corral where she was tossing hay to several horses inside. He turned his back on her questioning scrutiny. He didn't have any more answers for her than he did for his partners.

"Hey, Georgie."

"Don't Georgie me, Gage. We've got real trouble brewing here. You need to get in touch with Cooper. He's calling for an emergency meeting of all the stockholders. Since he can't do anything about the shares you own, he's going to push for them to call for your resignation."

"What? If not for me, we would never even have had a product."

"Yeah, well the last one isn't exactly doing anything good for our bottom line. It's going to cost us even more than we thought. We just had three more banks claim our system resulted in a major loss. This is costing us millions."

Gage pinched the bridge of his nose and inhaled slowly. "How soon?"

"He's trying to get everyone together two weeks from today, in the San Francisco office. The corporate bigwigs are all gung-ho to see the new office, and I think he's trying to use the opportunity to schmooze them and make sure you don't have any excuses as to why you can't show up."

Gage didn't miss the accusation in George's voice. In reality, he deserved every bit of it. For the first time, it was likely that the company would end the year in the red.

"I'll be there."

"Screw being there. What if you just make a decision and let us know, Gage? We're all waiting on you. You know what Cooper's going to do to this company if he can get your resignation, right?"

"Yeah, I do." Gage rubbed his hand over his eyes as he made his way down Leah's porch, pacing along the walkway between her place and Jessie's, the gravel crunching loudly in the quiet morning. "And the other shareholders will be happy about it because he'll make them a huge profit."

"This isn't just about profit. This is *our* company. We started it, together. They only joined us because they had the money to back us. Without our ideas..." George sighed into the receiver. "They're going to lay off four hundred people, Gage, all because they can hire kids out of college cheaper. These are people who have worked for us for years. Are you seriously going to just roll over and let all this happen? That's not like you. You know we can't let them do that."

The pleading note in George's voice tugged at Gage. George had known him since college. They'd written code together, graduated together, and created their first security program together. George had also been the first to warn him about the potential problems with Titanium, their latest security flop, but he'd ignored George and signed off on it anyway. He owed it to George to at least commit to showing up for the meeting.

"I'll call Cooper. If there's a meeting, I'll be there. I promise."

"Gage, man, what is up with you? It was a mistake. Move on before you bury yourself and the rest of us in this."

He knew George was right. He should just forget about it, move on to the next program, and immerse himself in code and their next project instead of dwelling on this one error. It happened to everyone. Except it didn't happen to him. It never had.

Growing up, he'd owed it to his mother and Dylan to be perfect. He'd made the choice to never let anyone to see what how much that precision cost him. Gage buried his concerns into a deep well, letting everyone see only the confident, successful super-human he wanted them to believe he was.

"I'm fine, Georgie. I just wanted to spend some time with my brother and my new niece." It wasn't a total lie. "Give me a few more days and I'll call Cooper and straighten this out. I'll call our lawyers, too."

"I hope so, Gage, because I wouldn't want to try to handle those two without you. We started this together. I want to finish it that way."

George didn't give him a chance to say anything as he disconnected the call. Gage wondered if George realized that it was just as likely as not that Iconics was finished, that Gage might not be returning at all.

"What the hell do you think you're doing?"

Jessie's voice snapped Gage from his concerns about Iconics and his partners. He looked up to see her storming toward him with some kind of whip-like object in her hand. She looked like a woman on a mission, and he was afraid that he'd just become her target.

"Nothing?"

The skeptical arch of her brow didn't leave any question as to whether she believed him. "You come strolling out of my new therapist's house before six-thirty in the morning and I'm supposed to buy that load of crap?" She poked a finger into his chest. "Let me make myself crystal clear to you, Gage. I like your brother and I like you, but don't think that means I'm going to let you screw around and chase off the person I've worked my tail off to find for Heart Fire. She is going to make this place into what I've dreamed it could become. If you ruin this—"

Gage crossed his arms over his chest, taking a deep breath. "I'm not going to ruin anything, Jessie. Nothing happened. We were taking care of the kittens and fell asleep watching a movie. It was completely PG, okay? Relax."

"Gage," Jessie said, her tone a warning. "I need her here."

"I get it, Jessie. Leah is going to take Heart Fire to the next level. Regardless of what everyone thinks, I'm not some player just out for a piece of ass."

"I didn't say that."

"You kind of implied it." He cocked his head to one side, slid his phone into his pocket, and turned back to Leah's place.

"Where are you going?" Jessie called.

Gage took a step closer to Jessie and lowered his voice. "Look, I don't know what you know about her, but that woman in there needs a friend."

Jessie glared at him. "Do you think I don't run background checks? Nathan's father was a politician, remember? If anyone knows how to dig up dirt, it's Nathan's guys." She pointed the short whip at him. "Just make sure friendship is all you have in mind."

As she pivoted on her heel and walked away, Gage realized he couldn't make that promise, even if he'd wanted to. His heart had already taken his friendship with Leah to the next level, in spite of his reminders to himself to keep it platonic. He was already a goner.

What in the hell are you doing?

Leah couldn't believe she'd kissed Gage, not once but *twice*. She had never, ever, been so driven to be near a man. In fact, she'd always gone out of her way to avoid any sort of intimacy unless it was absolutely necessary. She couldn't even blame it on being half-asleep since he'd caught her staring at him. Who knows what might have happened if he hadn't taken that phone call. She'd let her emotions take over, lost control, and she didn't like this feeling of helpless vulnerability.

She peered out the kitchen window to see him pacing the walkway with the phone to his ear. He didn't look happy, and she was curious about the early morning phone call, but she wasn't about to pry. He hadn't pressed her for information last night when she'd opened up about her past, and she would extend him the same courtesy of privacy. She saw him disconnect the call as Jessie made her way to him.

Icy dread slid through her veins as she prayed her boss didn't see him come out of her house. Jessie glanced at the house and Gage followed her gaze.

"Crap," Leah muttered. They had to be talking about her, and from the looks of it, Jessie wasn't happy. She debated going out and clearing up any misunderstanding Jessie might have but wasn't sure what she could say.

Fat chance, her mind whispered. *There is no misunderstanding. You spent the night with the guy, and the way you lost your head, you would have slept with him.*

Leah turned away from the window and ran a hand through her hair before heading to fill the coffeepot. Jessie had every right to fire her. Even if Gage was only family by marriage, Leah was a new employee. She'd very nearly crossed a line that would've been career suicide.

"Are you making coffee?"

His voice was husky. She turned and caught her breath. Between his voice and the stubble shadowing his jaw, Leah was having a hard time keeping herself from being drawn closer to the early morning seduction standing in her kitchen. His gaze caressed her and Leah had no doubt from the heat she could see in his eyes, he would burn her. She couldn't handle any more scars.

"I am. Have a seat and I can make some pancakes if you want." She reached into the cupboard for two mugs. "Cream and sugar?"

"Just sugar." She slid the box of small packets toward him across the counter, waiting for the coffee to brew. "Don't worry about the pancakes. I need to get to work."

She tried to ignore the stab of rejection, reminding herself that this was exactly what she wanted. There was no room for any sort of relationship.

"Leah, about earlier—"

She quickly raised her hand. "Don't even. I shouldn't have kissed you, especially after the things I said. Let's just pretend it never happened, okay?" Gage snapped his jaw closed and she saw the flicker of indecision in his eyes. "We can be friends, but I don't think either of us has time or inclination for anything more than that."

He took a step closer, letting one hand fall gently on her shoulder and slide down her arm. "Are you sure about that?"

Goose bumps broke out over her arms, and Leah fought back the shiver of response to his touch. She wanted to lean into him, to go back to that moment on the couch, where he stoked the passion smoldering in her. He was intoxicating.

"This is my job. I can't jeopardize it." The words slipped out before she could stop them.

One side of Gage's mouth curved up in a sad smile. "You saw Jessie."

His comment didn't tell her anything. It didn't tell her if Jessie was angry or appalled. It didn't tell her what he'd said.

"Yes." Her brain yelled at her to push him away, but her body ached for his touch, her blood pounding in her veins.

"Leah, I won't do anything to put you at risk. You are one-hundred-percent safe with me. I promise you." He took a deep breath and let it out slowly, letting his hand fall away from her as he took a step back. "Friends."

Gage poured himself a cup of coffee and took a sip. She wondered if he was aware of the sigh of pleasure that slipped from his lips. When he opened his eyes and met her gaze again, she recognized the desire she'd seen in them on the couch.

"For now," he amended.

Chapter Thirteen

LEAH WAS HAVING a difficult time standing still as the truck came down the driveway. She'd been fidgeting since Jessie pointed out Chase's truck, loaded down with four teenage boys he was bringing for the weekend. She'd worked with plenty of teen boys at her old clinic, but this would be the first time she was responsible for every aspect of the sessions. There were no guidelines, no requirements, and no paperwork. The freedom was as exhilarating as it was frightening. She was completely on her own to decide what would be best for each young man after meeting with him.

"Relax," Jessie said with a chuckle. "You look like you're about to throw up."

I think I might.

Leah didn't trust herself to speak. As the truck pulled to a stop at the corral, she saw a tall man slip from driver's seat, turning to open the back door for a large black shepherd. "Hey, knock it off, Cody, or I'm going to sic Gracie on you."

He pointed at the boys in the truck, and the dog barked happily as he moved around the front bumper. The four boys—young men, Leah corrected herself—poured out of the truck amid a cacophony of noise.

"Morning, ladies. I'm Chase," he said, holding his hand out to Leah.

She shook it firmly, eyeing the dog who sat at his feet. "Leah McCarran."

She wanted these young men to see nothing but confidence from her at the get-go.

"Our new therapist," Jessie added. She pointed to the cabin to the right of Gage's and addressed the boys. "Hey, guys, you'll be sharing that cabin right there."

Chase arched a brow and his mouth quirked into a quick grin. "You're trusting these guys to stay in the cabin alone? I hope you don't plan on it staying in one piece?"

"It had better." She leaned closer. "Gage already told me he'd keep an eye on them since he's next door."

Leah's heart immediately picked up its pace at the mention of Gage's name.

Stupid pulse, she thought, cursing the way her body betrayed her.

"Well, they should be fairly quiet. All four of these guys are in the same foster home, so it's not like they aren't with one another all the time. They're friends. Melody runs a pretty tight ship at her house, from what the boys have said." He turned to Leah. "Jessie gave you their files, right?" Leah nodded and Chase lowered his voice.

"Then you know about Miguel and Hector's abuse, and that Jude is the usually the mastermind of any trouble they get into."

Leah watched the four boys push and shove at one another playfully as they entered their cabin. To an outsider, they looked like any other group of friends enjoying one another's company. Looking at them offered no clue to the physical abuse they'd endured—two from their father, and one from his grandmother. But Jude was different, he was simply ignored by his family, until he'd hacked into the school computer system and sent a threat to his teacher. All four of these boys shared a common dysfunctional thread, which had brought them together in a foster home and bound them for life.

Leah felt an instant connection to the boys and a surge of inspiration. These boys were at a precipice in their lives. Not boys but not quite men, at least not in anyone else's eyes. She knew exactly what they could talk about tonight at the campfire, provided she could get them to open up and trust her in the next few hours.

She had to. There was no other option. If she couldn't do this, she might as well pack up her belongings and head out with her tail between her legs. This was her chance to either prove herself or fail miserably.

GAGE WATCHED LEAH and Jessie trying to give the four boys a riding lesson. Neither of those women had any idea that those kids had absolutely no desire to learn how to groom horses. They were far more interested with watching the curves of the two women trying to instruct them.

They might be troubled teens, but they were still teen boys, and like all sixteen-year-old males, they were walking, talking, raging hormones in semihuman bodies.

"She has no clue, does she?"

Gage turned to see Nathan walking to the small porch of his cabin, and he laughed with Jessie's husband. "I'm not sure who's going to get the more painful wake-up call, those women when they realize those boys aren't listening at all or those boys when either of those two figure out what the boys have been paying attention to this whole time."

"Yeah, what those *boys* are paying attention to." Nathan laughed, leaning over the railing. "What do you say we go save those poor kids before they get caught staring, too?"

"I don't know." Gage didn't really have any excuse to offer, especially since Nathan had just caught him ogling Leah. "I'm sure Leah and Jessie have some kind of agenda. I wouldn't want to mess anything up."

"Come on," Nathan coaxed. "Jessie said I'm supposed to lead them on a ride up to The Ridge. The more the merrier."

"She doesn't have enough horses saddled."

"I'll grab Grady for you to ride. Besides, I think those four boys need to see an example of how men should treat women. With respect instead of like pieces of meat."

Maybe, if he got to know the boys, it might make things go more smoothly later. Gage had already promised Jessie he'd keep an eye out for any trouble tonight, since he was sure to be up late with the kittens, although he wasn't really sure what she expected him to do other than report if they left the cabin. He didn't need any more trouble while he was here.

Gage stood up. "Okay, but only because those four need to learn a lesson."

"Yeah," Nathan said with a chuckle, as he eyed the group in the corral. "I'm sure it has nothing at all to do with the new, very single, therapist you rescued on the side of the road."

Gage let his gaze slide over Leah, from her high ponytail and flushed cheeks to her long legs, encased in denim and what appeared to be a pair of Jessie's cowboy boots. As much as he craved spending time with her, it was a dangerous proposition.

Leah was already winding her way around his heart, and he wasn't in a position to commit anything to anyone, especially someone who needed the kind of patient tenderness she would. It was already taking every bit of fortitude he had to hold himself together long enough to focus on the decision he had to make about his business. That didn't even take into account that now he had to prepare a rebuttal to the accusations Cooper would make to the shareholders.

"Hey, I was just kidding."

Gage realized he was frowning and smoothed his brow. "Sorry, just thinking about a project for work. I'll change while you get the horses, then I'll meet you in the corral in a few."

Gage hurried into the cabin, wondering why he was giving in to Nathan's request. He might not really have any work to do, but he should make a call to Cooper. He needed to find out what Cooper's intentions were and whether he was actually going to force Gage out of his own company. The scuttlebutt George had passed along wasn't looking promising. The quick email he'd shot off to his assistant hadn't done anything to make him feel any better, especially when his return email informed Gage he'd been reassigned to Cooper. Gage got the feeling that there was a coup in the works and being on the wrong coast wasn't helping him mount a defense.

He slid the boots Julia and Dylan had bought him last Christmas over his stocking feet and hurried back out the door toward the corral, cursing his stupid desire. Leah didn't want him on this ride, and Jessie wanted him there even less.

Then why are you going?

Because, regardless of his professional troubles and her request to keep things platonic between them—not to mention his assurance he would—Gage wanted more from Leah. He wanted to see her eyes darken again, the way they had when she'd kissed him this morning. He wanted to feel her melt against his body again, to have that warm desire slowly trickle through his veins when her hand pressed against his chest. He wanted to let his fingers run through her long waves again, to smell the sweet scent of her shampoo, and to hear her make that agonizingly sexy sigh while she slid her hand around the back of his neck and dragged him back down to her mouth.

Unfortunately, Leah had made it perfectly clear, she had no interest in any sort of relationship.

"WHAT THE HELL?" Leah didn't miss the aggravation in Jessie's voice when she looked up and saw Nathan heading into the corral with two saddled mounts instead of one. "Why is Grady saddled?"

"Gage is coming."

"Why?"

Nathan turned his back on his wife to loop the reins over the railing, avoiding the death-glare she shot at him. Apparently, Leah wasn't the only one hesitant to have Gage with them for the ride, although she doubted she and Jessie shared the same reasons for the feeling.

"Why not?" Nathan asked as he turned back toward her and arched an inquisitive brow.

Jessie took a deep breath. Leah could see she was trying to control the desire to spit out a quick rebuttal when Nathan crooked his finger at her, indicating she should come closer, and then he leaned forward to whisper into her ear.

Leah couldn't hear what he said, but she could tell from the way Jessie narrowed her eyes that she wasn't happy and someone was in trouble.

"Fine," she said, glancing at Leah then at the four boys laughing near the horses before she eyed Gage, now walking their direction. "But that better be all there is to it," Jessie warned her husband, jabbing her finger at his shoulder as she walked past him and to the boys.

Leah watched her walk away and turned back to Nathan. "Everything okay?"

"Yeah," he answered with a quiet chuckle. "Jessie just doesn't like it when things don't go exactly the way she wants them to." He glanced at Gage. "He's a good guy, you know."

Leah felt her stomach drop to her toes. Had Gage told Nathan about their kiss that morning? Or worse, told Jessie? She seemed too concerned with Gage's presence to not know there was something brewing between her and Gage.

Is there something?

Leah wasn't sure what to even call it. She could say it was friendship. Gage was a nice guy, someone she *could* be friends with, but friendship wouldn't cause this slow burn that traveled over her body, flushing her skin, nor would it cause the flutter in her stomach. But this wasn't simply sexual attraction either. That would imply that this was just a moment of lust, that there weren't tender moments or a shared emotional connection. Gage was far more than just a hit-it-and-quit-it kind of guy. Neither of them was interested in a one-night stand or meaningless sex. But as far as she was concerned, all of this was something she didn't have time be distracted by.

She opened her mouth to respond to Nathan, but his grin let her know he was assuming plenty from her silence.

"Hey, Leah, looking forward to a ride?" Gage asked as he walked past her.

Leah's eyes widened at his suggestive comment and was sure the blush that flamed her cheeks could have been seen from outer space.

Nice. That probably looks guilty as hell.

Either he enjoyed making her uncomfortable or he was the king of unintended innuendoes. She opted for the latter.

Nathan laughed. "She's riding a pregnant mare who barely moves out of a walk. Between her riding Pumpkin and you on Grady, the two of you are going to be eating a crap-ton of dust at the back of the pack."

Gage shot her a broad grin. "I'm sure we'll be fine bringing up the rear, right?"

She was on this ride to spend some time getting to know the four boys before the bonfire tonight or they'd have little to discuss while there. In fact, that might be the only thing that saved her from riding next to Gage the entire way. If not, then it was going to be nothing more than an exercise in raising her heart rate and making her feel like an idiot for lusting after some rich playboy who was out of her league. Leah wasn't about to be stuck at the end of a line of horses kicking up dust with no possible way out of the humiliation that she'd sentenced herself to.

"Sorry, I have to hang with the boys. Looks like you're stuck bringing up the rear on your own."

It came out more severe than she'd intended, and she bit her lip, as if that could draw back hastily spoken words. Gage lifted a daring brow and grinned at her boldness, looking amused by her comment rather than offended. Nathan clapped him on one of those bulging biceps.

"A strike out for the ladies' man? I thought I'd never see the day you got shot down."

Gage's gaze never left her face. "We'll see."

Both of her brows arched high in surprise before Leah bristled at his braggadocio. "I doubt it."

She didn't want to continue the tête-à-tête when she was sure it would only end in frustration, especially when she wasn't sure what she wanted, only what she *thought* she wanted. And that was something completely different from what she *needed*. That was what she was finding so confusing.

She'd come here to do a job, a great job, and instead was finding herself distracted by the one thing she had never wanted and had avoided at all costs for the last ten years. She was not about to fall for some rich playboy just because he was nice to her and made her feel a few tingles. Okay, maybe it was more than a few. Maybe it was more like an electric current charged from the top of her head to the soles of her feet.

"Leah," Jessie called. "You ready to mount up?"

Leah hurried toward her boss and the mare she held, grateful for the interruption. Reminding Leah to check the cinch before mounting up, Jessie held the reins as Leah slipped her foot into the stirrup the way Jessie had shown her. She reached for the saddle horn and swung her leg over the saddle, settling into the barely padded seat and mentally preparing herself for the ride ahead.

Jessie reached out a hand and patted her calf. "You've got this. Just relax and let Pumpkin have her head. She's as calm as they come. You focus on getting to know these four on the way up to The Ridge."

Leah slid her hands around the reins as she nodded, and Jessie reached up to loosen them and press her hand onto the mare's neck. "This will be a piece of cake. I promise."

While waiting for everyone else to mount up, Leah couldn't help the way her eyes strayed to Gage, watching him lift himself into the saddle effortlessly, the muscles in his arms and thighs rippling with the movement. She licked her lower lip, remembering how those arms had felt around her just this morning. When he looked her way, his gaze locking on hers, Gage smiled at her knowingly, and Leah quickly looked away, turning her attention to Cody, the clown of the group as he rode up beside her.

"Hey, Doc. Jessie said we're supposed to pair up for a bit." His wide grin was playful and he winked at her. "Does this mean you like me best already?"

"Sure, Cody." She rolled her eyes at him. "What it means is that you get to be my guinea pig."

"Really?" He picked at the leather reins with his thumbnail, looking slightly nervous. "What if I don't want to?"

She laughed quietly, relaxing into her therapist mode, that comfort zone where she wasn't the one on the defensive. Right now, she needed to focus on putting these boys at ease.

"Cody, I'm kidding. I'm not going to make you talk about anything you don't want to, okay?"

The young man beside her suddenly looked like a boy again as relief softened the worry in his face. "Really?" he repeated.

"I promise." She glanced up as Jessie opened the gate, and Nathan led the other three boys out of the corral with Gage behind them. "Looks like they're waiting on us," she said as Jessie waved to her.

Cody urged his horse through the gate and Leah followed, praying she could stay in her seat the entire way.

Jessie left the corral gate open behind them, and Leah saw her leap into the saddle from the corner of her eye, wishing she had even a quarter of Jessie's skill with horses.

"So, Doc, what d'ya want to know?" The boy slowed his horse to walk beside her. "I don't have a lot to tell."

"No?" She glanced over at him. "If that were true, you wouldn't be at Heart Fire, would you?" she asked bluntly. "But we don't have to talk about any of that. Why don't you tell me about the last prank you pulled on one of the other guys?"

Cody ducked his head, trying to hide his guilty grin. "What makes you think I pranked anyone?"

She cocked her head to one side. "Cody, you've been joking around since you guys got here this morning. Of course you prank them." She jerked her chin upward, directing his attention toward Jude. "Especially Mr. Serious there."

"Jude?" Cody's lips twisted to one side as he looked at his friend. "He's a good guy. He's just way too smart for his own good. It's kind of bull how he ended up here."

"Hacking into the high school computer and changing grades is illegal. So is threatening a teacher."

"Yeah, but that was only because Mr. Greene got mad and gave him an F because Jude proved his test question wasn't even solvable." He shook his head. "And he didn't threaten him, he just sent him a message that said he could get to him anytime he wanted. He meant he could aggravate him because he was smarter and could get into Mr. Greene's head."

Leah made a mental note to ask Jude about the incident with the teacher. "So, pranks?"

Cody laughed. "Okay, the other day, Melody had picked Jude and me up from school while Miguel and Hector were at track practice, and I knew he had a date with some chick from his AP chem class." That guilty grin tugged at the corner of his lips as Cody ran a hand through his shaggy sandy-blond hair. "He's really particular about how he looks. His clothes need to look just right, his hair...you know, really metro."

"I could see that," Leah said, glancing at Jude who, even now, was brushing horse hair from his jeans.

"So, he always uses this one particular hair gel and the container was half-empty."

He snickered and Leah couldn't help but laugh with him, guessing where this story was heading. "What did you put in it?"

"Hector's muscle ointment!"

Leah covered her mouth with her free hand, but her laughter bubbled past. "Cody, that had to sting."

"Probably, but the look on his face was priceless. He must have washed his hair at least ten times before his date. The best part was that when she saw him, she asked why he smelled like peppermint."

Cody fell forward on the saddle laughing at his own antics, and Leah smiled at him, silently congratulating herself on connecting with the kid. He was a nice boy with a wicked sense of humor. She looked toward where Jude slowed in the line so that he was closer to Gage, whose eyes were fixed on her. She felt the blush rising on her cheeks as he tipped his head toward her and smiled slightly.

"So, he's got a thing for you, huh?"

"What?" Leah's head snapped back to meet the boy's inquisitive look. "Who?"

"Body-builder guy." Cody pointed at Gage, not caring who might see him.

"No, we barely even know each other."

That's it, Leah. Deny, deny, deny.

"Uh-huh." Cody scoffed, circling a finger in the air at her face. "Those rosy cheeks of yours say something different."

Leah would've argued his point if she hadn't felt the blush burning her skin. What had happened to her ability to con people when it served her? She'd always been able to believably lie her way out of unbelievable situations but her attraction to Gage had her tripping over her own words and her body reacting in ridiculously stupid ways.

"Don't worry about it, Doc. Your secret is safe with me." He pressed his lips together and pretended to lock them.

She frowned at the kid. It was a bad idea for him to believe he had any personal information to hold over her. "There's no secret and nothing between me and Gage. Like I said, we've only just met and…"

"Ah, so you *want* him to notice." Cody winked at her. "Jude will be disappointed, but I can help with that."

Before she could argue, Cody bumped his heels against his horse's sides, and the animal took off at a jog. She watched as he hurried to where Jude and Gage walked ahead.

"Crap," she muttered, wondering what this kid with a very big mouth was going to say to Gage.

Chapter Fourteen

"WHAT DO YOU mean, you're a hacker?"

Gage was struggling to keep his face void of any emotion when right now he wanted to strangle this kid. Jude seemed almost proud of his accomplishment, hacking into his high school's system in order to change not only his grades but those of his buddies and half of his class, simply because he could. He was completely unapologetic when he laughed about the chaos it had caused as the administration scrambled to figure out the correct grades for each of the kids affected and tried to right the after-effects of this kid's "good time." The horse tossed his head, trying to pull at the reins Gage suddenly realized he was clenching in a fist that he'd rather use to throttle this arrogant genius.

"It's what I do." The kid shrugged, his blue eyes taking in Gage's barely controlled rage. "It's not like I hurt anyone, and before you say it, I did *not* threaten that teacher. You a cop or something?"

Gage loosened his grip on the reins and the horse relaxed beneath him. "Something."

Jude laughed. "Let me guess, you had your credit card stolen, and you think it was a hacker that did it? Got news for ya, Grandpa, living in a digital world is dangerous. People should be more careful."

Clenching his jaw and trying not to visualize pummeling a teenage kid, Gage inhaled deeply as the blond kid with the quick smile came up on his other side.

"Hey, Romeo, Doc's feeling lonely at the back of the pack."

"What?" He turned in the saddle to look at Leah, who was trying to look busy inspecting the landscape.

"What?" Jude followed his gaze, a frown pinching his dark brows together.

"Sorry, Jude. She's only got eyes for muscle-man here. You don't even register on her radar, Geek."

An irritable shadow crossed Jude's face. Gage saw him clench his jaw in anger and fought back a self-righteous smile. *Suck on that, you little prick.*

Okay, so his jealous, immature inner child was surfacing. Leah would have no interest in a sixteen-year-old boy. Logically, he knew it, but it didn't quell the animosity for this kid from rising up in his gut. This was a kid who did what he wanted just because he could, without any consideration for the people he might be hurting. Teachers and administrators could have lost their jobs, simply because he was mad about a grade.

"Whatcha waitin' on? The doc is calling; best get to runnin' over there." Jude sneered, his lip curling in derision.

A confident grin split Gage's lips. "Oh, kid, you've got a lot to learn about women." He slowed Grady, falling behind the group to where Leah rode. "Hey."

She didn't even look his way. "Hey."

"Enjoying the ride?"

"Yep."

These one word answers weren't going to get them anywhere. "You know, of all your curves, your smile is my favorite."

Leah rolled her eyes and looked at him, trying to hide her smile behind annoyance. "Really? You're going to try one of those stupid lines on me now?"

"It got you to smile, didn't it?"

She shook her head and ran a hand over her horse's neck. "I'm supposed to be working. I can't do that if I'm chatting with you. I should be talking to the boys."

"I have no doubt they'd love to be talking to you."

She prickled, sitting up straighter in the saddle. "What does that mean?"

"Oh, come on, Leah. You and Jessie had to notice how those four were watching the two of you instead of the horses in the corral."

"Yeah, watching us tell them how to saddle and ride."

"Sure they were," he scoffed. "Especially when you showed them how to clean a horse's hooves."

He tried not to visualize the rounded curve of her rear as she'd bent over, the jeans she wore accenting the length of thigh under the denim.

"You're sick." She bumped her heels against the animal's side, urging the mare to speed up, leaving Gage to watch her hips rock provocatively in the saddle as she rode up to the two brothers talking to Nathan.

Jude's mocking laughter rolled backward as the kid turned in his saddle. Gage felt the muscle in his jaw ticking like a time bomb as he tried to keep his temper from exploding on the smart-ass kid riding ahead of him.

"Thanks for showing me how it's done, Romeo. Or was that how *not* to get the deal closed?"

LEAH WANTED TO discount what Gage had said about the boys, wanted to believe that they wanted to talk to her so that she could help them, but the way their eyes kept straying, she knew Gage was right. Especially considering Cody's earlier comment about Jude.

It wasn't the first time a patient had flirted, so she always made sure to dress appropriately. There wasn't anything for the teens to see other than her jeans and a T-shirt. But, while their attention was focused elsewhere, they'd loosened their reservations and opened up to her. So far, Hector and Miguel had already confessed to her how much better their life was with Melody, their foster mother, than with their father. Once they'd been able to get away from the influence of their father, who was serving time in prison, they'd been able to do things they'd never dreamed. Like participating in track, even earning a chance to go to college and, feeling, for the first time, that they had a family.

She could hear the tender affection the boys had for the woman in their voices. "She sounds like an amazing woman. I can't wait to meet with her."

Hector laughed. "You will. She'll be coming to pick us up."

"At least we don't have to look at Chase until next week. He makes me nervous," Miguel said with a chuckle.

"He should after that call that you were loitering."

"You were loitering?"

Leah frowned. She didn't know the boys well, but they seemed to be well-adjusted teen boys from what they had said so far. Both B-students making the honor roll, both on the varsity track team at school, no real issues to speak of now that they were away from the gang that had tried to lure them in after their father's arrest.

"No, but I guess, because my skin is brown, someone decided I must be dangerous. They called the police, and Chase showed up to check it out. I was just waiting for Coach outside his office."

Leah didn't miss the angry hurt she could hear rising up at the prejudice the boys had faced, whether due to their race or economic status. She'd faced the same harsh judgment because of her mother, as well as her own poor choices, and could empathize. But, she couldn't explain that to these two. At least, not yet.

"Heads up. We're almost there," Nathan called, interrupting the conversation and the anger was snuffed from Miguel's eyes by his excitement.

Jude's voice carried to where Leah was, and she turned in her saddle to see the boy leaning toward Gage.

"Don't be such an arrogant ass, man. I didn't hurt anyone."

It wasn't the teen's comment that caught her attention. It was Gage. She'd never seen such open animosity in his face. His entire body was taut, like a coiled snake ready to strike, and looked just as dangerous. Without thinking, she tapped the horse in the ribs and hurried to move between them.

"Jude, head up to the front if you want to see The Ridge first."

The boy cast one last challenging glare at Gage. "Yeah, I think I will."

As soon as Jude was out of earshot, Leah turned on Gage. "What the hell are you doing?" she hissed through her clenched teeth. "We are supposed to be helping these kids, not instigating arguments and causing more trouble."

"He's a delinquent."

"No shit, Sherlock. That's why he's here." She shook her head. "You're supposed to be an adult. That means having your temper under control enough to help, not make matters worse."

"How can you deal with arrogance like that?" Gage flung his hand in the direction Jude had gone. "He doesn't even care if what he did was wrong."

"And how are you qualified to judge that?"

Leah couldn't believe this was the same man she'd gotten to know over the past few days. The same man who'd rescued her, as well as two kittens. The same man who'd been so tender with her the night before. She stopped her mount in front of Gage.

"What is this really about?"

The fire seemed to douse in him as he rubbed a hand over his eyes. "Damn it," Gage muttered.

Leah frowned, concerned. "Gage?"

"It's nothing, okay? I'll apologize to him when we stop. I shouldn't have…I'll apologize."

She looked back at the group as they made their way to the end of the path that climbed up the hill. "Look, we can stop for a minute. Talk to me."

"No, it's just work stuff. I just need to get my head on straight."

She eyed him skeptically. "Gage, you wouldn't act like this with a kid over work stress." She blocked the path, refusing to go any further until he gave her some answers. If this had something to do with Jude, or something he'd done, she needed to know. "You're pretty fired up over something that simple."

Gage sighed and stopped his horse. "He's a hacker."

"I know, I read his file. What does that have to do with you?"

"Look, you have a job to do. I promised not to interfere with it, so let's just catch up to everyone else and—"

"And what? Have you start another fight with a sixteen-year-old kid?" Leah moved her horse closer, wondering why he was being so secretive. Was it possible that Mr. What-You-See-Is-What-You-Get had a skeleton in his closet?

Gage growled low in his throat. "That *kid* was fighting with me." She heard the soft *clop* of hooves in the distance and saw Gage look past her. "Jessie's waving to you. We should go."

He maneuvered the horse around her, but Leah reached for his arm, her fingers closing over the hard muscle of his forearm, feeling it tense under her palm. "Gage, you can talk to me."

Leah meant it. She had no idea what might have him acting this way, but she wanted him to trust her. He'd been there for her last night, and she wanted to prove to him that she was ready to return the favor.

"Thanks, but there's nothing to talk about, Leah."

YOU'RE SUCH A *liar, Granger.*

He didn't like misleading Leah, but spilling the gory details about his stupid mistake, the way he'd allowed a few kids to nearly topple his company, or the fact that he still wasn't sure how to fix the situation didn't rank high on ways to get the girl. Once the situation was in control again, then they could have a laugh about how he'd been outsmarted by a couple of hackers like Jude.

Gage eyed the kid across the bonfire Nathan had built, watching him slide a few inches closer to Leah before smirking at Gage again. He was playing him, and Gage knew it, but he was helpless to squelch the wave of jealousy that swirled in his chest. He rose, making his way along the Sequoia logs that circled the fire to the overlook. He could still hear the conversation, but he wasn't forced to deal with a punk-ass kid trying to get a rise out of him.

"So, let's talk," Leah encouraged. A quiet groan sounded from the four boys and Gage looked back at the group over his shoulder.

"Seriously, Doc? I thought this was supposed to be different than regular therapy visits," Cody complained. "Chase said it was going to be fun."

Hector and Miguel exchanged knowing looks and rolled their eyes. Jessie fidgeted nervously across from Leah. Gage didn't miss the confident grin that spread over Leah's lips, and he could see that Jude hadn't either. He was the only one who looked intrigued rather than uncomfortable. Gage leaned his back against the railing of the overlook and watched Leah as her eyes sparked with an enthusiasm he hadn't really seen in her until now.

"Not you," she corrected. "Me."

"What?" Cody looked surprised.

"You guys don't know me, and who wants to tell their secrets to someone they don't trust yet?" Her eyes found Gage's gaze deliberately, and he wondered if she wasn't trying to drive home her offer to let him talk. She tore her gaze from his and looked at the four boys around her. "That means you guys can ask me whatever you want."

Gage was surprised by her offer. She'd been so closed off and secretive up to this point, he wondered if she would really tell the boys the truth or whether she had thought the idea through completely. They were likely to ask about things she might not want to talk about unless she set some boundaries. He glanced at Jessie who shifted nervously on the log.

"Really?" Jude looked suspicious.

"Yep," she answered with a nod.

"How old are you?"

"Are you really a doctor?"

"Where did you grow up?"

All of the boys spoke at the same time, and Gage nearly breathed a sigh of relief at the innocent questions. They might just be warming up, but he had no doubt she could handle any of these with ease.

"Why are you really here, working at this ranch, with a bunch of delinquents?" Jude's voice cut through the rest, and the other three fell silent.

If Gage hadn't already suspected it, Jude's question made it obvious he was the spokesman for the group and, likely, the ringleader for any trouble they got into. He looked at Leah, wondering if she realized the can of worms she'd just opened with these four.

Leah raised her brows and took a deep breath, glancing at Jessie who looked far too interested to know as much of Leah's history as she claimed. It made Gage wonder how much of her past Nathan had been able to dig up and how much more Leah had been able to keep hidden from her boss before accepting the position.

"My life wasn't really that different from yours."

Jude blew out a breath, easily rejecting her statement, elbowing Hector in the side. "Sure it was."

"My mother was a drug addict who'd do just about anything for her next fix. To say we were broke would be wishful thinking."

"You grew up in the system?" Cody's voice was hushed, as if he was almost afraid to ask but couldn't help himself, his usual light-hearted demeanor subdued.

Leah nodded, looking at each of the boys in turn, letting her eyes rest on Jude. "I bounced between my mom and foster homes from the time I was about ten. My teacher reported a bruise on my arm."

"Then you know what it's like," Miguel said.

"I do." From where he stood, Gage could see the fire flickering in her eyes and wondered if it was a reflection of the bonfire or simply the painful memories of her past. "And you can imagine what it must be like for a young girl."

Hector and Miguel exchanged a glance before looking at Leah again. "But all of the foster homes weren't bad. Some were good people who legitimately wanted to help. They just didn't know how to best handle someone like me, with the anger I tried to hold inside. Until Nicole. When I moved in with her, things changed. She made them change for me, made *me* change. She's the reason I graduated high school, went to college. She's the reason I'm here.

"At this ranch," Leah said, focusing on Jude as she used his own words back at him, "with a bunch of young men who just need to realize that someone believes in them and can help show them a better way."

The kid narrowed his eyes at her before looking at his three foster brothers. "Show *them.* I've got everything I need right here," he said, poking one finger at his temple. "I don't need your help."

Jude stood up and strode away from the fire toward the corral where the horses were eating, leaving Leah and the others to stare after him in silence.

Chapter Fifteen

"WHAT THE HELL is your problem? She's trying to help you." Gage was having a hard time holding back his temper with this ungrateful brat. "You do realize they could have just sent you to juvie instead, right? But Chase and Jessie and Leah are all—"

"It's not really any of your business, is it?" Jude barely gave Gage a backward glance. "Sorry if your girlfriend is on a mission to save the world, but I don't want to be a part of it."

"She's not my girlfriend."

Jude rolled his eyes. "Sure she's not, and I'm not a genius," he said sarcastically.

Gage leaned over the pipe corral fence. "Stop bragging, it's not that big an accomplishment. I should know."

Jude narrowed his eyes but didn't ask even though Gage could see the curiosity eating at him. "If you were half as smart as you think you are, you'd be doing something besides causing trouble. Obviously, you're a bright kid. Instead of being a criminal, why don't you try following the rules for a change and watch how much easier life gets?"

"Where has following the rules gotten you?"

Gage didn't miss the sarcasm in the kid's tone. The truth of the matter was that he'd always been a guy who followed the rules, did what he was supposed to, the right thing, but that wasn't helping him now. Kids like Jude, who hadn't followed the rules, had made him look bad, breaking the rules and pushing through an untested program had ruined his reputation, and a partner who wasn't following the rules might force him out of his business. Where had following the rules gotten him?

As if sensing Gage's misgivings, Jude pressed on. "You probably sit in some cubicle, filing papers, slaving away for every dime you earn while someone else is sitting fat and happy with the millions you earn him."

Gage almost laughed. If this kid had any idea how much money Gage actually earned each year, let alone how much he'd lost because of a kid like him, he'd pass out. "Not exactly."

"Whatever, dude." Jude waved him off, dismissing anything Gage might have to say. "I'm not going to work my ass off for someone else. I'm too smart for that."

"So you're too smart to work for someone else but not smart enough to avoid getting caught hacking into the school computer. Come on."

"I only got caught because they think I threatened Mr. Greene. I was just reminding him that I could get into his head."

Gage tipped his head to one side, focusing on the kid's face in the dying light of the sunset. "Bull, you wanted to get caught. Why?"

"Don't act like you know me."

"You just wanted to prove to the teacher and the admin that you could do it, right? That they'd underestimated you."

Jude looked up, meeting Gage's gaze with apprehension. He suddenly looked like the lost sixteen-year-old kid he was instead of the hard-ass he wanted everyone to think he was.

Gage moved closer, recognizing the struggle of a kid as bright as he'd been in school. "So, school is boring and teachers just can't teach to your level, right?"

Jude didn't answer, but he also didn't walk away. "And you don't even bother to do the homework, because it's as simple as basic addition."

"I'm in all advanced courses, and I feel like a freak because everyone around me keeps saying how hard the work is." He crossed his arms over the metal railings of the corral panels and leaned his chin against his forearms. "But it's not and they look at me weird when I say it."

Gage took a step closer, standing beside Jude, and hung his wrists over the railing. "So, you don't even bother doing the work anymore, right? Inside you want so much more than just existing, but there's nothing you can do on the outside."

"Only when our foster mom notices." Jude didn't say anything for a while. He just continued to stare at the horses. "How'd you know?"

Gage inhaled deeply, letting out his breath on a sigh. "Would you believe I was just like you?" He turned to face Jude. "Except I kept it on the right side of the law."

Jude glared at him, but there was little venom left in him now. He looked like a kid who wanted to believe in someone but had been burned too many times to trust anyone.

"I kept focused on school and grades, proving how smart I was. Following all the rules." Gage saw the corner of Jude's mouth lift slightly as he tried to hold back a smile. "In college, I found a great friend, George. We decided to start working together on programming. We wanted to show the world what we could do."

Gage shook his head, thinking back at how idealistic he and George had been. They wanted to make a difference, to reach the stars. They'd been naive enough to think that money and power wouldn't change them, or their ideas.

"Did you?"

Jude's question jolted him back to the present, to the circumstances he now faced: turn his back on George or fight the money and power they'd let control their business.

"We did, for a while. Now some people who decided it was better to ignore the rules are trying to ruin us."

Jude clenched his jaw and shook his head. "That's pretty fucked up."

Gage arched a brow at the kid's expletive but didn't say anything. He felt the same way. It was *fucked up*. To watch everything you'd believed in and worked for slipping through your hands.

"How do you think the school felt? You broke into their system, changed anything you wanted, and made them feel like fools. Even worse, instead of proving how smart you were, you just made them feel unsafe with you, like they couldn't trust you."

"But they won't forget me, either."

Maybe that was the point, for Jude to make his mark, but Gage read more into the comment. Maybe it was really a cry to have someone make him feel important, unforgettable.

LEAH LOOKED TOWARD the voices she heard coming from the corral. Part of her had wanted to get up and follow Jude, to explain to him how he could better focus his attention to stay out of trouble, how he didn't have to change his personality but simply his perspective. Instead, she'd watched Gage follow him, keeping her eyes on the pair as they talked. The last time they'd talked it had turned into a shouting match, but this time, they seemed to reach some sort of understanding.

Gage moved closer to Jude, and she saw the boy's stance relax slightly. She couldn't hear what they were saying, but she could see that Jude was listening, taking in what Gage was saying to him, and that, alone, might be more than she could do at this point. He needed someone to reach him, and Gage was a good role model, better than she was.

Cody, Hector, and Miguel plied her with questions about her past, her experiences in foster care and how she'd managed to go to college after graduating. She'd answered them as honestly as possible without going into too many details that no one needed to know.

As the fire blazed bright in the darkening sky, the boys set up their sleeping bags behind the logs, close enough for warmth while still being protected from sparks from the fire. She moved closer to the railing that marked the edge of the cliff, overlooking the river that cut a path through the meadow below.

Pine trees scented the air, circling the ridge like sentinels, and the soft gurgle of the water flowing over the rocks below was soothing. She glanced back at the soft snap of twigs underfoot and saw Jessie walking toward her.

"You didn't tell me."

"Would you have hired me if you knew?" Leah felt bad for keeping the truth from Jessie and Nathan, but she'd wanted this job—*needed* it—too much to risk being passed over due to a past she couldn't change.

"I already knew some of it. I just didn't expect you to talk about it."

Leah looked at her in surprise. "Really?"

Jessie laughed quietly. "Haven't you figured out yet that Heart Fire isn't like most places? Broken people fit in here, Leah. Maybe that's why I was drawn to your application from the start."

Leah looked at the river below, shrouded in darkness, avoiding the sympathy she could see in Jessie's gaze. "I'm not broken. Not anymore."

A warm hand fell softly onto her shoulder and squeezed slightly. "We're all broken, Leah, just in varying degrees. That's what makes us human. That's why we need other people."

Leah kept her eyes trained on the landscape in front of her as Jessie walked away, feeling more secure in her position at the ranch but less confident about the illusion she'd wanted to portray. She wondered for a moment how Jessie would react if she knew all the sordid details of her past. Would they still want her working for them? Would she still be so understanding?

She shook herself from her reverie as Gage appeared beside her, his hands hanging loosely over the railing. She hadn't even heard him approach. "I have to admit I'm a little surprised by how much you admitted to those boys," he said.

She forced herself not to look at him. Even with more than a foot between them, she could feel the heat coming from his body, as if he was a bonfire on his own. And that was the problem. Getting too close to Gage was going to end with her getting burned.

"They needed to hear it, to know they weren't alone here."

His hand slid to the side and covered hers, his fingers twisting through hers, and she stared at their hands. His was large, engulfing her smaller one as the firelight played over them. However, it was gentle in spite of the size and strength of it. She flipped her hand over so that their palms were together. For such an innocent touch, it felt incredibly intimate when Gage's thumb stroked the side of hers. Leah looked up at his face, lit only from the

dying bonfire, shadows and light playing over his cheek-
bones and eyes.

"Gage," she whispered in warning, but she didn't
remove her hand from his. She couldn't deny herself his
touch, any more than she could convince the warmth
emanating from his body not to seep into hers. Or maybe
this was some wildfire he'd ignited within her, sending
waves down her body to nestle low in her belly.

Gage let go of her hand, and she felt a moment of disappointment until he stepped behind her, surrounding
her with his body and curving his arms around her. "I
know, just friends." His chin rested on her shoulder as
her brain ceased to function. "I just wanted to let you
know you did great with those boys today."

His breath was warm against her neck, and her trai-
torous body responded of its own volition, leaning back
against his chest, letting the burn rage out of control.

"Jessie is lucky she found you." His lips found a spot
behind her ear and brushed against it, barely caressing the flesh as he spoke, sending a shiver of yearning
through her body. She dug her fingers into the railing of
the fence. "You should be proud of yourself."

"Gage."

This time her voice barely came out as a whisper of
sound, a plea on her breath, begging him. But she didn't
know what she was begging for. Her body ached for him
to touch her, to kiss her again the way he had in the early
morning hours, but her mind was ordering her to get as
far from him as possible. Her heart was caught in the
middle. She liked him too much to push him away, but

she was too afraid of the hurt he would bring to let him any closer.

His hands moved over hers on the railing, and he pried her fingers loose, twining their fingers and wrapping his arms around her again. "Leah, I won't hurt you."

"Yes, you will." She dropped her head forward. "You aren't staying."

His lips found the outer shell of her ear. "What if I did?" Gage slid the tip of his nose behind her ear, his lips sending jolts of white-hot lightning through her body.

She sighed, frustrated with him and herself for feeling torn. "I don't do relationships."

Gage chuckled quietly against her neck, dropping his chin to her shoulder. "Have you ever tried?"

He let go of one of her hands and ran a finger over the line of her jaw, gently turning her face toward him. His voice was a gravelly sound, making parts of her body throb. "You're asking those kids to step outside the box people have placed them in, to figure out another way to live the lives they have. Shouldn't you be willing to do the same?"

His lips hung just above hers. If she tipped her head even slightly, she could taste him again. And she wanted to, damn it. Every part of her body was practically crying out to be kissed by him again. But Gage wasn't moving any further. He'd conceded as far as he was willing. She wasn't sure how she knew it, but she was certain he was waiting for her to meet him halfway, to commit to wanting this from him. He wouldn't take a kiss, he wanted her to give it.

"Do you trust me?"

His words were a plea, whispering over her. She could feel his breath, moist and sweet, against her neck. It surprised her that after only a short time with him, she did trust him. She didn't *want* to trust him, but she did. Her life had been simple without the complication of friendships or lovers, but somehow this man had wormed his way past her usual impenetrable defenses.

"Yes." Saying the word aloud was almost painful, but it felt right. It was something she needed to do, and in that moment, Leah felt like she'd just taken a giant step away from her past and toward her freedom. "I do," she reiterated.

She stood on her toes, brushing her lips against his tentatively, unable to curb the smile that tugged at the corners of her mouth. "But I still have a job to do tonight, and you're distracting me."

Leah took a step backward, trying to put some space between them so she could think, but Gage pulled her close again, his palm cupping her jaw. She sucked in a quick breath just before his mouth slanted over hers. This time the kiss wasn't a sweet caress but a heated fusion. His groan rumbled against her chest, pressed against his, as his tongue sought hers in a duel that left her limbs languid and weak, swaying into him for support. He withdrew slowly, making sure she could stand on her own, but it was still too soon.

"Go do your job. We'll talk tomorrow when we get back."

Chapter Sixteen

LEAH CRACKED OPEN one eye and groaned as she pressed her toes into the end of her sleeping bag. Every muscle in her body ached again, but this time it was from sleeping on the ground, not the horseback riding. Even the foam pad Nathan had laid out under her sleeping bag hadn't helped much. If she was going to be doing this on a regular basis, she was going to need to figure out a way to make it more comfortable. She shivered as the cold morning air sliced through the padded bag. Tugging it up and over her nose, she debated whether it was worth freezing for the time it took to move closer to the fire she could see Jessie feeding back to life.

"Morning," Jessie said quietly. "I already have some coffee made if you're ready for it."

"You are a saint." That was enough temptation to draw Leah from her cocoon of warmth. She reached for one of the foam cups Jessie had set out beside a camp stove. "Do you always get up this early?"

Jessie smiled but kept her attention building the fire. "I'm always up early to get the horses fed, so this isn't atypical." She jerked her chin at the horses munching contentedly in the corral. "We'll let the boys sleep for a bit. Nathan will fix breakfast, so it'll be ready when they wake."

Leah snapped the lid onto her cup and took a sip, letting the coffee warm her from the inside out.

"What can I do to help?" She looked around at the camping equipment and realized she had no idea what to do with any of the items on the ground. She couldn't even tell what most of them were. "I'm feeling pretty useless at this point."

"Don't worry, you've got your work cut out for you today. What you did last night with them was a great start. They opened up to you because you connected with them." Jessie cut a glance in her direction, and Leah knew what was coming next. "You know, if you need to talk about anything…"

Leah couldn't imagine anything good that would come from telling Jessie about the payments that had been extracted from her for her mother's addiction. Even when faced with the emotional and physical scars she'd suffered, too many people had turned a blind eye and returned her to the very birthplace of her nightmares. No one wanted to see the truth. Talking about it now would only cause her to relive it.

Hard pass.

"Jessie, I understand if what I said last night makes you nervous, but realize that I've been through years of therapy." At least that much was true. "I've dealt with my past, and with help, those wounds were healed a long time ago." Leah prayed the blatant lie didn't show in her expression, that it wasn't flashing like a neon sign across her forehead.

Liar. Slut.

"What happened was bad enough that I don't want to let it impact my future any more than it already has."

Jessie nodded and glanced at Nathan, sliding out of his sleeping bag slowly. "Okay, but if you ever want to talk, about this or anything else, you can talk to me, Leah. I'd like to be your friend, not just your boss."

Fat chance, she thought, biting the corner of her lip.

Regardless of how much she liked Jessie and Nathan, they still employed her, paid her bills, and had the final say as to whether she stayed or went. Unless they had equal footing, which they never would as long as she worked at Heart Fire, they could never be real friends. There would always be a line in the sand.

"I appreciate that." Leah turned away as Jessie greeted her husband. She found herself walking back to the look-out area, tucking her free hand into the sleeve of her sweatshirt to stay warm.

As uncomfortable and out-of-place as she felt camping, she loved the tranquility of this place. Birds began to chatter in the trees, their warbling songs making the boys groan in protest, but she inhaled the sharp, clean scent of pine on the crisp air, making her nose tingle from the cold. Movement along the river caught her eye, and she watched several deer creep closer to the water for a drink. She'd never seen a deer in person. While the antlers were impressive, the animals were smaller than she'd thought they would be—smaller than the horses—and far more delicate boned; they moved with dainty grace.

"I must have died and gone to heaven in my sleep. Are you my personal angel?" Gage's voice was warm and seductive, like a caress or a sweet kiss, and it filled her with contentment.

Leah turned to see him approaching with his own coffee, steam spilling out of the small hole on top, trying to ignore the warmth spreading through her at his words.

"Ugh! That was awful, Gage." Jessie groaned from near the fire, drawing a chuckle from Nathan. "Are you still doing that? Give the stupid pickup lines a rest already. They don't work."

Nathan chuckled. "I told you, Gage."

The hell they don't.

Leah hid her smile by taking a sip of her brew as Gage bumped her with a hip. "Maybe my intention was to make Leah smile. And, there," he said smugly, pointing at her. "Mission accomplished."

Jessie rolled her eyes. "That's probably a pity smile because she thinks you're pathetically cheesy." She left the fire and shook one of the boys gently. "Time to get up, guys."

Leah laughed quietly at the protests coming from behind the log barrier, along with several requests for five more minutes.

"How'd you sleep?"

Gage's words were an innocent inquiry, but they felt more like an intimate suggestion. "I think sleeping on the ground is going to take some getting used to."

"It's not high on my list of things I love to do, but it's almost worth it for this view." He moved behind her, looking out over the terrain spread out in front of them, rubbing a hand over her arm when she shivered. "Cold?"

"A little," she admitted. Leah glanced back at the fire where Jessie was unconvincingly pretending to ignore them. "I was going to move back to the fire but then I saw them." She pointed her fisted hand at the deer by the water. "Look at all of them."

Gage's voice held the same wonder she felt as he followed her gaze. Without warning, he wound his free arm around her waist, the heat of his body warming her back. When another shiver traveled down her spine, she knew it wasn't from the cold this time. As much as she wanted to freeze this moment, to allow him to hold her while they watched the sunrise through the hills and savor his touch, Leah was here to do a job, and that meant maintaining a professional appearance to her boss and the boys she could hear climbing out of their sleeping bags.

"Gage," she whispered, slipping from his grasp, "I can't. Not with everyone here."

His eyes lit with amusement, but he moved to one side. "But you *want* to."

It wasn't a question, and she could tell from his overconfident smile, he didn't need for her to confirm he was right. She wasn't about to give him the satisfaction of admitting it, even if she could feel the cold creeping down her back where his body had just been.

"If I say yes, will you clean both litter boxes?"

Gage arched a brow and tipped his chin down. "If you say yes, I can promise a lot more than clean litter boxes."

Damn, if that didn't send more than a few butterflies into flight in her belly. Every nerve ending sparked to life and pulsed with anticipation. Just before he laughed quietly and walked away from her.

"GAGE, WOULD YOU come help me saddle the horses?"

The serious note of Jessie's voice didn't bode well for him. She'd warned him before this little field trip to stay away from Leah, and he hadn't missed the way she stopped whatever she might be doing to watch them every time Gage came within ten feet of Leah.

"Sure." He finished shoving the sleeping bag he was packing into the storage bag before slipping into the corral and locking the gate behind him. He crossed his arms as he turned toward her. "What now, Jess? Because we are both well aware of the fact that I barely know the difference between a stirrup and a saddle horn."

She glanced his way as she tugged at the cinch. "You know enough."

It was clear they weren't talking about saddles or horses. As much as he liked Jessie, he wasn't about to bow down and be bullied by her demands. "Is it really any of your business?"

She slapped the stirrup into place and turned toward him, laying one hand on the horse's neck. "It is when she works for me, and I'm the one who'll have to pick up the pieces when you decide to head back to your regularly scheduled life."

"What makes you think I'm going to leave her in pieces, Jessie? Leah is a big girl and I'm pretty sure she's been making grown-up decisions for a long time. Probably longer than either of us. I don't think she needs your permission, or your judgment, when it comes to who she dates."

Jessie's mouth pinched to a thin line, and he knew she was trying to control the fiery temper he'd heard rumors about, but he wasn't about to let this go.

"What's the real issue here? You didn't say a word when I dated Bailey."

"Leah isn't Bailey."

"No," he agreed, "she's not."

"Bailey recognized you for a player. She knew exactly where she stood, and if anything, I was worried about *you* getting hurt in that relationship." Jessie poked a finger against his chest. "Bailey wasn't starting a new job in a new city completely out of her element. She wasn't lonely, hurting, or fragile."

Gage wanted to laugh at the idea that Leah might be fragile. She was tough. Tough enough to stand up to a stranger on the side of the road, and tough enough to fight through the abuse she'd suffered. The image of her trembling in her kitchen, in the middle of a panic attack, flashed in his mind.

He couldn't deny she'd been fragile in that moment. The pain and the fear he'd seen in her eyes, the vulnerability she'd confessed. Leah wasn't weak, but she was breakable, and he knew that was what Jessie worried he might do.

"Jessie, I'm not going to hurt her."

"You can't know that." She pushed past him and lifted the saddle blanket to Grady's back where he waited, tied and already groomed. "You're leaving."

"About that. I don't think I am."

LEAH SAT AT the island in the kitchen while the kittens jumped and tumbled at her feet. After they'd arrived back at the ranch yesterday, Gage had disappeared, leaving her to clean the litter boxes and wonder what she'd said, or done, to make him want to avoid her like the plague so suddenly. One minute he was making promises that made her bones melt where she stood, and the next, he was riding at the front of the group with Nathan, acting like she didn't exist.

The kittens yowled from where they pounced on her feet, demanding breakfast. "Fine, you two," she answered with a sigh, scooping them into her arms. Both rewarded her with purrs of appreciation as Puma touched the tip of his nose to hers. "You two are spoiled brats."

Great! I've become that crazy lady who talks to cats.

"At least you monsters let me sleep last night."

"Knock, knock." Gage's voice sounded just before he entered the house.

"It's customary to wait until you're invited in. What if I wasn't dressed?" Leah asked with a scowl. It annoyed her that he was acting like he hadn't forgotten her existence last night.

"Then I'd have been a lucky man." He winked at her playfully, his gaze warm and languid as it slid over her.

She tried to ignore the fact that the tight yoga pants and the T-shirt didn't leave much to the imagination. At least she was wearing a bra. She turned her back on him and, standing on her toes, reached into the cupboard for another coffee mug, trying to still the butterflies that had taken flight the moment she heard his voice.

She should have felt outraged at his audacity. Instead, she just felt ridiculous, like a girl with a silly crush, not that it did anything to still the fluttering in her belly.

"Maybe I'd have skipped the coffee and headed straight for dessert."

His voice was low, reaching into her and heating her blood, as he stepped behind her, surprising her and causing her to bobble the cup in her hands.

"Here, I'll get it."

Gage slipped the mug from her fingers and moved away, leaving her feeling shaken and bereft, while he appeared completely relaxed. He poured himself a cup, spooning in the sugar, before taking a sip, peering at her over the rim.

"What?"

"You've got a lot of nerve."

She didn't like feeling defensive. It took her back to the time when she was a victim, helpless and waiting for the next attack. She'd spent too many years on the offensive, too many years planning ahead so that she didn't end up in this position. She'd spent too long making other people feel the way she did right now.

The kittens meowed a greeting and left their food bowls to wind themselves around his ankles. "I thought you were coming to clean the litter boxes last night when we got back. Instead, you just disappeared."

He arched a brow in question, and she realized how petty and needy she sounded. She hadn't felt this pathetic in years, since she'd first been escorted to Nicole's office and Nicole had pointed out that being helpless was a choice. She took a deep breath, vowing to be the strong woman she'd spent the past ten years becoming. She didn't need help from anyone.

"But whatever." She finished off the last of her coffee and put the cup into the sink. "I need to take a shower and get a few things together before I meet with the boys today. You're going to have to leave." She planted her fists on her hips, waiting for him to go. Instead, a slow smile spread over his face.

Damn him and that sexy mouth of his. She wasn't going to stand here and let him mock her. Leah brushed past him, but he reached out with his free hand and grasped her elbow, pulling her to his side.

"Why the rush to get rid of me? Are you trying to tell me that you missed me last night?"

Narrowing her gaze, she channeled all of the irritation she could muster, while his thumb was making circles on the inside of her forearm, sending a sizzle of heat up the limb and making it hard to catch her breath.

"I mean, did the kittens miss me?" He gave her a cocky grin. "Sorry, slip of the tongue."

He didn't look apologetic at all. For all she knew, he could have found some other stupid woman to watch movies with last night.

"Yes, well, you and that slippery tongue of yours can take your coffee to go." She tugged her elbow from his hand. "You know how to find the door."

"Come on, Leah. You can't be mad."

She spun to face him. "Who said anything about being mad? I just have a few things to get in order for my *job*. You know, that thing I do here to ensure I get a paycheck, so I can give you back the money for my car repairs."

She started down the hall, leaving him to watch her go. She might have thrown a little extra sway in her hips, but she'd never admit it to him.

"Which is exactly what I was doing last night." Leah stopped just outside of her office as he went on. "I had to take care of some…issues with work. There were phone calls and arrangements to make. I need to go to San Francisco tomorrow."

She turned slowly, facing him, trying to read him. He could be lying, but she didn't think he was. He'd already mentioned trouble at work, but what if this was just an excuse?

"Leah, I wanted to come over, but by the time I finished, it was really late." He ran a hand over his eyes. "Honestly, I wasn't sure if you wanted me to come over, and I wasn't in any frame of mind to be able to do…well, this." He let his hand fall to his side. "I was mentally exhausted and more than a little sore from the ride. I didn't want to take that out on you."

"Well, wasn't that thoughtful of you?" The ice in her tone even caught her by surprise. She turned her back on him and reached for the doorknob.

She felt him behind her even before his hand slid up the wooden frame of the door. He didn't touch her but he surrounded her—with his presence, his scent, the desire that rolled off of him in titillating waves. He brushed her hair away from her shoulder, his fingers moving over the curve of her neck exposed by her shirt, and she felt the longing coil tightly within her as his arm slipped around her waist, his palm lying against her stomach.

"You think I didn't want to come? It was killing me all day remembering how it felt to kiss you." His lips brushed over the sensitive spot behind her ear as he spoke. "I haven't been able to get the taste of you off my lips. You were part of the reason I couldn't come over last night. I couldn't stop thinking about you long enough to focus on the work I needed to be doing."

Leah let her head fall to one side with a sigh, giving him full access to the column of her neck. His lips found the pulse racing at her throat as he moved to one side of her, blocking her into the corner formed between the wall and the doorjamb. His hand slid around her back and curved around her waist. His thumb slid up over her ribs, teasing the underside of her breast; and his lips trailed hot kisses to her jaw. Leah's hands found his waist, clutching at the T-shirt he wore, wishing she was bold enough to slide her hands beneath and feel the flesh that was scalding her through the material.

"You're not ready for this. Any more than I am."

His words fell around her, each one stabbing her heart. He was saying exactly what she'd already thought, but hearing it come from his lips hurt more than she'd ever imagined.

Chapter Seventeen

"I should go." Gage sucked in a shaky breath. He didn't try to move away from her, and she didn't release her grip on his shirt. He could feel her palms heating his skin through the material.

Looking up at him through feathered lashes, her eyes sparked with desire. "No," she whispered. "You shouldn't."

He lifted his hand and brushed away the thick wave of hair that had fallen into her face, tucking it behind her ear. He pressed his forehead against hers and felt her tense. Gage took a deep breath and pressed a kiss to her cheek before reaching for her hands. "Yes, I should."

"Gage?"

He knew he should walk out of the house and head back to his cabin. He should be thinking about the meeting he'd set up with George, Cooper, and their fourth partner and CFO, Griffin Masters. He *should* be studying the spreadsheets to see if there was a way they could still pay out the court settlements without laying off loyal employees. Being at Heart Fire, watching Jessie adamantly champion Leah, made him remember that, not too long ago, before he'd fallen victim to the whims of corporate greed, he'd done the same for his employees. He wanted to be that man again. Leah made him want to stand up and be that man again, the one who defended those who couldn't fight for themselves, the one who would be an advocate for those who couldn't speak. He shook his head and walked back toward the front door.

She stopped at the edge of the hall, forcing him to pause and turn back to her. "Why?" Her voice was quiet but demanding.

He pulled her toward him, and she came into his arms willingly but kept her palms against his chest, as if she was ready to flee if she felt threatened. He put his finger under her chin and lifted her face to meet his gaze.

"Leah, you flinch whenever I touch you. I can feel you tense up. I don't want you to feel like I'm forcing this on you." Gage ran his thumb gently over her cheek. "I'm going to go for now. I'll come back later after you're finished with the boys today, and we can have dinner or something, okay?" He pressed a kiss to her forehead and started for the door.

"Every man who has ever touched me has hurt me, except you."

Her words stopped him mid-stride. Gage hung his head, praying she wouldn't go on, hoping that what he was sure she was about to tell him hadn't happened to her.

"The first time was when I was ten. He made me strip down, and she told him he could touch me. I can't even count how many times it happened after that. But when I was twelve…" Gage turned to see Leah shake her head, saw the ashen pallor of her skin, the coldness in her eyes. "She needed more money, so when he told her what he'd pay to have sex with me…she was too strung out to even know what was happening to me."

Gage didn't need to ask who. She'd already mentioned her mother. He felt repulsion at the nightmare Leah lived as a child, hating the one person who should have protected her. His fists clenched at his sides, and he could feel the bile rising in his throat at the perversion she'd been forced to endure.

"I couldn't do anything to stop it. Every time I ran away, they brought me back. If I told someone what happened, she told them I was lying."

Gage wondered if she even realized she was crying. The tears slid down her cheeks, unchecked, but Leah seemed distant, completely detached from the girl who suffered so deeply. Her arms hung limply at her sides, and although she looked at him, Leah's blank stare didn't see him. She was completely focused on the nightmare she was reliving.

"So, I finally decided that if I couldn't make it stop, I would at least control it. I started making them pay me directly, instead of her. At least that way, I could manage the situation and keep myself from catching something the way she did. I could hide some of the money for food and bills."

Gage felt like he'd been kicked in the gut by her revelation. She couldn't possibly be saying that she'd prostituted herself. But Gage couldn't work up the self-righteousness to judge her. As bad as things had been when his father was alive, he'd had his brother and his mother. He'd still had a family he could count on. Leah had no one. Everyone had failed her. The hardened exterior he believed she revealed to the world was formed for sheer survival.

He reached out to her, unable to control the instinct to want to comfort her.

Her eyes suddenly cleared, and she took a step backward in the hall, distancing herself from him. He could see her trying to build the wall between them, higher and stronger. She'd let him see her deepest vulnerabilities, and now she wanted to hide.

"How can you touch me? Don't I disgust you? I'm dirty. Contaminated by everything I did, and I'll never be clean again, if I ever was."

Her voice broke, and her strength seemed to disappear as she leaned back against the wall, sliding down it to curl into a ball on the floor. Her entire body trembled as tears poured from her. Gage fell to his knees in front of her, reaching out to pull her into his lap, wrapping himself around her, whispering words he wouldn't even remember saying, sharing the pain he could feel flowing from her like an infected wound finally cleansed.

He felt his own heart breaking for her, for the child she'd been, for the young woman who hadn't been able to figure out a better way, for the innocence she'd lost.

She'd opened up to him and revealed more than he'd ever expected. She'd entrusted him with a gift. And a curse.

They couldn't go back. Gage couldn't unhear any of this. It had changed things between them, but he wasn't sure to what extent. Contrary to what she'd expected, he wasn't turning away from her. He wasn't repelled by her past, just by what had been done to her. He found himself wanting to help her more than ever before.

Leah was a fighter, a warrior who battled odds that would have made most people drown in fear and self-destruction. She had continued to fight her way to the surface, and he respected her. He wanted to lift some of the burden from her shoulders, to give her a safe place to be weak, knowing someone else would be strong for her.

"Leah," he whispered against her hair, wishing again he could shoulder the pain for her, to change her past. "Baby, look at me. You're not dirty." His hands cupped her face, forcing her to look into his eyes, to see the truth in them instead of in the tainted words she'd been told by others. "You're beautiful and strong and...God, Leah, you're incredible."

Gage pressed kisses to her forehead, her cheeks, her eyelids, tasting the salty tears that continued to slip down her cheeks, as she shook her head in denial.

"Listen to me." Her eyes opened, and he could see she was. "What happened to you wasn't your fault. You did what you had to do to survive. You got out."

"But what I did..." She buried her face into his chest.

He could remind her that she would never judge one of her patients the way she was judging herself. Or point out that she hadn't had other options. Or point out to her how far she had come from the girl she'd once been. But none of those things would offer what she needed most—someone to hold her until the terror of the past faded, like a child waking from a bad dream. Leah needed him to be a rock for her to cling to while the waves of self-recrimination crashed around her. He would help her hold on as long as she needed him to.

LEAH WOKE AS the light streamed in through the window, while the dark brown curtain blew slightly as a light breeze fell into the room. She stretched out on top of the large bed, feeling spent and wondering how she ended up in her room.

She bolted upright in the bed as the memories flooded back—Gage coming for coffee, getting angry, telling him about her past—everything, including the mistakes she'd made. She looked around the room, searching for anything that might give her a clue where Gage had gone. Her eyes fell on the clock, and she realized the boys would be here in less than an hour for a final session before they left. Leah swung her legs over the side of the bed as Gage entered the room.

"What are you doing?" he asked.

"I have a session, remember? I need a quick shower."

"Leah."

She held up a hand, cutting him off. "Don't, Gage. We can talk about this another time." She turned her back on him, as she reached for a shirt in the closet. "Or not at all. Trust me," she said, turning to look at him over her shoulder. "I wouldn't blame you at all for trying to forget everything I told you."

Gage crossed the room in just a few strides and turned her so that she faced him, his hand curving at the side of her neck, his fingers burying themselves into her tangled hair.

"Don't." He closed his eyes. "Don't start hiding from me again."

Her hands rested against the wall of his abs, and she felt him tense. She wanted to deny everything, to fall back into the stoic persona she'd cultivated, but he'd already seen the truth. He'd seen how paper-thin that facade was. His thumb traced the line of her jaw, as he tipped her face up to his, and the familiar shiver of heat spread through her limbs.

"I don't know how to do anything else," she confessed. "I've been hiding all my life. From my mother, from people who wouldn't believe the truth." She let her forehead fall against his chest, hiding her face and her shame. "I shouldn't have told you."

"You have no idea what your trust means to me." His voice was thick with emotion, sounding like he was holding back his own tears. "I never meant to make you feel the way…" He didn't finish the thought, but she didn't need him to.

"Gage, you *never* hurt me or made me feel afraid. When I'm with you, when we…" She took a step back so he could see her face. "I don't feel the way I did. That's what's so confusing for me. It scares me." She felt the blush cover her cheeks and turned away before he could see it, walking to the end of the bed. "Everything in my life has taught me that sex is a tool, either a bargaining chip or a weapon to hurt. Use or be used. But with you…it's not like that."

Gage took a step toward her, but she held out her hand. She wanted to finish saying this before her nerve left her, before she let fear or common sense swallow up her courage.

"Wait, let me finish. I'm not saying I expect anything from you in return, especially after everything I told you. Obviously, I'm not as far removed from my past as I like to believe I am, but you make me feel like I could be, like I could get to that point where it can't affect my future."

Gage stopped where he was, about two feet from her, and tucked his fingers into the front pockets of his jeans. She could see the tension in his shoulders, but she couldn't tell if it was because what she said encouraged or upset him.

"I don't know what this is," she said, waving her hand between them, "but thank you for this morning. I have never had anyone but Nicole who would just be there for me."

"How long were you with her?" His question was quiet and not the one she'd expected, giving everything she'd confessed.

"She was my high school counselor and eventually became my foster mother for two years." Her eyes misted with tears. "She's the reason I wanted to become a therapist. I wouldn't be alive if it weren't for her."

Gage's shoulders seemed to relax slightly as he closed the distance between them, letting his hands fall to her upper arms, pulling her back into his embrace. "I'd love to meet her someday," Gage said as he tucked her head beneath his chin.

She smiled sadly against his throat. "You can't, but she'd have liked you."

"I'm sorry. She must have been a great woman," he whispered against her hair, and she realized he must have guessed by her use of past tense that Nicole was no longer in her life. "And I will be there for you whenever you need me."

"You can't promise that. You don't know me that well." In spite of her cynical nature, Leah wanted to believe him, to take him at his word and trust his promise. After what he'd seen and heard this morning, he was still here. That alone said a lot about Gage's character.

"What? You don't think spending twelve hours a day together for the last week is enough to know you?" She felt his smile against her hair, felt him relax as he ran his hand over the back of her head. "Leah, I don't know everything about you, but I told you I would be your friend. I wasn't lying then and nothing you've said can change that. I care about you."

Relief coursed through her, sapping whatever strength she had left, and she leaned into him, tightening her arms around his waist and enjoying the moment. For the first time, she felt like she could trust someone else to be strong for her and allow herself a chance to release the fear that had dogged her for so long. He hadn't tried to fill her head with pretty words, he didn't try to pretend her past didn't matter, he didn't try to convince her that he loved her or ask her for something she couldn't offer him.

All of those things would have been lies. Instead he gave her his honesty, and that made her feel safer than any lie ever could.

Chapter Eighteen

"Nathan, I need your help." Gage didn't know who else to turn to. If nothing else, Nathan would have the connections to help him get the ball rolling on the idea he'd been contemplating since his conversation with Jude.

"What's up?" Nathan looked up from the computer in the office he shared with Jessie. "Recovered from the campout yet?"

"Yeah, that was fun." Gage rolled his eyes as he took a seat in one of the plush, leather chairs situated in front of the mahogany desk. "How do I go about setting up a nonprofit organization? I want to start a school."

Nathan's brows shot toward the ceiling. "A what?"

"Well, maybe not a school exactly, but a place where kids could go learn skills, either mechanical or technical, something that might help them feel like they weren't just wasting their brains being bored in a classroom all day. It needs to be for at-risk kids, not some pandering day-camp." He ran a hand over the top of his head as he continued to think aloud. "I want it to be challenging but something that will help them learn how to do good instead of using their genius to get into trouble."

Nathan folded his hands in front of him. "You mean Jude."

"Not just Jude, but kids like him. He's smart, a freaking genius, and he's lashing out because he's bored, and no one is giving him an outlet to use that brain. What if I could create a place where he could?"

Nathan leaned back in his chair, crossing his arms. "Well, for starters, you'd have to decide who you'd help. Just smart kids? And how would you set the standard, IQ tests? Or would it be for anyone who wanted to attend? Then you'd have to set up some sort of curriculum or educational plan. Once you have that, you're going to need to write out a business plan and start finding investors willing to participate. All while you're trying to get your 501c3 status. It's going to be a lot of work."

"I'd be one of the main investors." Gage had no problem forking out money for a cause that would teach kids how to be a positive influence on the future of technology rather than a hindrance.

"You or Iconics Industries?"

"Does it matter?" He trusted Nathan's input. The man was highly intelligent and one of the most sought after financial analysts in the United States, but more than anything else, Gage knew he was a good person. Nathan had fought against corruption more than once to make sure the right side prevailed.

"You can give your money to any cause or person you choose. However, Iconics Industries can't. There are meetings and shareholders to convince, documentation to provide if they are going to be major contributors." Nathan paused, as if unsure how to proceed. "This wouldn't have anything to do with bolstering Iconics' image after the latest less than stellar product release, would it?"

Of course, Nathan would know Iconics was at fault for the recent system breaches. But that had nothing to do with Gage's interest in starting a foundation. He missed getting involved in the creative process, honing his skills, and figuring out problems. He was tired of letting everyone else create while he just checked the product and signed off on it. He didn't want to answer to stockholders and worry about what their shares were selling for. He needed to feel like he was making a difference again. He had lost his passion for his work at some point in the past ten years, and somehow, in the last week here with Leah and Jude, he remembered what it felt like to have that again.

He would pay the price for his error, and he would step down from his position at Iconics, but he could only do it if there was something better waiting. This was his "something better."

"It has to do with Iconics, but not in the way you think. Can you help me do this? Help me find the best people to make this successful?"

A slow grin spread over Nathan's face, his eyes brightening. "I can make some calls. For the record, I think this is a great idea."

LEAH WAVED GOOD-BYE to the boys as Melody backed her SUV down the driveway. She was going to miss them. At the clinic where she'd worked before coming to Heart Fire, it was a relief when one of her clients moved on. It meant they'd progressed to a point where she was no longer needed, or they found someone else. In reality, she'd never had time to miss anyone. Her patient load was far too heavy, and complex, to wonder what might happen in the future. But with these four boys, she hoped they'd return, even as she wished they wouldn't.

"I should probably head out tonight, too." Gage's hand reached for Leah's as Jessie turned to face them.

"Oh, are you *leaving*?"

Leah could feel the tension spark between the two of them and wondered what had caused the sudden animosity.

"I have a few meetings in the Bay Area. I should be back in a couple of days."

"I thought you were leaving tomorrow," Leah said.

Leah glanced up at him, standing behind her, and was struck again by his dark, expressive eyes as he gazed down on her. She could see more in them than she wanted to— concern, respect, desire. If they were alone, he'd kiss her, she had no doubt. And she wouldn't stop him.

"I had to schedule a few more meetings than I thought I would. It shouldn't take more than a few days."

"Uh-huh." Jessie obviously didn't believe him, and Leah wondered why it mattered. "We have a group coming next Monday, so you have this week to prepare. They'll be here for ten days, and it's going to be about eight girls, ranging from fourteen to eighteen." Jessie shot Leah a nervous glance. "They've been recommended to us from a women's shelter in Sacramento to help them deal with abuse."

Gage's hand squeezed hers reassuringly. This wasn't the first time she'd been expected to counsel women who'd been abused; however, it was the first time since sharing her experience with someone who knew that it might affect her. With Gage, she couldn't pretend that it wouldn't be difficult or that she wasn't relating to their experiences. He could read her, whether she wanted him to or not.

She met Jessie's gaze, saw the way she examined them. This was also the first time she would have someone watching her closely, scrutinizing her every reaction.

"I have a few ideas that should get some conversations started. We can't do it the way we did with the boys, but I think a night on The Ridge would be a great idea. Without Nathan and Gage." She cast an apologetic glance at Gage. "No offense."

"None taken. I'm sure men are the last thing they need around. I just hope you're not too jealous of the nice, comfy bed I'll have," he teased.

Jessie glared at him. "For the girls, I'll bring blow-up mattresses and tents. You can stay in your nice, comfy bed, alone." She turned her attention to Leah. "I'll set it up for Tuesday, after they've had their first riding lesson. We can get my sister and Bailey to come, maybe bring a few of the therapy dogs as well."

It was actually a brilliant idea. The animals worked wonders for helping people find comfort and to loosen their reservations enough to talk, especially knowing that their secrets were safe, since the animals wouldn't judge. For those that might be intimidated by the size of the horses, the dogs could provide a welcome substitution. Leah had tried to convince the clinic to try therapy animals with several of her clients, but they had never approved her requests.

"I love the idea."

"We should take a ride to Julia's place this week, and Bailey can help you figure out which dogs would work out best for our program. I'm sure Moose would love a friend or two around here to play with." At the mention of his name, the giant shepherd nudged her hand. Jessie looked from Leah to Gage before her eyes fell on their clasped hands, and a frown formed on her brow. "I have work to do."

"What was that about?" Leah turned on Gage when Jessie had left earshot.

He shrugged nonchalantly and reached for her waist. "Who knows?"

"*You* know and don't pretend you don't." Leah pulled her hand from his grasp. "She is my boss, Gage. I can't risk losing this job."

"You're not going to lose your job." He sighed as he slipped his hands to her hips and drew her close. "First of all, you're great at your job and Jessie can see that. She's not going to let you go because of me. Second, this isn't her decision to make."

Leah's hands slid up his arms, coming to rest on his biceps, flexing slightly under her fingertips. "And what *decision* is that? What exactly is *this?*"

Gage's eyes smoldered, growing darker with each second that ticked by. "I honestly don't know what to call it, Leah."

The way his voice dropped, the husky sound that seemed to caress her skin as he drew her close, his arms moving around to her back, the musky scent of him surrounding her, made her pulse race even as her blood pooled in places she never thought it would.

Desire, longing, need—she'd never experienced any of them. The ability to feel any sort of sexual attraction had been stolen from her before she'd even understood that it was a natural experience, one that everyone *should* have. Years of sexual abuse had killed any sense of excitement and replaced it with fear. She'd secretly been envious of the women who felt anything, convincing herself that she was above her most base instincts, but the fact that she never experienced them reminded her of the pain of her past, making her feel used and wasted.

Even now, instead of relishing every moment with Gage as her pulse fluttered in her chest and the heat spiraled through her body, she fought the natural instincts Gage drew out in her. She fought the yearning to touch him, to feel his skin scorching her, to trace the valleys and ridges of muscle she could feel under the waffled Henley shirt he wore, to let his hands explore her.

A flush rose over her, and she licked her lower lip before biting the corner. Gage groaned quietly, deep in his chest.

"Aw, hell, Leah, stop looking at me that way, or you're going to get us both into trouble." She lifted her gaze to see his deep brown eyes nearly black with desire. Gone was the look of concern and sweet kindness she usually saw. She saw him clench his jaw, felt his fingers dig into the soft flesh of her hip slightly. "Let's go for a walk."

"A walk?" she repeated, unable to force her brain to function and spit out words that made sense. Leah wondered if every bit of her brain's blood flow hadn't been rerouted.

"Yes," he growled. "Because walking will force you to stop looking at me like I'm your next meal and you've just decided you're starving." He reached for her hand and dragged her toward one of the walking paths that led to the paddocks behind the barn. "And it will give us some privacy."

"So will my house." She made the offer without thinking.

"Dear God, you're trying to kill me," Gage muttered under his breath.

GAGE HAD BEEN desperately trying to figure out a way to keep a safe distance between him and Leah since her revelation. Not because he wanted to, but from the sound of things, she'd never had any healthy relationships, even friendships, other than one she'd shared with her counselor, and his heart ached with the loneliness she must have felt over the years. He didn't want her to feel like he was pressuring her into anything. She'd been coerced and violated enough in her life. He would force his body into submission because he would not rush this with her.

He wanted to make sure she knew what it felt like to be cherished, what it should have felt like to be loved.

Easy there, Ace. Love is a strong word.

He couldn't argue with his own logic, and he wasn't admitting he was in love with Leah, but he cared about her, a lot, and it was different than it had been with any other woman he'd dated—not that the two of them were even really dating. What the hell were they doing, anyway?

So far she'd been silent as they walked behind the barn, and he was grateful she hadn't pressed him about what Jessie had said. He hadn't told her yet about Jessie warning him to stay away. He would prove Jessie wrong, so that the entire issue was a moot point. What Jessie didn't know yet was that he wasn't going to be another man who hurt her, nor was he leaving. Watching Leah with the boys helped him make that decision.

He'd been tied up for far too long in the drudgery of corporate politics. He and George had started the company in order to help people. Somewhere along the way, that purpose had been lost. After their camping trip, he'd quickly realized that he was blaming the wrong people for his slide into shame. It wasn't the hackers who'd trashed his reputation; he'd done that well before they ever found the backdoor into the security program. He'd sold his soul, and he was going to make it right. If not for the woman beside him right now, he would have never recognized it.

Leah sighed heavily from beside him, and he looked down at her. "Gage, if you are trying to tell me something, just say it."

He frowned at the uneasiness in her voice. "Like what?"

"Like that this was fun while it lasted, that you're moving on, that this didn't mean anything...Just go to San Francisco."

"Leah, I—"

"I'm a big girl, Gage. It was a few kisses." She tried to sound nonchalant, but he could hear the wounded note in her tone.

"You're a terrible poker player."

She stopped and leaned her back against the wall of the barn. "I am a terrific poker player. Trust me, if I wanted to hide something from you, I could, and you'd never find out."

"Could you?" His hands reached for her hips, sliding up to the curve of her waist, his thumb tracing a circle over her flat belly. He heard her slight gasp and his gaze focused on her mouth, the way her lips parted slightly as her teeth bit softly into the flesh.

"You can't make me fall for you, Gage."

His surprised gaze crashed into hers, but she looked away just as quickly, and he could see the retreat she was trying to make. He tucked the side of his finger under her chin, lifting her face up again and dipped his head closer, his lips barely brushing against hers.

"No?"

She rolled her lips inward and shook her head. He could feel the hesitation radiating from her, even as her fingers clenched in his shirt, drawing him closer.

"Have you ever fallen in love?" She shook her head again. He'd figured as much. "Falling is the easy part. The rest of it, the putting someone else's needs and desires above your own, allowing yourself to trust another person enough that you relinquish control, that's the hard part."

"I can't do that." The admission quietly slipped out as her lashes fluttered closed, fanning on her cheeks.

"Leah, look at me." She obliged, and he could see the yearning in her eyes. She might not think she could, but he could see she *wanted* to.

Trust and control, the two things she clung to with a death grip. But Gage could see a passion in her begging to be released, and he wanted to be the one to prove her wrong, to show her she *could* trust someone without getting hurt.

"Maybe you can't, but I can." His finger traced the line of her brow, down her cheek and over her jaw to her chin. "I trust you. You can take whatever you want, whatever you need, from me."

Leah's breath caught, and Gage lay his cheek on the top of her head, waiting. He couldn't let his own yearning cloud his judgment, and this had to be her decision alone, not something she felt coerced into. She needed some time to make a choice out of her true desire, not one clouded by lust that she would regret. Gage refused to be something she would look back on with sorrow.

Leah hesitated and he could see the indecision in her eyes. Just as he saw the way her breath hitched as his fingers moved down the side of her neck. Leaning forward, he pressed a kiss to the racing pulse at her throat, inhaling the sweet scent of her.

"Tell me what you want," he whispered against her skin.

"Just once, I want to know what it feels like to be loved instead of used." She looked deeply into his eyes, her whiskey-colored eyes warm with raw emotion. "I want you."

Gage had never heard sweeter words in his life.

Leah tugged on his hand, pulling him between the barns in order to get to his cabin around the corner faster. Once they arrived at the door, she turned toward him, her eyes warm and inviting as she waited for him to open it.

"Leah, are you sure you want this?"

Her hands landed against his waist, pressing him against the door, the worn planks biting into the center of his spine. Leah's hands slid up to his shoulders and around his neck, pulling him toward her while his arms circled around her back with answering urgency.

She stood on her toes, pressing her mouth against his, hungry, needy, the sweet kisses they'd shared gone. Her hand skimmed over the back of his head, his short hair rasping against her palm as she slid her tongue into his mouth, tasting him, teasing, taking what he so willingly wanted to give her, and Gage knew there was no way he could refuse her. Leah would know what it felt like to be loved for the first time.

Chapter Nineteen

LEAH REFUSED TO allow her past to color what her body and her heart were demanding from her. If she allowed herself to think too much, to question the logic of her decision, her past would creep in and suffocate her. It was easier to just feel, to let Gage's words wash over her, relieving her fears.

She *could* trust him. Hadn't he proved that every day of the last week she'd spent with him? He wasn't like any man she'd ever known. The mere fact that she'd allowed him this close to her proved that. He'd seen her worst: the dark, damaged, fearful girl inside the woman, but instead of casting her aside, he'd pulled her close. Leah didn't want to consider what tomorrow might bring or even the consequences of this choice. Right now, she wanted to know what it felt like to have someone care, to feel a man's gentle touch instead of a painful one. She wanted to know what it felt like to be made love to, even if it was only this one time.

Gage's hand reached behind him and turned the doorknob, his other wrapped around her waist, keeping them from both falling into the room. He lifted her slightly, enough that he could move into the cabin with her and shut the door behind them, and she smiled slightly against his lips.

"That was sort of 'cave man,' don't you think?"

He settled her back on her feet. Panic began to rise in her as she wondered if he'd just locked her inside, if she could get away if needed.

As if reading her mind, Gage released her and moved to sit on the arm of the sofa in the middle of the room. "We need to talk for a second. I want you to be sure."

It was so surprising, so unlike anything she'd expected from a man who had a willing woman in his arms, that she took a step back. "Gage, I—"

He held up a hand. "Leah, I want to make love to you. You have no idea how much I want to make love to you."

His voice was strained, and he closed his eyes for a moment. Leah saw his fingers digging into the leather, as if he was trying to hold onto his control. He shook his head, his chest still rising and falling with ragged breaths. "But I won't take anything from you. I can't. You've had too much demanded, forced upon, and taken from you. I don't want you to feel like you have to…" He ran a frustrated hand over his head. "I don't want this to be something you look back on and regret."

His words were so tender, so heartfelt and honest, that they settled over her like a warm blanket, wrapping around her heart and sheltering it from her doubts. She'd only had one person in her life who'd cared about how she felt, or thought beyond what she could do for them. To have Gage, the only man she'd let close enough to see the reason for the bitter shell she'd become, care for her was more than she could have dreamed to hope for. It was that realization that ignited the smoldering embers of her heart.

This was the difference between having sex and making love.

Leah moved forward, reaching for his hand and slipping her body between his thighs. "Gage, I won't regret this." She wrapped his arm around her back, cupping his jaw and tipping his face so he would look into her eyes. "I told you. When I'm with you, it's not like before. You don't take, you give." She kissed his forehead and felt his other hand on her thigh, heat bursting white-hot in her belly. "You've been giving to me since you saw me stranded."

Leah ducked her head and kissed him then, letting go of the restraint she'd been clinging to. Gage's palm slid up her thigh to curve around her rear as he stood, his fingers gripping her, the friction of his chest brushing against hers stoking a fire in her that she'd never experienced before. She swept her tongue into his mouth, desperate for more of him, tugging at his shirt in an effort to get it off.

"Oh, no, you don't." Gage pulled her hands together at his chest before kissing the knuckles of one hand. "In every way that matters, this is your first time. I want this to be special, not rushed."

He silently drew her with him into his room, stopping at the edge of the massive bed and turning on the bedside lamp before tugging at the back of his shirt, pulling it off, and casting it aside. The man standing in front of her made her mouth water. He was perfect. His caramel skin was flawlessly sculpted muscle and flesh. Every inch of him practically glowed in the soft light, and she reached her hands to his chest, allowing herself a moment to finally relish the experience of his skin under her palms as they slid up to his shoulders.

"Leah," he growled deep in his throat, both plea and warning. "Do you have any idea what you're doing to me?"

"Is it anything like what you're doing to me?" He stared down at her, and she could see the concern in his eyes. She ran her thumb along the edge of his bottom lip. "Whatever is making you worry, stop. I want this, with you."

Gage caught her hand and pressed a kiss to the inside of her wrist. His eyes, so expressive, were filled with hunger for her, and she wanted him to know she felt the same way. Leah slid her hand from his and began unbuttoning her shirt, revealing herself to him, something she'd never done before.

As much as she wanted to shut out her past from their present, she couldn't help but acknowledge the differences. With Gage, she wanted him to see her, all of her, to be open and vulnerable with him. She wanted to give all of herself because she trusted him not to take from her anything she didn't willingly offer.

His earlier words about falling in love rang through her clearly. She hadn't thought she could trust anyone enough to let go, didn't think she could care about any-one enough to put their desires above her own. But she wanted to with Gage. She'd fallen for him, in spite of her adamant unwillingness, and for the first time, she felt desire to be with a man. Not just any man. Gage.

Gage watched her slip the shirt from her shoulders, his eyes so dark they were almost black, but it was easy to read the longing in his face. His fingers moved to her collarbone, tracing the line of her bra strap to where her breast swelled, aching for his touch.

"You're so beautiful. It almost makes me hurt."

She reached behind her and unclasped the hooks, letting the garment slide down her arms and fall to the floor. "Gage?"

Leah reached for him, desperate to touch him, and sighed as her hands landed on his chest. She pressed a kiss to the muscled wall, the heat of his body scorching her, making her want more. She wrapped her arms around him, pressing her body into his, her breasts crushing against him, feverish with yearning.

Instead of laying her down on the bed, Gage wrapped his arms around her and turned so he sat on the mattress with her between his thighs, his hands on her hips, and he looked up at her. Pressing a kiss in the valley between her breasts, Gage slid one hand up, tracing the curve before his thumb brushed over the sensitive peak. She gasped as pleasure shot through her, making her knees weak and her limbs liquid. His thumbs stroked her belly, and she whimpered at his touch.

"Please?"

The word fell from her lips, unbidden, as her head dropped forward and she reached for the button on her jeans. Gage smiled slightly as he brushed her hands aside and worked the button himself. His breath was moist and hot against her skin, causing a shiver to break out over her. He took her breast into his mouth before letting his tongue swirl over her. Leah gasped as his hands slid her jeans from her hips, dragging her underwear off as well, as he ran his fingers inside the denim material and down her thighs. Gage pressed kisses to her stomach as he helped her out of her pants, letting his fingers brush up the back of her thighs, holding her steady when her body wanted to collapse in the maelstrom of heady desire making her feel faint.

When he slid a finger into her core, where her need burned hottest, Leah cried out, clinging to his shoulders as he caressed her. Her body arched against him as he found the center of her desire, stroking it into a flaming inferno until she cried out again, her nails digging into his shoulders as her release washed over her, leaving her spent and limp in his arms.

Gage rose, laying her onto the bed and jerking the rest of his clothing off in one swift motion. Her eyes slid over him, taking in every hard ridge and taut muscle. As he lay beside her, his finger traced the curve of her thigh, over her hipbone, skimmed her waist, and settled over her ribs. As much as she loved his hands on her, she wanted to touch him. Leah pressed him onto his back, leaning over him.

The corner of his mouth tipped up in a grin. "What are you doing?"

"I know you want this to be slow and special, but I need to touch you."

She ran her fingers down the ridges of his abs, feeling them flex as she moved her hand lower and she bent toward him, her lips hovering just above his. His fingers clenched against the rounded curve of her rear. "I need *you*."

Gage buried his hand into the mass of waves falling around their faces like a curtain, sheltering them from everything around them. Right now, there were no doubts, no fears, no past, and no future. He kissed her, a groan of sweet agony slipping deliciously into her mouth as her fingers wrapped around him, stroking him to the same heights he'd taken her.

Gage reached for her hand, stilling it and breaking their kiss. "Enough." He rolled her beneath him, hovering over her. "I'll be right back."

He headed into the bathroom. She heard a cabinet close before he returned. Then he tore open the foil packet between his fingers and sheathed himself. His gaze skimmed over her, so hot and intense, she could feel herself growing warm all over again.

"Are you staring at my chest?" she asked, holding his jaw in her hands as he slid up the length of her body, pressing kisses along the way and making her squirm with delight beneath his ministrations.

A wicked grin tipped the corner of his mouth, and she felt her heart skip a beat. "No, I'm staring at your heart."

Laughter fell from her lips but died on a sigh when his tongue circled the peak of her left breast. Her fingers dug into the muscles in his back, and she arched into him. Gage was solid and strong, his body cradled between her thighs. Leah opened beneath him, wrapping her legs around him and urging him closer. He didn't withhold anything from her, pressing himself into her, and she couldn't stop the sound of pure bliss that escaped her.

"Gage," she whispered against his shoulder, as she buried her face into him.

He paused, his body filling her. "Don't hide from me, Leah. I want to see every bit of what you feel in your eyes." His voice was a growl, and she knew he was fighting for the same control over his desire.

His hand slid down to grip her thigh and drag it up to his hip, inching himself deeper into her. What little control Leah had over her passion snapped. She bucked beneath him, rising up to meet each thrust, driving her closer to the brink of ecstasy, until she crested the pinnacle with him. She drew him down for a deep kiss as her climax burst within her, afraid that he would see more than she wanted him to in her eyes. Afraid he would see how deeply she'd come to care for the one man who had shown her what it was to be loved.

GAGE LAY SPENT with Leah lying against his chest. A fine sheen of sweat still covered them both, but he didn't want to move. Her fingers played over his heart where his pulse was finally slowing. Making love to her had been incredible, and far more devastating than he'd expected.

It had nearly killed him to try to hold back, to keep from letting his feelings for her consume him, but in the end, it had been useless. Leah had reached inside him and gripped his heart with both hands, marking him forever as hers. And she had no idea what she'd done. She would figure it out if he stayed though, and he couldn't have that. Not yet. Not before he'd told her everything.

What he should do was put some distance between them, to get into his car and get his ass to San Francisco. He needed to get his own life settled. Then he could come back and tell her the truth about who he was and what he could offer her. Once he had this mess with his partners settled, he could be free of the chokehold his mistakes had over him and take the first steps toward his future, with Leah. A fresh start with a woman who needed him. But until then…

His fingers trailed over her back, running along the curve of her shoulder blade, the silken smooth skin, as her breathing slowed and steadied. Her hand had stilled, curled under her chin, and he was almost certain she'd fallen asleep. Yet his brain still couldn't quite convince his body to move, something that had never happened to him before.

Gage wasn't the kind of guy to sleep around just to get his rocks off, but he also wasn't the kind of guy to commit himself to anything too serious. He'd seen the disaster that had been his parents' marriage, and he wasn't about to fall into that trap either.

But Leah made him want to stay here, to let the rest of the world continue to turn without his involvement, to remain in this bed with her letting her heart beat in time with his own. She made him want to create a safe place where nothing from the outside could reach them, where her past and his present troubles couldn't touch them.

She stirred slightly, curling closer to him, sighing softly. The sweet scent of her shampoo seemed to envelop him, making his chest ache. He wasn't sure exactly what he felt for Leah, but it was a more powerful passionate attachment than he'd ever felt with any other woman.

That's called love, you idiot.

Shock seemed to ripple through him. He couldn't possibly be in love with Leah; he barely knew her. But this wasn't the first time the word *love* had run through his mind in connection with Leah.

He may have only met her a little more than a week ago, but spending almost every moment together had a way of throwing a monkey wrench into the normal dating experience. He knew she'd shared more with him in the last week than she probably had ever shared before.

Guilt slid into his chest, twisting and coiling around his lungs. He owed her the same. Especially if he cared about her as much as he claimed. But he didn't want to see the disappointment in her eyes. He wanted to fix the situation first so that when he told her, he'd see admiration instead.

Gage took a deep breath and pressed a kiss to the top of Leah's head before carefully sliding out of the bed. Grabbing his clothing from the dresser, he dressed quickly and tossed a few items into the duffel bag he'd packed the day before.

"You're leaving?"

Gage froze. He'd hoped to make his escape while she slept. To get to San Francisco and back without having this conversation in person. Not yet. Not after last night. He needed just a few days longer.

"I have to go to San Francisco, and I'm running late, but Leah…" Gage paused, trying to gather his courage. "When I get back, we need to talk."

Pansy-ass. Suck it up and spit it out, already.

She rose onto one elbow, the sheet falling away from her shoulder, and yearning shot through him, making his body hard and his chest ache. He saw the worry in her eyes and hated that he'd caused it.

"Gage?" Her voice caught on his name, and he could hear the doubt in her tone.

He turned with a sigh, not giving himself an opportunity to run from this again. "You know my last name is Granger and that I run an IT company, but I didn't tell you it was Iconics Industries."

"Iconics? The company that made Titanium?" A frown creased her brow, and she sat up, pulling the sheet around her.

"I'm also the reason for our current legal troubles. I signed off on a security program that I knew wasn't ready. The company was under pressure to perform, and I knew we couldn't take the hit releasing it late would cause."

He rubbed his hands on his thighs, unable to look her in the eye. "It was a mistake that cost the company millions. Then I found out that our COO is trying to get rid of me if I don't fire enough people to cover the cost of the settlements. That way, it won't affect our bottom line and the stockholders can still be appeased." Gage pinched the bridge of his nose.

"How many?"

"About four hundred employees, maybe more."

She shook her head, hiding her face behind a curtain of caramel-colored waves. He didn't want to see the loathing in her face. Leah fought for the underdogs, those who couldn't fight for themselves. He didn't want to think about how she'd feel about a man who didn't do the same. "And you're okay with doing that to them?"

"No, but I'm not sure what the options are." He was going to try his best to convince the other partners, but things might be entirely out of his hands at this point. "I may not have a choice."

"You always have a choice."

He threw his hands up. It was futile trying to make her understand. "I'm doing everything I can to fix it. But the fact that I ran away instead of facing it head on doesn't exactly instill confidence in my decision making to the rest of the partners."

"What do you mean, 'you ran away?'"

"I needed some time to get my head on straight." He reached for his bag. "I have to go, Leah. They're expecting me and I'm already late." He didn't look at her, couldn't stand to see the accusation in her eyes. He would fix this and prove he was the man she thought he was. Somehow.

"What makes you so sure that's not exactly what you're doing again?"

He paused with his hand on the door, unable to answer, because he couldn't be sure she wasn't right.

Chapter Twenty

THE SUNRISE CAST the entire room in a deep orange glow as Leah watched Gage leave. She heard the loud roar of the Challenger's engine before the gravel crunched under his tires.

Gage was gone. Not just physically, but the man she thought she'd come to know over the past week. He'd kept so much of his life a secret, even after she'd confessed so much of her own. He'd been her rescuer and now, to see him in the role of villain, ready to fire hundreds of people to protect his own interests, made her doubt her own judgment. She wasn't sure what to believe. Who was the callous man who'd just walked out of this room without a backward glance or a promise to return?

He'd heard her question. She'd seen it in the way his shoulders hunched. Instead of answering, he'd walked away.

The room was quiet, completely still as she waited for an answer to materialize. When none came, she took a deep breath and flopped onto her back, staring at the ceiling and wondering how she could have been so stupid. She had allowed herself to fall for him, the one thing she'd sworn to never do. She'd opened herself up completely and had been rewarded with rejection.

He'd gotten what he'd wanted and disappeared.

You should have known better than to trust a man, she scolded herself.

She couldn't blame Gage entirely. She'd been a willing participant in their relationship, more than willing. Leah reached for the quilt at the foot of the bed, tugging it around her, wanting to insulate her heart as easily from the pain that seemed to chill her. She'd been weak, and Gage had simply used that weakness to his advantage. A single tear slid from her eye into her hair, but she quickly swiped it away. It was only sex, and it wasn't the first time she'd been used and cast aside. She'd survived before, and she would survive this time as well.

Leah slid from Gage's bed and retrieved her clothing from the floor. She wasn't looking forward to making the "walk of shame" to her house, but if she was careful, she could sneak into her back door without anyone the wiser.

She looked around the room. Gage's presence could still be felt. He hadn't taken everything—there was a pair of jeans and a T-shirt slung over the corner of the bed, clothes hung behind the slightly askew closet door—which mean he'd be returning. It also meant that she needed to snuff out her emotions before then. She couldn't make this same mistake again, regardless of how her body responded to him. Even now, her insides began to hum at the thought of his hands.

Leah silently tugged on her clothing and snuck out the front door, hurrying to her own house. Once inside, she closed the door, leaning against it.

"It was just a mistake," she whispered in the silence, trying to ignore the ache throbbing deep in her chest the admission caused her. "One I'll never make again."

Puma and Lynx came skidding around the corner, meowing loudly, demanding breakfast. Leah was grateful for the distraction they provided, but she knew, like Gage's disappearance, it was only temporary.

"HEY, LEAH!" BAILEY waved from the doorway of the dog kennel. "What brings you here?"

Leah tucked her hands into her pockets and headed for the outbuilding, casting a wary glance at the main house, wondering if Julia was inside waiting but not wanting to be rude by ignoring Bailey.

"Julia and I were going to see if some of the dogs might be ready to work with a group of girls Jessie has coming." She stepped inside and was greeted by loud yips and barks, enough to rattle her senses for a moment.

"Quiet down, you guys," Bailey said firmly to the animals. Surprisingly, most of them obeyed immediately.

"They listened."

"I have the magic touch," Bailey joked. "They only get like that for two reasons: visitors and feeding time." She walked down the aisle between the large indoor runs and led Leah into a small kitchenette area, motioning for her to have a seat at a small pub table at one end of the room.

"Julia should be out in a bit. She was just finishing feeding Emily." Bailey reached inside a refrigerator and pulled out two bottles of water, holding one out to Leah. "Want one?"

"Sure." She took the bottle and eyed the woman taking the seat across the table from her.

So far, she hadn't spent much time talking to Bailey, but the little she had at the barbecue had made it clear that Bailey was a straight shooter. She said whatever came to mind. As Leah watched her now, lips twisted to one side thoughtfully, eyes hesitant, it made her wonder what Bailey was thinking and why she didn't just say it.

"What?" Leah asked, taking the offensive.

Bailey sighed. "You look upset and Jessie mentioned that you and Gage—" She shrugged. "Never mind. It's none of my business. It's just, Gage is a good friend."

"I'm sure he is. Not to mention, he's Julia's brother-in-law. I'm not sure what Jessie told you but—"

"Are you two together?"

"What?" Leah was taken aback. Bailey was right; her relationship with Gage was none of her business. But she got the distinct impression this family didn't operate under normal personal boundaries. "Gage and I are…we're friends."

"Friends?" Bailey repeated.

Leah wasn't even sure the word quantified what she and Gage were. Friends may have been a good explanation before the latest complication. Now, she wasn't as sure. But, at least it was a safe explanation and far better than the truth.

Bailey didn't give her the opportunity to respond. "Because I know this really great guy, and I think the two of you have a lot in common." She went on without waiting for any encouragement. "He's a doctor in town, a pediatrician."

"I don't know, Bailey, I don't usually—"

"It wouldn't be anything serious, not even a date. But Jessie said you haven't really left the ranch since you got here, and I know Blake needs a night out to unwind. I just thought having a few more friends around town wouldn't hurt."

Leah might have imagined Bailey's emphasis on the word *friends*, but she didn't think so. What could she say without arousing Bailey's suspicions?

"I guess."

"Why don't we hit The Watering Hole tomorrow night? I'll double check with Blake, but I'm pretty sure he's got the night off. Chase will be there, too, since I'm singing an early set. There you are, Jules," Bailey said, looking toward the doorway where Julia leaned against the frame, her daughter on her hip. "You and Dylan want to join us tomorrow evening for a night out?"

Just the idea of going out with Bailey and Chase made Leah nervous, but adding in Julia and Dylan made her heart skip a beat. Dylan looked so much like Gage, and the pain of his departure was still too fresh. Leah wasn't in any hurry to spend an entire evening with him.

"And who will I get to babysit?"

Relief flooded Leah, just before guilt set in. How could she begrudge the couple a night out? Suddenly an idea surfaced. "I'll watch her. You four go out."

"I've got a better idea. What about Aleta? She'd love to watch her."

Julia looked like she was considering the idea. "She doesn't have any night classes right now, and I'm sure she'd love the extra money, since she's trying to save up for her own place." Julia shrugged. "Maybe Jessie and Nathan want to come?"

Leah felt caught up in a whirlwind and wondered how this had gotten out of her control. Bailey pulled her phone from her back pocket and tapped her fingers against the screen. "I'll let everyone know. This is going to be a blast."

Julia smiled as Bailey hurried out of the kitchen. "Ready to find a couple of dogs?"

"What just happened?" Leah asked, unsure how she'd just gotten roped into a blind date with three other couples.

"Hurricane Bailey blew through." She laughed and rubbed her nose against Emily's. "Don't worry, you'll get used to it."

"Gage, what the hell is going on?"

Looking up from the laptop he'd set up in the office he'd appropriated in their San Francisco building, Gage frowned at George. He'd been busy putting the final touches on his plea to the shareholders, but he wasn't sure how much he wanted to reveal before the meeting this morning. However, he knew he couldn't keep George in the dark about his plans. He owed it to him, especially when Gage took into account what this change was likely to cost George.

"Come inside." He motioned to George to shut the door behind him. "We need to talk."

"You know that this is going to get ugly, right? Cooper is ready to hang you out to dry."

"I know, and I'm going to give him his way."

Shock registered on George's face, just before his eyes clouded with anger. "Are you kidding? You're going to leave me to deal with this mess?"

"You don't want this any more than I do." Gage held his arms out, indicating the massive office. "This isn't what we set out to do, Georgie. We were going to make a difference. All we've done is make Cooper and the rest of the stock-holders richer. We haven't helped anyone. Not really."

George shook his head, letting out a heavy sigh. "You didn't seem to mind before these lawsuits."

"Bullshit. We've both been complaining about what this company has turned into. We turned into 'yes-men,' and it got us into this mess. If I hadn't been the one to cave and sign my name to that program, they would've got-ten you to do it." George crossed his arms, but he didn't deny it. "We've let the shareholders take what we started, our company, and destroy it. They've turned it into some corporate monster only satisfied when it's churning out profits."

"So, your solution is to run away?"

"My solution is to wash our hands and start over. Do it our way this time and really make a difference." It felt good to say the words aloud. Just the act of saying them gave Gage more determination to see his idea to fruition. "I want to start a program for gifted kids."

"What?" George laughed, nervously. "Okay, for a second, I thought you were going to walk away from all of this in order to play games."

Gage shrugged. "Sort of, I guess. We were nearly destroyed by a bunch of bored kids. What if we taught them how to turn those skills into something marketable, if we taught them to make a difference for their futures?"

"How is that going to make Iconics money?"

"It's not." Gage laughed at the ridiculousness of what he was proposing, but it didn't stop him from knowing it was the right thing for him to do.

George rose from the chair and stalked to the door, ready to storm out of the room, but he turned back suddenly. "Are you joking? Take the same kids who cost us millions and teach them to do worse?"

Gage leaned back in his chair and crossed his arms over his chest, shaking his head. "No, help them learn to focus their skills, to hone their abilities into something good. Think about how much more we could have done, even before college, if someone would have helped direct us, helped us find our niche. I've already got most of the funding lined up, and I have several professors from local colleges willing to donate time to teach these kids."

Gage saw George clench his fists at his sides before jamming them into the pockets of his slacks. "You're really going to go through with this? Leave Iconics and teach kids? What if I say no?"

"Then I'm going to do it alone." Gage rose from behind the desk and, walking to the front of it, leaned his hip on the corner. "But, Georgie, I don't want to. I want you in this with me, man. Like the old days."

"You're crazy." George sighed heavily, before walking out of the office and leaving Gage completely alone.

"YOU REALLY THINK these three will work?" Leah sat on the stoop in the yard where she and Julia had just finished working the dogs. Tango, Julia's massive Great Dane, trotted around the yard, while a long-haired shepherd mix sniffed at Julia's feet. A Lab and border collie played tug-of-war with a long rope nearby. "They don't even seem...I don't know, interested?"

"Bingo, Chaz, come." The two playing in the yard dropped their rope and hurried to Julia's side. "Sit." All three dogs planted their rear to the ground and looked up at her expectantly. She turned toward Leah. "Now, bury your face in your hands like you're crying."

"What?"

"Just do it."

Leah shrugged slightly and hunched her shoulders, covering her face with her hands. She was just about to make sobbing sounds when Razor, the German shepherd nudged her hands with his nose. Bingo, the border collie, laid his smooth head against her thigh, and Chaz laid a paw on her leg, his dark eyes concerned. Even Tango came trotting over to see what was going on.

"See?" Julia grinned. "They're grounding, and each one does it differently. They might act like regular dogs, but the fact that they'll drop what they're doing instantly is a good sign." She reached out to pet the dogs. "And that was with you faking it. Imagine if it were real."

Julia cued the dogs to move, releasing them into the yard to play again and sat down beside Leah. "You realize you're probably going to need to keep them with you most of the time. These aren't going to be typical outside pets."

"I have two kittens in the house already. Now I get to add three dogs?" Leah shook her head and leaned her chin into her palm.

"Not what you signed up for, huh?" Julia chuckled.

"Not exactly. It's a good thing Gage—" she stopped, the mere act of saying his name making her lungs constrict.

Julia eyed her suspiciously, and she immediately regretted mentioning him at all. Now that she had, she was better off finishing her thought than leaving it hanging and letting Julia guess about their relationship.

"He's been helping me with the kittens. I have no clue what I'm doing."

"Gage has? I'm surprised he knows how to take care of kittens."

"Justin helped us get them settled and vaccinated, but they love Gage."

"Most animals have a sense about good people. He's a good guy."

Leah wanted to change the subject. She didn't need to get into a discussion with Gage's sister-in-law about what kind of man he was. Leah didn't want to be the one to crush his "good guy" image by telling Julia how he'd left her in his bed without even a good-bye.

Chapter Twenty-One

CHAOS ERUPTED IN the boardroom as soon as Gage offered to step down as CEO of Iconics. He hadn't expected this kind of response, since he'd assumed that Cooper had turned most of the major stockholders or already had them in his pocket. By the look of shock on Cooper's face, so did he.

"We can't discuss this until it's quiet." George's voice boomed over the ruckus, as several investors rose, threatening to sell their shares immediately if Gage stepped down.

"Values have already taken a hit. If you sell now, we'll tank and never recover." Griffin Masters, their CFO, pointed out the financial risk.

Cooper rose, slamming his fist onto the table, and pointed at Gage. "Granger is the problem. He's the reason we're already paying out millions in settlements."

"That wasn't all him and you know it, Cooper," George said.

Gage was surprised to see him stand up to Cooper. Gage had always been the voice behind the pair. Usually, George was too timid to say anything, but maybe knowing the majority of stockholders were backing him gave his friend the confidence he usually lacked.

"We told you that program wasn't ready. You pushed until Gage finally relented and signed off on it. You knew there were unresolved issues. You said we'd deal with the bugs when someone found them. Guess what, someone did."

"You knew?" Griffin stood up, his fingers tented on the table as he stared at Cooper with his mouth open. "You told me you had no idea."

"What kind of operation are the four of you running?" One of their biggest investors stood up, shoving papers into her briefcase. "You know what? Don't tell me. I don't need the culpability."

"Are you happy now?" Cooper spun on Gage. "Just because you're finished and your reputation is shit doesn't mean you need to drag the rest of us through the mud with you."

Griffin slid back into his chair and shook his head, disgust written plainly in his face. "Shut up, Cooper. You've said enough." He looked at Gage and George. "Can you fix this?"

Gage nodded. "The program is fixed. Publicity is taking care of spinning the media, and once the settlements are finalized, we have a public apology prepared. But as long as this pressure on production continues, this is going to happen again."

"And where does that pressure come from?" one of the investors asked.

Gage turned to see that the investors were still seated around the table, waiting for an outcome. He lifted a brow, waiting for Cooper to admit that it came from him.

When he didn't respond, Griffin supplied the answer for him. "Mr. Cooper is our COO. He's the one bringing all information to Mr. Granger."

"Then I suggest, unless we want to see Iconics completely crumble, Mr. Cooper be replaced, immediately," said the investor.

This entire meeting had deteriorated from Gage's original intention. He'd come in to request Iconics invest in his new project, Apotheo, before agreeing to step down as CEO. He'd never imagined that the shareholders would insist on Cooper's resignation, nor that Griffin and George would back that demand.

"Ladies and gentlemen, please, everyone come back in and sit." Gage attempted to bring this meeting back on track. "There is still the matter of Apotheo to discuss."

He had the attention of the investors now. "It's a nonprofit organization you'd like to start for kids showing a high aptitude for technology and programming skills, correct? What's to discuss? If nothing else, it would be great publicity and take some of the focus off the errors of the past year. I'm all for it."

Several of the shareholders concurred before putting it to a vote. With only two of the twenty voting against it, two million dollars was appropriated toward the start-up of Apotheo, with Gage overseeing the efforts. It was also unanimously decided that Cooper should step down and be replaced as COO. Until his replacement could be found, George would step in as the interim COO. As far as Gage was concerned, it couldn't have worked out better if he'd planned the scenario.

Now, he just had get back and make things right with Leah.

LEAH STARED AT her reflection in the mirror and smoothed down the front of her button-up shirt before reaching for a long chain and draping it over her neck. She pulled her hair from under it and cocked her head to one side.

"It's going to have to do."

She didn't look bad in the jeans and knee-high black boots, but she didn't look great either. Razor sat at her feet, cocking his head from one side to the other, while Chaz blew out a sigh of exasperation from the end of the bed.

"Well, I'm so sorry to have bored you with how long I took getting ready." She rubbed each of the dogs' heads in turn. "But if I'm going out, at the very least, I should look decent."

Bingo yawned widely and rose, trotting out of her bedroom and into the kitchen, his nails clicking against the tile.

"Great, now even the dogs find me boring." Leah could hear the kittens tearing down the hallway as they chased one another. "Remind me again when I signed up for this zoo?" she asked Razor.

In less than a week, she'd gone from taking care of herself and never having pets to having a houseful. She welcomed the dogs' company, and the kittens hadn't been nearly as enthusiastic as the first night, and they had all kept her mind from straying to Gage. She sighed.

Well, maybe they hadn't actually *kept* her from thinking about him, but they'd kept her from thinking about him as much as she would have otherwise.

He hadn't even called to apologize for running out. It had been several days with no word from him at all. If that didn't speak volumes, she didn't know what did. He'd couldn't make it much clearer. She was a one-night stand and hadn't even been worth the breath to tell her good-bye. She might have fallen for him, too hard and too fast, but she could find someone else to fill his place just as quickly.

Or not.

She'd been better off when she'd been alone. Except, no matter how many times she tried to convince herself of the fact, it just didn't ring true.

She missed Gage. Missed the way he could make her smile with his cheesy pickup lines and compliments. Missed the way he would push her buttons just to get her talking. Missed the way he could heat her blood with just a look from those dark eyes. She might not want to admit he'd broken her heart when he walked out, but that didn't change the hurt that echoed through her body, making her chest ache and sleeping difficult.

The knock at the door jolted her from her pity party. "Leah, you ready?"

Hurrying to the front door, Leah nearly tripped over the dogs as she reached for the knob and jerked the door inward. "Yeah, if these hairy beasts would move out of my way."

Jessie laughed. "It'll never happen. They live to be underfoot, I swear."

She moved into the entry as Leah stepped into the kitchen. "Let me just get them some food and we can go." She measured out the dog food and staggered the bowls around the room before reaching for her purse.

"Um, you might want to…" Jessie pointed at the lint roller on the counter, where it had taken up permanent residence in the past two days, since bringing the dogs back to the ranch.

Leah looked down to see clumps of dog hair on her jeans. "Ugh! Do you realize this is the fourth time I've had to do this?"

"Have you not met Moose yet?" Jessie reached down and rubbed behind Razor's ears. "But, when he cuddles with you, it's all worth it."

Lynx yowled loudly from behind Jessie, and she turned and scooped her up. "So, this is one of the kittens, huh?" She scratched under her chin, eliciting a loud purr. "You've definitely got your hands full, but the kids will love it. You might never get them to go home."

"Speaking of the kids, maybe I should stay home tonight and go over the case files again."

Jessie shot her a dubious glance and tipped her head to the side. "This wouldn't have anything to do with Gage, would it?"

"No." Leah realized she answered far too quickly and adamantly for Jessie to believe her. "I…I'm just not really into blind dates, and I get the feeling Bailey is setting me up."

"Then don't think of this as a blind date. You're just going out to listen to Bailey sing."

"With my boss?"

"Yes," Jessie agreed, pushing Leah toward the door. "And a bunch of other people. You need to make some friends, Leah. You can't stay holed away on this ranch only talking to teens. You need to live a little, too."

Jessie tugged the door shut behind her, allowing Leah to lock it before waving for Nathan that they were ready. "Now, stop second-guessing everything and enjoy yourself for a change, okay?"

Leah slid into the backseat of Jessie's truck and took a deep breath. Jessie was right. She'd spent every moment of her life waiting for something to go wrong, and it had, but she'd come to Heart Fire with the intention of starting over, living a different life. Now was the time to prove to herself that she would not only live differently but she could think differently as well. Tonight, she was going to have a great time for a change.

"BAILEY, YOU'RE INCREDIBLE." Leah couldn't believe the way Bailey had the crowd eating out of the palm of her hand. She was a born entertainer, and it made Leah wonder why she was singing in bars and working at the vet clinic with her cousin. "Ever thought of getting a manager and taking your show on the road?"

"Nope, just not in the cards." Bailey leaned into the crook of Chase's arm and stood on her toes to press a kiss to the corner of his pursed lips. "I've got everything I want right here."

"Get a room, you two," Blake said, laughing as he slid another pitcher of beer and frosty mugs on the table. "I swear, Leah, these two make out more than teenagers."

"Jealous?" Bailey shot back with a wink. "Blake's just mad because he's not the hottest doctor in town anymore."

Leah smiled slightly at their friendly banter, but in truth, the entire situation was making her uncomfortable. She didn't know anyone well enough to hold up her end of the conversation, and she didn't know Blake at all. He seemed friendly and nice, but there was an air about him that suggested his amicable laughter was a cover, a diversion from the sadness she could see in his eyes. She knew better than most how deep still waters ran, leading her to believe there was far more turmoil beneath the surface than anyone realized. Or, maybe it was the therapist in her just reading too much into things.

Blake rolled his eyes and turned toward Leah. "You want to dance?"

His question surprised her. So far, he'd been slightly standoffish, as if he didn't want to let his guard down, but she didn't want to make a snap judgment about Bailey's friend. Leah bit her lip. She didn't want to seem rude and refuse, but she'd never learned how to dance. She'd never had the opportunity growing up.

"I don't know how." She shrugged apologetically.

Blake reached for her hand and pulled her toward the far side of the dance floor. "Don't worry, I'll teach you."

She looked up into his stormy eyes, praying for just a moment that the handsome doctor would make her pulse race or her heart flutter. She wanted to feel a sizzle of heat travel down her spine. Something to indicate that the way her body reacted to Gage's nearness could happen with another man, that it was simply a matter of attraction. But even when Blake slid his arm around her waist and rested his hand on her low back, there was nothing.

"Damn it," she muttered under her breath.

"Pardon?"

She hadn't meant to say anything out loud. "Nothing. I was just afraid I stepped on your toes."

Blake smiled and she could see why, according to Bailey, he was the "it" guy in town. A handsome doctor with blue eyes you could drown in and a disarming smile that could charm even the most prudish woman from her panties. Just enough scruff to be rugged and just enough mystery to be intriguing.

Come on, butterflies. Wake up.

"So, where'd you go to med school?"

"UCSF, Fresno. I grew up down there and was lucky to be able to stay. What about you?"

"Davis, in Sacramento."

"So, this isn't too far from home for you."

"I moved to the Bay Area for my internship and then worked there for a few years before coming here."

"What made you move? The Bay Area is beautiful."

He stumbled, tripping her up, and mumbled an apology. "It was just time to leave."

Leah didn't miss the pain that flashed across his blue eyes, or the regret. When another slow ballad began to play, Blake's arm tightened around her waist, pulling her closer. Leah let him take the lead in their conversation and the dance, tucking her head under his chin and resting it against his chest. They had something in common, more than Bailey had known when she decided to set up this get-together. Leah recognized the acute agony of loss in Blake, felt her own recent anguish respond as she laid her head on his shoulder. It didn't take a therapist to realize there was something far darker than leaving his home eating at Blake. Nor did it take a doctor to realize he didn't want to talk about it. She was willing to be his shoulder to lean on, especially since he was willing to be her distraction from her thoughts of Gage for the evening.

He wasn't Gage, he wasn't even a friend, but for a moment, they shared a common bond of heartache and that was enough.

The music swirled around them as the rest of the crowd seemed to fade. Blake swayed slowly to the sad song that spoke of sorrow and love lost. They didn't need to speak. For a few minutes, she could pretend she was in Gage's arms, listen to Blake's heart beat in time with the music and convince herself he was someone else, and she would assume the role he wanted her to play, of the woman he wished he was holding, the one he'd lost.

As the last strains of the song died, she heard Bailey take up the microphone. Leah took a step back as Blake looked down into her face, and she could easily read the gratitude in his eyes as they misted over.

"Thank you," he whispered, his voice choked with emotion.

Empathy ripped at her for the anguish she could see in his face as she gave him a sad smile, cupping his cheek. "I know you probably don't want to, but we can go outside and talk."

Blake shook his head, dropping it so she couldn't see his face. "Some blind date I make, huh?"

"I'm not exactly in a dating frame of mind either." She glanced back at the table where Jessie, Nathan, Julia, Dylan, and Chase all waited, watching Bailey. "You sure you don't want to just skip out and leave them behind?"

"Bailey would never forgive me." He looked at the woman on the stage. "She thinks she's saving me from myself. She has no idea." His blue eyes cleared suddenly, as if he slipped on a mask, and he smiled brightly at Leah. "I think we need drinks."

"I don't think—"

Blake pulled her toward the bar. "Then I need one. I'll get you a soda."

Leah clearly recognized an attempt to drown misery. She couldn't fault him, she'd done it enough in her life. "Okay."

He wrapped an arm around her shoulders as they approached the bartender. "Bart, I need a Coke for my girl here, and give me a double Gentleman Jack neat."

"Now that's a drink I can get behind."

Leah felt her breath catch in her throat. She could pick that husky voice out in a crowded room. What was he doing here?

Gage turned around, letting his gaze slide over her slowly. "Don't the two of you look cozy?"

Chapter Twenty-Two

"GAGE!"

He didn't miss the surprise in her whiskey-colored eyes, the same as the drink he was about to finish. Gage tossed it back in one swift motion, trying to dull the pain of finding her on a date with Bailey's friend.

He'd hurried back to Jessie's after his meetings, hoping to find her at her place so that they could celebrate his success. Not only had he been able to keep his company intact, but he'd also been able to acquire four new investors in Apotheo, more than enough to get started before the first of the year. He was finally going to tell her the truth about why he was at Jessie's and tell her he was going to find a house in town, and he wanted her to stay with him.

But when Dylan texted him and told him to meet everyone at The Watering Hole to watch Bailey sing, he figured the conversation could wait until they were alone.

He just wanted to see her and hold her in his arms again. The last thing he'd expected to see was Blake dancing with her, the two of them snuggling on the dance floor like lovers.

Okay, so maybe *snuggling* was a bit of an exaggeration. But that didn't stop the raging jealousy from knotting and twisting his stomach. Bile rose in his throat making the whiskey taste sour as he slid the glass toward the bartender.

"Bart!" He pointed at his glass, motioning to the bartender that he wanted another. "Put the drinks for the happy couple on my tab, too."

"Gage." Her voice was as cold as his was. "I'm surprised to see you back so soon."

"Obviously." He glanced at Blake. "Good to see you again, Blake."

Blake looked from Leah back to him. "Do you want me to go?" he asked, directing his question to Leah.

"Yes," Gage answered.

"No." She glared at Gage. "Would you like to join everyone at the table? I'm sure your brother would like to see you."

Gage slid from the barstool and looked up at the stage where Bailey sang. She'd just finished a fast-tempo song that had most of the dancing crowd heading back to their tables to quench their thirst and launched into a melody he recognized as a slow ballad, her voice rich and sweet.

"Mind if I steal your *date* for a dance, Blake?" His gaze never left Leah's face, even when her eyes shot flames at him. He could see more in the depths, something that looked more like pain. Why would she be hurt? She'd been the one to make love to him and go out on a date with a stranger just a few days later.

Blake looked to Leah for confirmation. Gage didn't miss her slight nod just before Blake took his drink and leaned toward her, whispering something he couldn't quite make out.

"Aw, is lover boy mad about sharing?" Gage asked as Blake headed back to the table. He reached for her hand to lead her out to the dance floor, but she jerked it away from him, following him without touching. "You're going to have to let me touch you if we're going to dance, Leah."

She let her hands drop onto his shoulders, but she kept her distance. He wasn't about to let her off that easily. He hadn't forgotten the way she melted in his arms, so he slid his hands around her waist, drawing her close, until the front of her body was crushed against his.

"What do you want, Gage? Another romp in the sack, so you can bail at first light? Once wasn't enough?"

"Excuse me?" He looked down at her and could see the betrayal in her eyes. "I wasn't the one practically humping someone else's leg on the dance floor."

"You're disgusting." She shoved him away and went back to the table, retrieving her purse. "Tell Bailey I'm sorry, but I can't stay."

Jessie stood up quickly. "Do you need a ride home?" She looked at Nathan. "Come on."

"I'll take her home," Blake stood up.

Chase waved him off. "You've been drinking. I can't let you drive right now."

"I'll take her home," Gage moved behind her, refusing to let her move past him.

"Go away, Gage. You've been drinking, too." Leah tried to shoulder her way through, glaring at him.

"Here," he said, slapping his keys into her hand. "Then you drive *me* home."

"Gage," Dylan warned. "Just let her take your car, and I'll drive you back later."

Gage narrowed his eyes at his brother. "Fine." He looked around the table at the others. "Fine. Take the car, enjoy your drive."

He leaned close to Leah so that only she could hear, his lips brushing over the spot behind her ear that he knew would make her shiver with yearning. "But I hope that every second you're in it reminds you of the last ride we had together."

"Trust me, Gage," Leah said, smiling up at him sweetly. "It's been easy to forget."

JESSIE JAMMED A finger into his chest. "I told you this was going to happen. I warned you to stay away from her."

She threw her hands into the air, and Nathan reached for her wrist, pulling her toward him, trying to calm her tirade. Gage just clenched his jaw and looked around the table at the group. Jessie was furious, but Julia and Dylan looked concerned. Chase and Blake simply looked amused.

"What the hell's going on over here? You guys were louder than the band. Where's Leah?" Bailey asked as she wandered over.

"Ask this guy," Blake said, tossing back what was left of his drink and jerking his thumb at Gage. "He took her out for a dance and pissed her off. Although your cousin seems to know more than she's letting on." He pointed at Jessie, deep in conversation with Nathan in the corner as he tried to settle her.

Bailey tipped her head to one side and gave Gage a reprimanding glare. "Please, tell me you didn't do what I think you did."

"I didn't do anything." Gage wasn't about to be put on trial in the middle of the bar. He looked for his brother to back him. "You think you could take me back to the cabin now?"

"Oh, no, you don't." Jessie came rushing back to the table. "You can collect your things and stay with them." She waved her hand at Julia and Dylan. "I'm not having you throw my entire operation into chaos because you can't keep it in your pants."

"Wait a minute, Jessie," Julia began. "You don't know what happened."

Gage wanted to hug Julia for her desire to believe the best about him, but unfortunately, this time her trust was misplaced. He'd done exactly what Jessie was accusing him of, except he'd been the one to get screwed.

"Gage?" Bailey frowned in his direction. They'd been friends since he and Dylan had stayed with Julia while his brother trained his therapy dog. They'd even gone out a few times. She knew him better than this, but he wasn't about to remind her of the fact.

"No." Bailey shook her head. Relief coursed through him. Finally, someone who would be the voice of reason. "Gage might be a flirt but he doesn't sleep around."

"It doesn't really matter though, does it, when I have a therapist who's too pissed off dealing with romantic drama to work? You did this, Gage, you fix it." Jessie jerked her purse from the back of one of the chairs and stormed out, leaving Nathan no choice but to follow.

"Well, this was fun." Chase chuckled as he leaned back, hooking one arm over the back of the chair. "Why in the world would you even consider crossing Jessie? Her temper is the stuff of legends."

"I guess this signals my night as a total bust." Blake stood up and slid several ones onto the table to tip their waitress. "My *date* gets chased away by another guy who I now find out may or may not be sleeping with her."

Gage glared at the other man. Blake waved him off. "Don't even sweat it, man. She wasn't into me anyway."

"That's not how it looked while you two were dancing."

"Yeah? Well, trust me. Looks can be deceiving. She wasn't the woman on my mind, and I certainly wasn't the man on hers." He gave Gage a pointed look. "I don't know what happened between the two of you. I'm not sure I want to. But I do know that Leah is a nice woman with a kind heart and a soft spot for people hurting."

Blake started to head toward his car when Chase offered him a ride. "I'll be right back," he promised Bailey.

When the pair had left, Bailey turned to Gage. "You really know how to make an entrance, don't you?"

"Gage, what the hell were you thinking?" Dylan ran a hand over his eyes. "Now the whole family is picking sides. Everyone is mad."

"I get it, okay? I fucked up." The euphoric high from his successful meetings was long gone. "I guess that's just what I do these days."

"You can say that again," Dylan muttered.

"Dylan, stop," Julia warned. "Gage is getting enough crap from work, he doesn't need you shoveling it on, too."

Gage jumped up, the chair skittering out behind him as he slapped his hands on the table between him and Dylan. "What does that mean?" he growled.

"It means, we aren't stupid, Gage. We watch the news and read the paper. We know about the trouble Iconics is in. I also know that final approval would have come from you, so that mess falls onto your shoulders." Dylan shook his head, looking frustrated. "Why didn't you just tell us what was happening? Why stay at Jessie's? You could have stayed with us."

Julia shot him a sympathetic smile. "You know we would have loved to have you."

Of course he hadn't been able to hide it from Dylan. As usual, his brother was still trying to take care of him. Gage felt the guilt wash over him. His brother had a wife and child to worry about. He shouldn't be wasting his energy worrying about Gage at this stage in his life.

"You have a new baby, and you haven't been married that long. I didn't want to add any more pressure to your situation."

"Gage," Julia scolded, "you're family. You should have let us know, so we could help."

"In case you haven't noticed, Jules, there are a lot of times when this family can help *too* much," Bailey chimed in. It wasn't exactly the way Gage would have said it, but it got the point across.

Gage dropped his face into his palm. "There was nothing anyone could do, Julia. I had to handle it, and being at the cabin gave me time to figure out a solution without any outside pressure."

"And create some more trouble," his brother said under his breath. Gage simply glared at him.

"What solution did you come up with?" Julia asked.

"To quit," Gage admitted. "That's why I went to San Francisco. But it didn't work out that way. In fact, it couldn't have gone better. Not only am I staying, but we replaced the COO, and I'm spearheading a new project, a program for highly skilled teenagers."

"Then what's with the long face?" Bailey asked, wincing when Julia elbowed her. "Seriously? You should be thrilled. You got more than you hoped for, and in spite of what you thought you saw, Blake says Leah wasn't into him." She slapped his shoulder. "Probably because she's into you, you jerk."

"Is this your idea of a pep talk, Bailey? Because if it is, you suck at it." Gage ran a hand over his head. He didn't need her to tell him he'd been a jerk and an idiot. He'd come back and immediately assumed Leah had played him, that he'd made yet another mistake. "What's your point?" Gage asked with a sigh.

Bailey rolled her eyes at him. "My point is that you need to get your ass to Jessie's and fix this with Leah. If I'd known there was anything between the two of you, I'd have never pushed her into a blind date with Blake. You and all your secrets have done nothing but create issues where there didn't need to be any."

Leave it to Bailey to be blunt, and right. "Dylan, can you give me a ride? There's a woman who I owe an explanation."

"If you were smart, you'd start off by apologizing to Jessie," Bailey said. "She's going to be harder to convince than Leah. She'd also be the one likely to throw your shit at the end of the driveway and kick you off the property as soon as you show up."

LEAH SAT CURLED in the corner of the couch with both kittens purring contentedly in her lap. Bingo was sprawled out over her feet, while Razor and Chaz lay on the floor, watching her intently. She was trying to stay unemotional, as detached from what had happened at the bar as she could, but so far she was barely holding back her tears.

She'd never expected to hear the bitterness she had in Gage's voice. Until tonight, other than his argument with Jude, she'd never even heard him raise his voice. But it wasn't just the anger in his voice, it was what she'd seen in his eyes—the raw, agonizing betrayal. She had no idea why he'd looked at her that way.

He'd been the one to walk away without a word, to not reach out after the night they'd spent together. She'd opened her soul to him, the first person she'd let close in almost ten years, and he cast her aside, making it clear how worthless he thought she was.

She'd pegged him right from the start. Gage was a playboy, accustomed to getting what he wanted and throwing it away when he was finished. Leah swiped at the tear that managed to escape down her cheek.

Chaz stood up, laying his head into her lap and nudging her hand. Razor, however, turned toward the door, a low growl rumbling in his throat.

"It's fine, boy. Lie down." Razor did as she commanded but leapt back to his feet as a knock pounded against her door.

"Leah, let me in. We need to talk."

She should have expected him to show up, especially now that he'd had plenty of time to self-medicate. She glanced at the clock. It'd been nearly an hour since she left him at the bar. Unburying herself from under the animals, she scooped Gage's keys from the kitchen island and opened the door, slapping them against his chest.

"Here, you have your keys. Now go." She tried to shut the door but he took a step forward, not forcing his way in but not letting it close either. "Go away, Gage."

Leah wasn't about to fight with him about the door, so she turned and walked back into the living room. Immediately, Chaz and Razor moved to flank her, the shepherd baring his teeth at the stranger who dared come inside.

"What the hell?" Gage froze at the entry. "Can you call off your guard dogs?"

"Sit," she commanded, crossing her arms over her chest and glaring at him. "I don't remember inviting you in." As if on cue, Razor growled quietly, his lips curling up slightly.

"How did two kittens manage to morph into three dogs?"

"These three are therapy dogs. Jessie agreed they'd be a good asset to the program with the horses, so I brought them home."

"I'm not so sure about that one." Gage pointed at Razor.

Leah reached down and rubbed his head. He immediately glanced up at her, his tongue lolling to the side. "The feeling seems mutual." She met his searching gaze with her own. "Or maybe he's just picking up on how I'm feeling."

Gage arched a brow. "Like you want to tear me to shreds?" A grin tugged at the corner of his mouth, but she wasn't going to take the bait.

"Maybe."

His smile died as quickly as it surfaced. "Leah, I'm sorry." He ran a hand over his head, looking more frustrated than she'd ever seen him. "I shouldn't have assumed the worst at the bar, but after what happened before I left, I thought we—"

"I'm not sure I see why you even care who I was with, Gage. You left. You didn't call. You were the one who walked away." She took a step toward him, but Razor moved ahead of her, keeping his body between them.

"Is that what you thought? I told you I had to go to San Francisco. You knew I had to go."

"You couldn't call while you were there? Not even a text? After the way you left…"

"Leah, can we sit?"

"Tell me why you just walked out." She wasn't about to bend. One more time and she would probably break.

Chapter Twenty-Three

GAGE SAW THE fire snuffed in her eyes as disappointment filled them. She'd trusted him, believed in him, and he'd let her down.

"I was trying to fix things."

"So you left?" Her voice caught on the words. "After we…I thought…"

She paused, shaking her head and shutting herself off from him, as if she was afraid she would say too much. Gage took a step closer, wanting to soothe the hurt he'd caused her. His hands found her waist, drawing her to him. He needed to touch her, needed her to understand that leaving her had been the only way he could salvage any part of the man he wanted to be for her, and he couldn't do that with this distance between them.

Leah pushed against his chest, and Gage felt the dogs circling around their legs, moving between them. They weren't growling now, but the big shepherd whimpered quietly while the Lab pawed at her calf. The third dog pressed its head against her leg. She turned to walk away from him, and he reached out, grasping her fingers in his.

"I can't." She half-heartedly tried to pull her hand from his grasp. "Why did you come back? I don't have anything else for you to take."

"I only want you, Leah. It's the only thing I've ever wanted. You know that."

"How?" She spun on her heel to face him. "I don't even *know* you."

It was like a knife to his heart. The distrust he could see in her eyes, the suspicion, the lack of faith in him.

"I thought I did. But then, you tell me about what you planned to do. How could you do that?"

"I didn't do it, Leah. I couldn't hurt people that way because of something I'd done."

Gage pulled her back toward him, letting his hands work their way up her arms and to her shoulders. He felt her shiver and prayed it wasn't revulsion at his touch.

"I didn't have a childhood like you did. Sure, my dad was an alcoholic, but I had a mother who loved me and a brother who took care of me. School came easily to me, and Dylan made sure I used it to my advantage. He made sure I was the one to go to college, while he went into the military. He never complained about it, but in my mind, I had to repay that debt to him and my mother, to take care of them. I didn't take that responsibility lightly and fate has smiled on me. My success hasn't just been luck, but there was plenty of it. Until recently."

She opened her mouth to argue, but he placed a finger over her lips. "Wait, let me finish."

Leah licked her lower lip, causing her tongue to barely brush against his finger and making every thought flee from his mind. He took a deep breath, closing his eyes, trying to regain control of his senses. Gage let his hands fall to either side of her neck, his fingers delving into the soft waves of her hair.

"I made a mistake with my company, and instead of facing it, taking responsibility the way I usually did, I ran away from it. I was about to make another mistake, to turn my back on who I'd always been and let all of those employees go. Then I met you."

Her gaze lifted to his, trying to read him, read his soul. "I used to always do what was right, regardless of what it cost me. It was part of who I was, as much a part of me as the blood in my veins. People believed me, believed *in* me, because I didn't lie; I was someone they could trust. Somewhere along the way, I got bogged down beneath the stress and the demands. When I was here, with you, I wanted to be that man again."

Her eyes misted, and he could see she wanted to believe him. But he could also see something in her eyes again that he hadn't seen since the first day they'd met on the side of the road—distrust. He'd worked so hard to be a friend her, to earn that gift, only to throw it away.

"I was stupid, and I should have told you everything before I left, but I had to find a way to go back and fix things first. To show you I *am* the man you think I am." He lowered his face, wanting nothing more than to taste her lips, to remind her of what they had together, make her see how much he cared, but Leah ducked her head.

"Don't walk away from this, Leah."

"What *is* this, Gage?" Her lashes were dark against her cheeks, and when she looked up at him, her eyes shimmered with the pain he'd caused her. "Because I'm not sure what I believe now."

He could hear the accusation in her voice. "I know, and I let you down. It won't happen again. I swear."

Really look at me.

He silently willed her to hear his heart. He knew it wasn't the right time to say anything aloud, but every beat of his heart, every breath in his lungs was crying out for her to hear the truth he couldn't quite confess.

Can't you see I'm falling in love with you?

Leah looked away again, and Gage knew it was too much for her to forgive. She was never going to be able to move past the fact that when she'd finally trusted him, he'd hidden the truth from her. He laid his cheek on the top of her head.

"I should have called you while I was in San Francisco," he said into her hair. "I should have told you everything from the start and kissed you good-bye that morning. I didn't mean to hurt you, Leah. If I'd just stepped up, you wouldn't have thought—"

"No, I shouldn't have just assumed…"

"You wouldn't have if I'd just told you how I felt before I left."

Leah looked up at him, resting her chin on his chest.

"I should have told you that what I feel for you is nothing like I've ever felt before." Gage brushed her hair back from her face. "I'm falling in love with you, Leah."

LEAH HOPED THE shock she felt didn't register in her face. Her heart felt like it actually stopped for a moment. Her breath caught in her throat and she couldn't say anything. He must have seen something in her eyes because he cleared his throat quickly.

"I know it's too soon, and it doesn't make any sense to me either, but I can't explain it."

"Gage," Leah couldn't hide the uncertainty in her voice. "You can't love me."

He gave her a sad smile and shrugged. "Leah, I can't help it."

She turned her back to him in order to avoid seeing too much in his eyes. Leah ran a hand through her messy waves, pulling them to one side, shielding her face from his penetrating scrutiny. His finger traced the curve of her shoulder, trailing over her upper arm. Desire rippled through her, spreading slowly, sapping any resistance she had. *He loved her?*

"Leah, because of you, I was able to fix my mistake, without letting go of my company or laying anyone off." He turned her back toward him. She could feel the heat from his gaze, could almost hear him willing her to look at him. "I was able to secure funding for a foundation for at-risk kids, like Jude, who are tech-savvy but need an outlet. That's what took so long."

Her gaze snapped back to him. "You what?"

"When I talked to Jude, and was able to get past his anger and resentment, I realized that if someone just listened and let him use his skills in a safe environment, he'd have been less likely to cause the trouble he did. I want to give kids like him a place to do that, a place where people will listen. Nathan's helping me, and I convinced the board that Iconics should provide most of the funding for the start-up."

She'd accused him of being too motivated by money to do the right thing for his employees, when in reality, he'd not only taken care of them, but he was trying to take care of the same kids she wanted to help. She'd completely misjudged him. She could blame it on being disillusioned because of her past, and that was likely true, but Gage had never deserved her doubt. He'd never done anything to cause her to assume he was anything less than generous and kind and giving. He'd already proven it with her.

"Gage." Tears filled her eyes, choking her, making it impossible to finish what she started to say.

He gave her a half-smile and shrugged. "After talking to Jude, I realized he didn't have much to look forward to. Maybe something like this would help. It's not going to be cheap, but with the investors Nathan and I've been able to line up, it'll be great. I told you, I wanted to fix things."

Leah frowned and shook her head. "Fix things?"

"Him, his life."

Fix him? Leah felt an icy shiver fall over her, freezing the blood in her veins. She'd heard those words a million times growing up as she bounced from home to home. People always wanted to fix *her*, not the problem.

"The way you did with me?"

"What?"

"Jude isn't some *thing* you can fix, Gage. You can't just throw money at everything and think that will solve the problem. *He* isn't broken." She backed away, and the dogs jumped to their feet, immediately rushing to her side, quickly tuning into her agitation.

"That's not what I meant." Gage's gaze hardened.

"I think it is, Gage. You see Jude as a problem to be fixed. You have a hero complex."

Gage closed his eyes and dropped his head forward, his shoulders slumping in defeat. "I did this because of you, Leah. You were the one who made the plight of these kids real to me. Jude just helped me connect it to something *I* could actually do to help."

"Why me?"

"What do you mean, 'why you?'"

Gage took a step toward her, but the dogs stepped between them. Razor focused on Gage, and a low growl sounded from deep in his throat.

"Back," she ordered Razor.

The dog quieted immediately but remained vigilant between them, for which she was grateful. She couldn't let Gage touch her. She'd fall into his arms again if he did. She'd been a victim for far too many years, and she wasn't about to return to feeling helpless and weak. She'd left that woman behind when she left Bakersfield and swore she'd never go back. The fact that she'd allowed him to fix her car, buy her groceries, and even let him crawl under the house for the kittens, had just eaten away at the independence she'd fought so hard to win over the years.

"Leah, don't do this. Stop trying to find a reason to push me away." He ran his hand over his head, the way he did every time he grew frustrated, and her heart ached to comfort him, but the doubts that had been raised by his words refused to flee, even in the face of his denial. He walked around the dog and reached for her hand. "Why do you keep searching for something wrong that doesn't exist? I told you I'm falling in love with you. We should be excited now, making love again, not arguing about why I'm trying to do something good."

"Don't. Don't touch me, please." Her voice broke on a sob she couldn't hold back, and all three dogs would have rushed toward her if she hadn't signaled them to *stay*. "I'm not broken, not anymore."

She couldn't be. To admit she was meant the past still owned her, still controlled her actions, that she was still a victim. But she knew she was lying. She could feel it in the depths of her soul.

"Baby," Gage whispered, cupping her face between his palms, forcing her to look into his eyes, "it's okay." He pressed kisses to her forehead, her eyes, her cheeks, as the hot tears she hadn't realized she'd been holding back, burned a trail down her face. "You're not broken," he agreed.

Except she knew he was lying.

She'd known better than to let anyone close. Not only was she broken, but she was about to break him. It was the only way to keep herself safe, to keep any more of her heart from chipping away. She needed to be alone, because if she was alone, no one could hurt her.

"Leave." Her voice was frigid. The anguish he'd seen written in her face moments ago were gone, replaced by chilly apathy. "And don't come back."

"Leah." He couldn't believe after what they'd shared, after everything said, this was really what she wanted. "We need to talk about this. You can't possibly believe that I'm trying to change you."

"No, you think you can save me from what happened." She pushed him away. Again. "But you can't. It happened, and nothing is going to *fix* that."

She walked into the bedroom and shut the door. "I'm asking you to leave before I come back out," she said from behind the door. She cleared her throat. "Good-bye Gage. I hope the foundation and your company do well."

He'd been dismissed, and there wasn't a damn thing he could do about it. Gage stared at the closed door, wondering what had just happened, how it had escalated from telling her he loved her to being shut out of her life.

"Leah?" He knocked on the bedroom door, but she didn't answer. Twisting the knob slightly, he felt the lock catch. "Leah, come out and talk to me, please."

He wasn't sure what to do. If he left, it would be admitting she was right, and he didn't believe that. Not for one second. But to stay and try to force her to talk would only make this situation worse. If there was one thing he'd quickly figured out about Leah, it was that she didn't respond to force. It would only cause her to shut down. Probably because it reminded her too much of her past.

The Lab came to scratch at the bedroom door, dragging Gage out of his thoughts. He noticed the border collie curled in the hall and both kittens lying on top of him. The shepherd stood at the end of the hallway, watching him warily. He might as well feed the animals and wait for Leah to finally come out.

He wandered around the kitchen, trying to figure out what he'd said or done that had triggered such an emotional reaction. He'd told her he was falling in love with her, and damn it, he meant it. He'd been excited about Apotheo and the good that would come of it, the way they would be able to direct kids away from the criminal activity and help them become more than just hackers. They were already setting up several scholarships, and she had been the inspiration. He'd seen the way she was with the boys, the way they listened to her, the way she was able to help them. Watching her, he realized he wanted to make that kind of difference, to use what money and power he had to do something good.

Gage wanted to do it for her, to be the man she thought he was. He thought she'd be happy about it, too.

His heart crashed, and he suddenly realized why she was so upset, why she accused him of having a hero complex. She thought he wanted to change the kids, not their circumstances, which led her to think he wanted to change *her*. He hurried back to her room, stepping around the three dogs and the kittens trying to pounce on his feet, and knocked on the bedroom door.

"Leah, come out."

"Go away." He heard the hiccup and the watery tone of her voice and knew she was crying.

"Baby, this is really about trying to help these kids. Yes, I wanted you to be impressed, I guess, but that's not the only reason."

She opened the door, looking furious and gorgeous. His pulse quickened, but he was smart enough to know this wasn't the time for desire.

"I came here to start over. I finally had a chance to put my past behind me, and I thought I could. But more than anything else, I was going to use what happened to me to make a difference, to show others how they could overcome the trauma, to prove to them that it didn't have to define them." She shoved her way past him and headed into the hallway. "But then you come along and you're so great. You're kind and generous and just…" She turned and met his gaze, her own watery again as she threw her hands into the air. "Wonderful."

Leah cleared her throat, and he could see the resolve settle over her. Alarm tensed every muscle in his body.

"And now you're saying that you're falling in love with me." Her voice choked and he rushed to her. "Don't." Leah held a hand up, refusing to let him closer.

He'd seen this side of her, the adamant, stubborn woman who was far too independent for her own good.

"What happened to me is over. I've moved on as much as I can. Yes, I still have occasional anxiety attacks. Yes, it has affected my relationships, and probably always will."

"It doesn't have to." His voice was thick with emotion. He already suspected what she was going to say, and he didn't want to give her the opportunity to say it.

"What I have gone through has made me the woman I am. It gives me insight that most other people would never have. I know how these kids feel, growing up in the system, unloved and unwanted. They don't need to be fixed. *I* don't need to be fixed."

"I'm not—"

"Yes, you are." She threw her hands into the air. She took a deep breath and another step away from him. "Start the foundation. It's a great idea. But I can't be a part of it with you. I can't be with you, Gage, because you don't love me. You love the idea of being my savior."

"No, that's not it."

Leah crossed the room to the front door and grasped the handle. "You want to rescue me from my past, Gage. But this isn't a fairy tale. I'm not a princess you're going to rescue from an evil queen. You're not my prince. There is no happily-ever-after. Not for me."

She opened the door.

"Leah, can't we just talk about this? You're not even giving me a chance to say anything."

He could see by the look in her eyes that arguing with her was getting him nowhere. He wasn't sure how to make her see how mistaken she was, but standing here, in her entry, he knew that nothing he said would help. He walked toward the door, knowing that once he walked out, he might never get another chance to touch her, to say what he wanted to say. His hand rose to caress her cheek, his fingers trembled as his thumb brushed her lower lip.

"I'm not sure why you're doing this, but I'm not going to give up. I'm not turning my back on us. I care about you too much, Leah."

She closed her eyes, unwilling to look at him any longer. He brushed a gentle kiss to her lips before she could protest and felt her tear slip between the seam of their lips. Salty and bitter. It tasted like good-bye.

"For the record, it was you who saved me, Leah."

———————————

Chapter Twenty-Four

LEAH STOOD ON the front porch of the house, watching as the group of girls arrived. Most of them had the frail, skittish appearance that characterized teen girls who hadn't lived typical, prom queen existences, but there were two who looked more intense than the rest. Leah couldn't tear her eyes from them and knew she would arrange it so both were in her first group when she, Jessie, and Julia split the girls up this afternoon. She could already tell that the pair was going to be difficult by the way they were refusing to follow Jessie's directions, trying to hide their anxiety and fear behind masks of defiance. It was like looking into a mirror.

It had been four days since she'd told Gage good-bye, and she'd tried to throw herself into her work, preparing for this group of girls. It had been therapeutic during the day, but at night, when the ranch was quiet, she couldn't help searching out the cabin, watching for lights, hoping for just a glimpse of him, even as she prayed that she wouldn't see him. Her heart had shattered when he'd walked out the door. But it hadn't been because he walked away, she was used to that. It was the last words he'd said to her: *You saved me.*

She'd been so certain that he was trying to change her, the way everyone else had, that once again she'd made the assumption that he was the same. She still wasn't sure she was mistaken.

Hell, *she* would have tried to change someone like her.

Wasn't that exactly what she was trying to do as a therapist? Was there really a difference between helping someone and trying to change them?

She watched the two girls again, as everyone else crowded around the corral, where Jessie had brought in a pair of geldings for them to become acquainted with and where the girls would be able to rid themselves of any fears they might have with the horses. Jessie had suggested it as an opportunity for her to watch them without the girls feeling like they were under a microscope. But Leah knew, as a foster kid, you were always aware of people surrounding you, looking for ulterior motives and waiting for the next bomb to drop.

As if sensing her scrutiny, the older of the two girls looked directly at her and arched a brow, nudging the other and pointing.

Busted.

Now that she'd been spotted, she'd let Jessie introduce her to the group. The counselors already knew there was a therapist on staff, but she doubted they'd shared that information, and she didn't want the girls to see her as someone trying to get into their heads. But she didn't want to keep her role on the ranch a secret either. She and Jessie had already talked about not pressuring this group to reveal anything, considering their abusive backgrounds. She made her way down the steps, leaving the dogs in the house.

"Here comes Leah," Jessie said as she approached. "She's going to be helping us with some of the exercises. She's a therapist, but she's mostly here to make sure I don't screw up." Jessie winked at Leah.

"Hey, guys." There were a few mumbled greetings, a couple of eye rolls, and the girl who'd spotted her leaned to the side to whisper into the other girl's ear. Leah could only imagine what was said. "I have a feeling you guys will be better than I am with the horses within just a few days, since I barely know anything about them."

She turned to Julia standing outside the corral quietly holding Emily. "And Julia has been great to help us with some dogs that are probably tearing up my kitchen right now, but I'm hoping I can at least help a little bit. Just know my door is always open." She pointed to her house and saw Gage standing on the front porch of the cabin, watching her.

"Who's the stud?"

Leah's head jerked back to the group to see the voice had come from the girl who had spotted her. She was definitely more like Leah had been at her age than she wanted to believe—crass, impulsive, and probably hiding behind the hard-ass persona for protection.

Julia was the first to speak up. "That's my brother-in-law. He was just visiting and is heading out today."

Leah felt her stomach plummet to her toes. He was leaving? Julia met her gaze, and Leah didn't miss the sympathy in them. She wondered if Gage had told Julia what happened.

"Too bad," she heard from the same girl. She met the girl's eyes, making a mental note to tell Jessie that she wanted plenty of time with the pair after the lesson.

"Anyway," Jessie said, dragging the word out, directing the girls' attention back to her. "I'm going to have all of you come into the corral slowly and check out these two boys. They're both very gentle and have spent a lot of time being handled from either side. They're big, but they're more like big dogs than horses."

Julia opened the gate and let the girls inside, while Leah tried to ignore the heat of Gage's gaze on her back and focus her attention on the group, trying to pay attention to who seemed timid or unsure around the large geldings. There were only three who exhibited any sort of hesitation, and it didn't last long once the rest of the group had surrounded the animals. Her gaze strayed away from the group back to Gage. He was already heading back into the cabin.

"You know," Julia said, "he's getting a place in San Francisco for a week or so to tie up some loose ends, and then he's going to move in with us until he can find his own place in town."

"Oh," Leah said, flushing. "I don't really…"

Who was she trying to fool? She was sure everything was written all over her face. "He's still planning on staying here in town?"

Julia nodded. "He's pretty adamant that's what he wants."

If Gage stayed, she was bound to run into him from time to time, either in town or at Julia's place. She couldn't avoid him, even here on Jessie's ranch. As much as it was going to pain her to see him, knowing that she had to remain distant, she had to put these feelings aside if she was going to do her job. The only other alternative was to leave Heart Fire and this place where she'd finally felt like she belonged, where she had a purpose.

"You should talk to him."

"There's nothing left for us to say."

The words sounded hollow. Leah knew there wasn't one ounce of truth in them, and for someone who'd demanded the truth from Gage, she wasn't sure why she couldn't face it coming from her own heart.

GAGE STARED AT the San Francisco skyline as the sunlight reflected off the glass of the nearby buildings, nearly blinding him. He should be looking over the locations his real estate agent had marked as possible building sites for Apotheo. But, as much as he wanted to make it a reality, San Francisco held no appeal. It seemed ridiculous now, but he'd hoped Leah would want to do it with him, had visualized them building it into something special together. Without her, his life seemed like a vacuum, sucking the energy out of him.

He'd left the ranch four days ago and had filled every waking moment with meetings, agendas, and proposals. Anything that might distract him from thoughts of the woman he wanted to be holding. He couldn't even crawl into the hotel bed without remembering the way she'd curled into him, as if he was her shelter in the storm of life. She'd clung to him like a lifeline and he'd loved it. Loved feeling like he was the only man who could reach her, the only person she let close.

A savior.

Maybe Leah had been right. Maybe he did want her to see him as a hero. But if that was all he'd wanted, he'd have been able to walk away without feeling like his heart had been crushed. There was nothing keeping him going right now other than the hope that with some time and space, she'd realize what they'd had was special.

It wasn't about changing or their pasts or mistakes. It was about becoming the best they could be, and he didn't think either of them could do that without the other. He just wasn't sure how to convince her that he was trying to make himself better, for her. He *did* want her to see him as a hero, but not by changing her—by changing himself.

"Mr. Granger, it's six o'clock and, if it's all right with you, I'd like to head home."

He waved off his assistant, a young man who had attended UCSF, majoring in business leadership. He'd shown promise, and George had mentioned that they should consider him for a position better suited to his skills.

"Jeremy?" Gage turned away from the window and faced the young man.

"Yes, sir?"

"Are you happy working here?" A look of confusion swept over him and Gage didn't miss the hesitation in his answer. "I'd like the truth."

"To be honest, sir, I *have* been happy here, at times, and I think with you back in charge again, it will be better."

It wasn't the answer Gage expected. He folded his hands together and pressed them against his lips, thoughtfully. "What did you want to do when you were young?"

The question seemed to throw Jeremy off guard, but he recovered quickly with a half-smile. "Besides a professional football player or a superhero?"

Gage returned his smile. Such was the dream of all boys, he supposed.

"I wanted to be a teacher."

"Really?"

Jeremy nodded. "I even spent my summers tutoring." He shrugged. "And then I realized that I'd never make a good living at it. So, I focused on business instead."

"Do you regret it? Not teaching, I mean."

"Sometimes," he admitted. "But I had to make a choice and used the information I had at the time. Who knows how things might have turned out? I can tell you that I've been able to help my parents put my little sister through college thanks to this job. I couldn't have done that as a teacher."

"If you could teach and keep your current salary, would you do it?"

Jeremy paused, thoughtfully. "Honestly, I don't think it helps anyone to play a 'what if' game, sir. My dad always said life was like his job driving a bus. If you look back too long, you're going to wreck, and a whole lot of people are going to be hurt."

Gage thought about what Jeremy was saying. Maybe that had been a big part of the problem with him and Leah. They were both so focused on their pasts that they weren't able to see the future ahead that was calling, ready for them to let go and stop looking back. They'd wrecked.

Jeremy smiled slyly. "Now, if you're offering me a position with Apotheo, that's a different story."

"You'd want to be involved?"

"Mr. Granger, I'd be honored." He turned to leave and paused in the doorway. "Sir, I'm not sure what has you questioning yourself, but I will tell you that your employees trust you. We all respect the way you stepped up after the last... well, you know. You may have made a mistake but you owned up to it. There are a lot of tech companies in the Bay Area we could have worked for. You've reminded a lot of us why we chose to work for you. You're a man of your word, sir, and there aren't many men like you around anymore."

Gage stared after his assistant and thought about his parting words. Jeremy might be quiet, but he was wise beyond his years. He'd make a fantastic teacher at Apotheo, but Gage owed the man far more than simply a job and would find a way to thank him. He'd helped Gage realize exactly what he needed to do to show Leah how he felt about her.

KAITLYN SHOT LEAH a "hell no" look that made it clear she wasn't climbing on any horse they put in front of her, regardless of how many people told her it was safe. At seventeen, the girl might be the oldest of the group, but that was also part of Leah's problem. Kaitlyn held a lot of sway with the other girls, and several tended to follow her lead. If she refused to ride, calling it a stupid waste of time, the others might do the same, and the entire week would be shot.

"Jessie, why don't we break up in three groups today with the dogs," Leah suggested.

It had been something they'd planned to do tomorrow, but it was better to change their plans than let Kaitlyn think she could derail them altogether. Jessie didn't look happy about the idea, but she trusted Leah's opinions. And it was working. In the last three days, they'd been able to get four of the girls to open up about their lives, including the abuse they'd suffered. One of them had never told anyone, and they had already alerted her social worker.

"I'll go call Julia and see if she can come help."

"Dogs?" Kaitlyn rolled her eyes. "You mean those flea-bitten mutts in your house?"

Leah laughed quietly. "What? You're not a dog person either?"

The girl glared at her, but Leah didn't miss the unease in her ice blue eyes.

"I'm not an anything person." She sighed heavily and leaned against the hitching post. "Why can't we just go back to the cabin and sleep? Or go swimming in the pool?" She complained, looking toward the other girls, trying to encourage a few to stand behind her minor rebellion. "I thought this place was supposed to be fun."

"And what would you consider *fun*?" Leah looked around the group. Several of the girls looked nervous. Her gaze flicked to Jessie, walking out of the main house on the cell phone.

"Anything other than being here, out in the middle of nowhere," Melanie, Kaitlyn's sidekick, replied quickly, looking to Kaitlyn for approval.

"Anything?" Leah eyed several of the older girls in turn, giving Kaitlyn a pointed look. "Because I doubt you'd like to consider the options. If I'm not mistaken, the next step for several of you is juvie. Or into yet another home?"

"What do you know?" Kaitlyn pushed herself to standing and leaned toward Leah. It wasn't threatening, but it definitely wasn't friendly. She was posturing, taking a defiant stance, and wanting to remind the others who they could count on to stand up for them. Leah had to use this opportunity to give them something to believe in, someone they could trust. Someone Kaitlyn could lean on without losing face.

"I grew up in the system. By the time I was eighteen, I'd been in seventeen foster homes. Until my last one, I never stayed in any of them longer than two months." Leah saw shock register in the faces of several of the younger girls, but she focused on Kaitlyn.

"So? You think that makes you like us?" Leah noticed that while her stance didn't waver, Kaitlyn's voice had lost some of its defiance.

"My first memory is being verbally abused by my mother. I was only about two and a half. It didn't stop until I moved into my last foster home when I was about your age. You name it, it's probably happened to me."

Leah's voice and her gaze were steady. Several of the girls turned away, tears filling their eyes. The reality of Leah's childhood didn't need to be spelled out. These girls could imagine without any details. Even Kaitlyn had taken a step backward. Leah could see the truth had forced them to view her in a different light. She was no longer an outsider telling them what to do without any real knowledge. She was one of them, a survivor in a common war.

"Why don't we head into my house? It's not exactly what Jessie and I had planned, but let's have a carpet picnic." She looked around at the girls, who now looked at her with vulnerable eyes. "Come on." Leah pulled out her phone and texted Jessie, since she was still on the phone, letting her know about the change in plans.

This was the kind of flexibility she'd have never had at the old clinic. She opened the front door and was greeted by Bingo spinning in circles excitedly, yipping happily at the guests. Razor sat at the edge of the carpet, supervising the group entering, and Chaz barely lifted his head from his place on the couch where Puma and Lynx were curled between his front paws.

"Oh!" Destiny, the youngest of the group, squealed and hurried for the couch, scooping up Lynx and rubbing her face against her downy fur. "You have kittens?"

"Kaitlyn, why don't you push the coffee table against that wall, and I'll get some snacks. Anyone want to help?"

"Me!"

"I will."

Girls who hadn't volunteered for anything in the last five days hurried to follow her, while the others began to shift furniture in the living room while the dogs romped around them. Leah glanced at Kaitlyn who, for the first time since her arrival, was smiling. It was just a ghost of a smile, but it was there as she bent down and rubbed her hands behind Bingo's ears.

A warm sense of purpose filled Leah. This was why she had come, what she had hoped to accomplish. She looked out the window to see Jessie coming to join them, and her gaze fell on Gage's cabin, dark and abandoned.

She felt her heart break a little more. Damn it. Thinking about him sucked every bit of joy she felt at finally reaching the girls out of the moment because he wasn't there to celebrate the success with her.

Chapter Twenty-Five

"WANT TO GO for a ride once the girls head out today?" Bailey asked, leaning against the side of the barn where Leah was supervising the girls and counselors as they said good-bye to the animals. Most of them were trying to hold back tears, and Leah could already feel herself choking up. Bailey leaned closer, lowering her voice. "You and Jess are both going to need to decompress."

"I don't know, Bailey. I need to get some notes jotted into the girls' files."

Bailey nodded empathetically, but Leah could see that she knew it was an excuse. Bailey took a long drink from her coffee mug, eyeing Leah over the rim. "You don't really think I'm buying any of this, do you?"

"Bailey, leave her alone." Jessie made her way into the aisle of the barn with Moose, her German shepherd following at her heels, pausing to lick the hand of one of the girls as he moved past. Jessie leaned close. "For the record, I think a ride is exactly what we need, though."

Leah sighed, trying to think of one good reason not to go. She hadn't had a chance to take a ride that wasn't with the kids since she'd arrived a few weeks ago. While she was still a beginner rider, she loved the feeling of freedom of letting the horses go where they wanted and just wander for a little while without feeling like every aspect of life needed to be controlled.

"See, your boss agrees with me," Bailey said. "How about a trail ride down to the river, just to hang out?"

"Okay, okay." Leah held her hands up in submission, and Bailey smiled at her victory.

"I'm going to head over to the clinic and help Justin for a few hours, and then I'll be back."

"We'll be waiting, Bailey," Jessie teased. "But you're saddling your own horse."

"Good, then I don't have to use that crappy barrel saddle you always stick me with." She winked and headed back to the motorcycle in the driveway, tossing the cold coffee into the shrubs.

"You know, you can tell her no if you want to," Jessie said.

Leah smiled. "Bailey is easy to tell no. It's you who doesn't take no for an answer."

Jessie returned the grin with her own. "You know, I've been told that a time or two."

For the first time since her arrival, Jessie felt more like a friend than an employer, and Leah realized that it wasn't because anything at Heart Fire had changed. She had. She'd realized her worth here and that she offered something special, that *she* was special.

"WHAT ARE YOU doing here?" Bailey arched a brow at Gage as he walked through the front door of the clinic.

"I told you I was coming back." Gage moved in to give his friend a hug, but she took a step away from him.

"Why?"

"What do you mean, 'why?' I told you I was moving back here."

"Oh." She tried to hide her surprise, stuffing several papers into a file and rising to put it into its place on the wall.

"What's going on, Bailey?"

"Nothing." She answered far too quickly for him to believe her. "Julia just said you were moving out of the cabin and back to her place, but I didn't expect it to be this soon."

He crossed his arms over his chest. "You're full of crap and we both know it. Spill it. What's going on?"

She bit her lower lip and glanced toward Justin's office, making sure the door was closed, before leaning forward. "Fine, but you didn't hear anything from me."

Gage nodded his agreement.

"Are you heading back to Jessie's anytime soon? Because I'm not sure how welcome you'll be. Jessie's pretty pissed about you bailing on Leah."

He clenched his jaw. None of his relationship with Leah was any of Jessie's business. A fact she seemed to forget, regardless of how many times he'd tried to make it clear to her. Gage crossed his arms over his chest.

Bailey laughed out loud. "Whoa, easy there, tiger. Getting kinda worked up for a fling, aren't you?"

Gage glared at her. "It wasn't a fling."

She looked triumphant, and he realized he'd just played into her hands. "So, there *was* more to this than just Jessie's suspicions?"

"Bailey," Gage warned. "I'll tell you what I told Jessie, don't get involved."

"Too late." She gave him an overconfident grin. "I like Leah. Not sure she's the woman I would have guessed that you'd fall for but—"

"Who said anything about—"

She rolled her eyes. "Please, Gage. Are you really going to try to convince me? The queen of denial?" She shrugged. "Besides, I know you better than that. I've seen you date plenty of women, and I've never seen you have that look on your face," she said, circling a finger toward his face. "That is the look of a man in love."

"Bailey." He ran a hand over his head, letting it fall over his face in frustration. He was tired of denying his feelings for Leah. "Yeah, okay. Just…yeah."

"Then you need to listen to me, lover boy. You need to do something big, something to impress them both."

"Leah doesn't want me to impress her, trust me. We've been down that road, and it didn't end well."

A drawer slammed in Justin's office, and Bailey leaned over the counter to see if he was coming out. "Just trust me," she whispered. "Go back to Julia's and I'll call you when I get finished at Jessie's. Then we can hit The Feed Lot for a drink. I'll even buy dinner, okay?" She glanced

at the door again and shoved a hand against his bicep.
"Now, go."

"Hey, Bailey, has Mr. Booth called about that damn
pig? I hate that thing," Justin called from behind the door.

"No, but I can get him on the phone for you." She
glared at Gage again as she came around the counter and
pushed him toward the door. "I will get this set up for you
and give you a call. You just show up when and where I
tell you to. Trust me."

He paused with his hand on the door. "Bailey, I hate to
say it, but I *don't* trust you."

She winked and shoved him out the door. "That's
because you're a smart man."

LEAH LOOKED OVER her shoulder, making sure that no
one saw what she was about to do, and then pushed open
the door of the cabin. It was chilly, especially for June, but
she knew it wasn't the weather. It was the lack of vibrant
presence from one man. Taking a deep breath, she
stepped over the threshold and closed the door behind
her. She should be changing her clothes, getting ready for
her ride with Bailey and Jessie, but as she'd walked back
to her house after the girls left, she couldn't help herself
from coming inside.

She missed him. More than she thought was possible.

She let her fingertips trail over the couch as she made
her way toward the bedroom. As soon as she stepped
through the doorway, the smell of him surrounded her.
His masculine scent hung heavily in the room, as if he
had just vacated it, and she inhaled deeply, trying to

conjure him from thin air. When it didn't work, she sat on the edge of the bed, reached for one of the pillows, and lay down on it, closing her eyes and pretending he was there, just for a moment.

She felt pathetic, but at the same time, it made her feel close to him.

"Knock, knock. Oh!" Bailey appeared at the doorway, and Leah sat up quickly. "The door was open. I'm sorry, I…" She moved to sit at the foot of the bed. "Are you okay?"

Leah nodded and took a deep breath, sitting up and squaring her shoulders. "Yeah, I just came by to find…" She looked around the room, praying that an excuse might come to her.

"Don't even bother." Bailey rolled her eyes. "I was once in the same position with Chase."

Leah opened her mouth to ask, but Bailey waved a hand.

"Trust me, it's a long story." A smile spread over her lips. "I'll make you a deal. Let's go to dinner and drinks instead of for the ride. I'll tell you all about it."

Leah shook her head, laying the pillow aside. "I'm not really in the mood for drinks, Bailey. It's been a busy week and…" Leah shrugged, as if that was the only explanation needed.

She wasn't about to confess that she hadn't been sleeping most nights because she was too busy thinking about Gage, wondering where he was and what he might be doing, or worse, who he was doing it with. She hated the fact that she felt like a lovesick teen girl and just wanted to go back to the confident woman she'd been before. Before she'd met him, before he'd gotten under her skin. Before she'd fallen in love with him.

"That's makes it an even better idea. Let's go out, just the two of us. I haven't gotten to know you like Jessie and Julia have." Bailey's voice held a plaintive plea Leah had never heard from her before. "Come on, you know you want to. Besides, maybe I can offer you some insight into Gage." She bumped Leah's leg with her knee. "We are friends, you know."

It was hard to resist Bailey when she insisted. And, to be honest, Leah wasn't sure she wanted to resist. The idea that Bailey might know something about Gage's inner workings intrigued her. Maybe Bailey could explain what he'd been thinking and whether he'd really been wanting to change her.

"Okay, let me change."

"I'll tell Jess that plans have changed. I'm sure she won't mind a night home with Nathan anyway."

For a moment, Leah thought about changing her mind and just telling Bailey she was going to stay in and go to bed early. Except she knew she would end up the same way she had every other night this week: staring at the ceiling, cursing herself for the argument with Gage, and wishing she'd done things differently.

THE FEED LOT was packed, and there were no parking spots to be found. Leah almost regretted agreeing to come, but seeing the excitement in Bailey's eyes had been a boost to her morale. Maybe it would be nice just to get out, the two of them, and have a good meal and get to know one another. She adored Jessie and Julia, but more often than not, they were both busy. She'd never had many friends, so Leah wasn't about to turn down the opportunity to make one when it arose.

Bailey slid her truck into a parking spot and jumped from the driver's seat. "I'm so glad you came, in spite of everything."

"Bailey." The word came out more like a warning than Leah had anticipated. "I don't want you to get the wrong idea about what you saw today."

Bailey arched a brow, slinging her purse over her shoulder. "What kind of wrong idea could I get? I know a broken heart when I see one, Leah. I've had my own. But we're not here to talk about that tonight." She frowned. "Unless you want to."

Leah pulled open the front door as they approached the hostess. "Trust me, I don't."

She didn't miss the suspicious way Bailey eyed her, but Leah was grateful she didn't push the issue. That would only lead to questions Leah didn't have the answers to and a conversation about Gage she didn't want to have. "I am here to have fun and for us to get to know one another better."

The hostess greeted them warmly. "Bailey Hart for two," she said to the hostess before turning back to Leah. "Here's to a girls' night to remember."

"Follow me," the hostess said.

Walking through the crowd, Leah was glad Bailey had called in a reservation. In spite of the bustling dining room, they were escorted to a table set away from most of the noise. According to Bailey, the owner owed her a few favors for filling in as a lead singer for his band on several occasions. It was a good thing she'd called in one of the favors because the building was packed with wall-to-wall bodies gyrating on the dance floor, blocking the view of the band onstage.

"We'd like some water and a pitcher of margaritas, please," Bailey said as the hostess slid menus in front of them. Turning back to Leah, she said, "You really can't go wrong with any of the food here. Everything is good."

Leah heard the band kick off a set and turned around to watch the crowd on the dance floor for a moment. When she looked at Bailey, she could see the longing in her eyes. "Why aren't you singing, Bailey? I've heard you and you're fantastic."

Bailey sighed and laid her menu down. "I could be. I even had a record deal, but I walked away from it. It wasn't right for me."

Leah nearly choked on the water she'd sipped. "Not *right*? What singer wouldn't want a recording deal?"

"Me," Bailey said with a shrug. "When it came down to a choice between that or Chase, he won, hands down."

Leah shook her head, finding it hard to believe anyone would turn down a dream like that for a man, even if she was in love. "Why?" she whispered.

Bailey laughed. "Because I had to decide which choice I could live with in the long run. Don't get me wrong," she said, folding her hands on the table. "I feel good when I sing, I enjoy every second of it."

"You're a natural."

"Thanks." Bailey returned her smile. "But I couldn't walk away from Chase when it came down to it, and I couldn't ask him to face his deepest regret in order to go with me." She cocked her head to one side. "Although he did without my asking."

Setting her glass to one side, Leah leaned forward, but Bailey answered her unspoken question. "His partner was killed on a call, and he blamed himself."

Leah was surprised that the man who'd laughed so easily had been fighting with survivor's guilt. Not to mention that someone as independent and free-spirited as Bailey had ever considered being tied down. She seemed like she'd suffocate. "If you don't mind my asking, how'd you know Chase was the one worth giving it up for?"

Bailey paused for a moment, watching the crowd before her gaze focused on Leah, her eyes shimmering with hope and happiness. "Because I wasn't really giving anything up. He was the only one who saw me for who I was and loved me in spite of it all. He'd seen me at my worst, all my fears and demons, but he never gave up on us."

Leah let Bailey's words fall over her, and guilt rose up as she thought about the argument with Gage. He'd been the only one she'd allowed to see her at her most vulnerable, to reveal her past to, and he'd never wanted to abandon her. She'd forced that upon him, not giving him an opportunity to explain himself. He'd insisted he wasn't trying to change her and that she'd made him want to be a better man, for her, but she'd only heard what everyone else had told her over the years—that *she* needed to change. She'd lumped him into the pack of people who had failed her and ruined their relationship because she'd hadn't stopped long enough to listen, hadn't trusted him enough to *hear* what he was really saying.

I'm falling in love with you.

He'd offered her his heart, but she'd been too busy not wanting to face her own brokenness to see that he filled the emptiness inside her that had been left behind by her past and her refusal to let anyone reach her. In spite of the fact, Gage had.

"I need to find him."

Bailey smiled across the table at her. "Gage."

It wasn't a question. She didn't need to confess anything to Bailey, she'd known all along.

"Did he tell you?"

"He didn't need to." Bailey took a deep breath before pressing on. "Leah, he's a good man. Not perfect, trust me," she said with a roll of her eyes. "He's made plenty of mistakes. We all have. But he's still a good man, and that's hard to find. I think you know that."

Leah's gaze met the intense blue stare across the table.

"You don't have to tell me what happened, but I know pain when I see it, and it's there in your eyes. You think it's hidden beneath years of acting, but for those of us who've hurt and been hurt, we recognize it." She nodded to the waitress as she brought the pitcher and glasses, pouring a drink and sliding it across the table to Leah. "But you can't allow whatever has gone before to color your future. I nearly did, and it would have been a huge mistake. The future is yours to design."

Bailey held up her glass, waiting for Leah to do the same. "To a bright future ahead, full of love and happiness."

"I—"

"Excuse me," a husky voice interrupted.

Leah looked up in the dark eyes of the man she wasn't sure she could face. The same man she wanted to wrap her arms around.

Chapter Twenty-Six

"I WAS HOPING you'd let me take your picture. I want to show everyone exactly what the woman of my dreams looks like."

Gage knew it was sappy, but it didn't make it any less true. Leah had changed the way he looked at his life. It was no longer about the image he needed to portray publicly; it was no longer about providing for his family. He wanted her to love him, flaws and imperfections be damned.

"Gage." Her voice was barely a whisper, as if she was afraid speaking his name would make him disappear. "What are you doing here?"

Bailey smiled up at the two of them, her grin broad and victorious. "I think I'll just go…somewhere else."

"You planned this, didn't you?" He didn't really need to hear her answer to know he was right. Her smile said it all as she patted his cheek. "I love you and I want to see you both happy. You're good together. I couldn't watch the two of you stupidly throw away something good because of a bump in the road."

Gage slid into Bailey's vacated seat. "If this is what she calls a bump, I'd hate to see a mountain."

Leah simply stared at him, not giving him the smile he'd hoped for. He needed to see something other than shock on her face. The surprise didn't tell him anything. He needed to know how she felt about his return.

He reached across the table for her hand. "Leah, say something."

"I don't know what to say."

Gage felt his heart drop to his stomach. This wasn't the response he'd hoped for from her. He needed to touch her, to remind her of how good they were together. She couldn't really mean for this to be the end.

"Dance with me." He rose and twisted his fingers through hers. "Please?"

Leah's eyes misted, and she looked away, but he took a step toward her, brushing the back of his fingers at her jaw. "Leah, please? One dance, that's all I'm asking for."

"Okay."

She stood up and let him lead her to the dance floor as the band played a slow ballad. Instead of sliding his hands to her waist, he tucked the hand holding hers against his chest, pressing a quick kiss to their linked fingers. His other hand found the center over her back, and he ducked his head, inhaling the sweet scent of her, letting it fill him and make his heart race. As the music filled the room, he swayed with her, her body fitting against his, making him ache with need. Holding her, the rest of the crowd disappeared. No one existed but the two of them in this moment.

The lights from the stage fell over her face; her cheek pressed against his chest. As if she could feel his gaze on her, Leah looked up at him, her eyes innocent, begging him for answers he wanted to give her.

"God, Leah, I'm sorry. I never wanted to make you feel like you needed to change."

"Gage, don't."

He couldn't stop the words from spilling out of him if he tried. It was like the dam had broken open, and he had to tell her everything or he'd fade into nothing.

"No, don't stop me now." He pressed his forehead against hers. "I need *you*, not the other way around. You are perfect the way you are. There is nothing about you I would change except one thing—that I'm not with you."

He stopped in the middle of the floor and cupped her face in his hands, lifting her chin so that she couldn't help but see the truth in his eyes. "No matter what was going on in my life, there has always been something missing. You. You are what I can't live another day without."

A single tear slid from her golden brown eyes, and it broke him. He wanted her to know how he felt about her, but he couldn't hurt her, and that was what he was doing. He pressed a kiss to her forehead and realized the music had ended and the band had picked up the pace, while they still stood in the middle of the floor.

"Let me take you home."

"Gage," she began. He didn't want to hear her reject him again.

"Just a ride home, Leah. Nothing more. You don't have to say anything."

Please, don't say anything.

He'd made a big enough fool of himself. Gage went back to the table, where Bailey was waiting, a triumphant smile on her face.

She passed him Leah's purse. "We girls watch out for one another." Bailey arched a brow at him in warning. "I got you this far, now take her home and don't screw this up."

LEAH'S INSIDES WERE a whirlwind of turmoil. Her brain kept telling her to keep her mouth shut, that Gage was far better off finding someone else. Someone he could show off in public, someone whose past wouldn't come back to haunt him, someone untainted. But her heart was breaking at the thought of letting him go for good. She wanted him; she loved him. And wanted to be loved by him in return.

You are perfect the way you are. There is nothing I would change. I need you.

The words she'd longed to hear from someone her entire childhood. Gage had given her the one thing she'd given up hope of ever getting. But in her heart, she knew now the words weren't enough, no matter how much she tried to convince herself that they could be. The words only meant anything if they were coming from Gage.

The car was quiet as he drove her back to the ranch, but Leah's pulse pounded in her ears. She wanted to say something, but she knew that they couldn't have a discussion this way, in the car. She wanted to see his face, his eyes, to know that he understood her.

As if feeling her gaze on him, Gage reached his hand across the console of the Challenger, winding his fingers through hers.

"Leah, it's okay. Your friendship means more to me than anything else." He glanced her way, his dark eyes shadowed from the blue lights of the dashboard. "No matter what, I'm always your friend."

Tears flooded her eyes, and she turned toward the window before he could see them. In twenty-seven years, only one person had stood by her, even in the face of her self-destructive tendencies, but now Gage was willing to take up the torch Nicole had held proudly.

Gage slowed as he drove past the spot where they'd first met, when her car had overheated. What she'd considered bad luck at the time had turned out to be one of the luckiest moments of her life. Had she not been stranded on the side of the road, he wouldn't have been there to help her. Their initial miscommunication had turned into something they could laugh about, especially knowing him as well as she did now. Leah couldn't help the smile that spread her lips as she thought about their first meeting.

"Don't think I can't see your smile reflected in the window." He chuckled from beside her as he turned off the highway and headed down the road leading to Heart Fire Ranch. "I stand by my original comment. I was talking about the car. How many times do I have to tell you?"

If he could see her reflection, then he'd also seen her tears. As usual, there was nothing she could hide from him. She wiped a hand over her cheek before turning back to him. "I know you were."

"You do?"

She nodded and smiled sadly. "If you'd been talking to me you'd have said something like 'Did you sit in some sugar? Because you've got one sweet ass.'"

Gage laughed out loud, the sound rushing over her, filling the hollow places in her heart. "I would *never* say that."

"No? Then it would have been 'Was your dad a baker? Because you've got a great set of buns.'"

Gage groaned and rolled his eyes, but his smile grew wider as he turned down the long gravel driveway, passing the sign that announced their entry at the ranch. "Not even close."

Gage slowed the car in front of the cabin, pretending he didn't notice Jessie as she came out on the porch of the main house, watching, ever-vigilant. He shut off the car and faced Leah.

"You deserved one I've never used before."

She could see the desire in his deep brown eyes as they swept over her, and she held her breath, unable to even ask him what it would have been. Gage gave her a half-smile, the one she'd always thought of as his playboy grin, but that, she now knew, was just Gage. Fun-loving, sweet, kind, gentle, flattering Gage. The man she wanted to throw her arms around and beg to love her forever.

He raised his hand and brushed her hair back from her face with a finger, barely caressing her as he tucked it behind her ear. "If beauty were time, you'd be an eternity."

Her breath caught at the sweet seduction of his words, but before she could even respond, he got out of the car and walked around to open her door, holding out his hand to help her.

"I'll walk you to your house." He laced his fingers in hers and walked her to the front door, waiting as she unlocked it. Now was the time for her to finally tell him to stay, to tell him how she felt, and to apologize for the way she'd acted.

"Mind if I see the kittens one last time?"

Her heart sank when she heard the finality in his voice. It sounded too much like a good-bye. Her pulse picked up speed again, her heart pounding against her ribs. She either had to give up trying to control this situation, give in to the feelings she had for Gage, or let go of them altogether and lose the one chance at finding love with someone who accepted her for who she was.

Leah looked at Gage, trying to force her mind to make the decision her heart had already made. His eyes glowed in the light from the porch light, but he looked sad, troubled, as if he wanted to say something but wasn't sure what to say.

Leah's heart raced in her chest as they stepped into the entry, her pulse beating out the words in a frantic rhythm. *Don't do this! Stop now! Don't say anything!*

Part of her felt like a caged animal, desperate to run away, to hide from the man who held her captive as surely as if he had handcuffed her to his side. She wanted to hold onto her belief that he wanted something from her she couldn't give, that he wanted to change her. But Leah was having a difficult time reconciling that man with the one who'd crawled under her house to rescue kittens. Or the man who'd held her as an anxiety attack wracked her body, leaving her a trembling mess. Or the man who'd made love to her with such reverence.

Part of her couldn't turn away from him, couldn't deny what he'd been making her feel since she'd met him on the side of the road what felt like an eternity ago. How could this man have reached into her soul the way he had in so short a time if he wasn't the man she thought he was? Wasn't it more likely that the fraud, the lie, was Gage trying to act like the cold-hearted businessman he'd forced himself to become?

There's no going back.

Leah didn't care. Her hands found his waist. Instead of pushing him away, she wrapped her arms around him, bracing her chin against his chest. "I said you couldn't make me fall for you."

"I remember."

His voice was uncertain, as if he expected her to disappear, or ask him to leave. His hesitation was a contradiction of the confident, self-assured man she'd seen up to now.

"I lied." She lifted onto her toes and pressed her lips against the curve of his jaw. "I already have. I love you, Gage. I think I've loved you since that night you stayed here and listened to me talk about my past. I didn't recognize it as love then, but it was. You've seen the darkest parts of me, and you've never even batted an eye. I can't help but love you."

"Leah." His voice was gravelly as his fingers buried into her hair, capturing her mouth with his, making desire curl through like morning fog, rolling in slowly, invading every crevice of her heart.

Her hands slid up his back, her fingers digging into the flesh desperately, unsure whether her heart was finally leading her toward her dreams or steering her directly into the face of disaster. With Gage's body pressed against hers, she honestly didn't care.

In a short time, he'd taught her to hope again, to quit listening to her doubts and fears. She needed him, needed to believe in him, because he believed in her. And if what he'd taught her to believe was a lie, then she really was the woman she'd tried to leave behind in Bakersfield, the woman she'd been outrunning since she was sixteen.

She needed to believe he was good and honorable and trustworthy, in spite of his mistakes, because then she could be as well.

GAGE DIDN'T WANT to question her, didn't want to ask if she was sure. But doubts niggled at his conscience. Even as she tugged at his shirt, as his tongue swept into her mouth, the taste of her stripped away his sanity.

"Leah, wait." He took a step back from her, his back hitting the door and just missing the paw of the Lab who had curled up behind him, realizing Gage was no threat to Leah. On the contrary, he was sure she posed a threat for his psyche. "You said—"

"I know what I said." Her voice was breathless as she stepped into him again, pressing her lips against his neck, his jaw, and his lower lip. "And you were right, the falling part is easy. You promised not to hurt me, and I'm choosing to trust you."

Gage ran his thumbs toward her chin, tipping her face so she could see the promise in his eyes. "I remember, and I still mean that, Leah."

"I know you do."

Gage slid his hands over her hips, lifting her so she could wind her legs around his waist as he carried her further into the house. He heard the growl from the living room before an excited whine sounded from the kitchen.

"Down, Razor," Leah ordered.

The growling stopped immediately, but the whine closed in on them as Bingo began circling in front of Gage's legs in a blur of black and white fur, nearly tripping him up and forcing him pause at the kitchen.

"Why do you have these dogs again?" Gage muttered against her lips as he flipped on the light to see both kittens sprawled along the back of the couch while Chaz lay in the middle of the living room on his back, spread-eagle and sound asleep.

"Because they're therapy dogs to help with the kids. They've been good company for me when you were gone."

He turned, settling her rear on the kitchen counter. "Leah, you know I only left because you told me to. It was something I never wanted to do." He brushed the hair back from her face and kissed the tip of her nose. "I've been trying to figure out a way to convince you to let me back in since the morning I woke up with you in my arms. Nothing in my life has ever felt as good as you do."

"But my past—"

"Is behind you. Just like mine is behind me." Gage shook his head. "We both know you're moving beyond it as well as you can. Look at what you've been able to accomplish. You're a doctor. You've turned something awful into a way to help people."

"I'm still kind of a mess," she admitted, hanging her head.

Gage tipped her chin up with a finger. "I've made a few messes of my own. Maybe we can help each other clean them up."

"I don't know how to do relationships, Gage."

"I'll help you figure it out. You're good enough at it to make me fall in love with you." He bent down and brushed his lips over hers. "You're something special, Leah. Just because you don't see it, doesn't mean no one else does."

She sighed, leaning into him and letting him take her into his arms again. Now that she was his, he couldn't get enough of her. His hands wanted to touch every inch of her, his lips needed to taste her. He wanted to wrap himself around her and bury himself within her.

"Ow! Son of a bitch!" Needle-sharp claws dug into his ankles as both kittens climbed up his pant legs. Leah tried to hold back her laughter as he bent to pluck them from his jeans by the scruff of the neck. "You two are monsters."

"I think they missed you, too."

"You missed me?"

She nodded, tugging him closer by the front of his shirt as he set the kittens on the counter next to her. "I even missed your cheesy lines."

"Hmm, you mean like how I'll never have to see the sun again because of the light in your eyes?" He pressed a quick kiss to her temple. "Or how I'd like to write a love song on your body with my lips?" His mouth found the hollow behind her ear, and he felt goose bumps break out over her arms.

"Yes, those cheesy lines." He felt her shiver against him, and her voice was breathless.

"You know what I missed?" His hands slid up from her hips to rest on her ribs, his thumbs grazing the swell of her breasts, his lips finding the curve of her collarbone. "The way you whisper my name and the way you lean into me when I kiss you. And the way I can see you choosing to trust me in spite of your reservations."

"Gage?"

"Hmm?"

Her fingers dug into the muscles of his back, pulling him closer, and she arched her body toward him as he slid his hands around to her back. She wound her legs around his thighs and dragged him a step closer, so that they were practically fused from shoulder to hip. His body throbbed, protesting every stitch of clothing they wore.

"If you really love me, you'll take me into that bedroom and show me right now."

He smiled against her flesh, thrilled that she no longer felt the need for pretense between them. "My pleasure."

Gage wrapped one arm around her waist and let his fingers trail over her shoulder as he brushed her hair to one side and pressed his lips against her heated skin.

He lifted her legs around his waist and carried her toward the bedroom. "Besides I don't want any kitten claws digging into my skin."

She arched a brow and gave him a wicked grin. "We'll lock the cats out, but I can't promise anything."

Gage groaned and settled her on her feet again, turning her so her back was against his chest, his lips trailing kisses along her shoulder as he removed her clothing, letting it fall to the floor around their feet. Leah sighed and let her head fall backward, leaning against him as his hand moved up to cup her breast, his fingers brushing the sensitive peak. She arched into his touch, and it was his undoing.

His hand trailed over her belly, lower, and Leah whimpered as his slid a finger into her folds, his own body straining to be free from his clothing. She spun in his arms, reaching for the button of his pants, but he beat her to it, ridding himself of the confining garments quickly. He wanted to feel her body against his, with nothing separating them.

They fell onto the bed together, a tangle of arm and legs, hands and lips, eager to touch and be touched. Gage couldn't get enough of Leah—her heated skin, the sweet honey scent of her, the taste of her on his lips—and tried to control the tempest of desire raging through him. She rose over him, straddling his hips.

"Wait, Leah."

She smiled softly and, as if reading his mind, she carefully leaned over the side of the bed to retrieve his pants. "In the pocket? Or do you need your wallet?"

"Wallet."

Gage wasn't sure how he was even able to form a coherent thought with the wet heat of her sex pressed against him. His body throbbed in response, twitching against her, and Gage prayed he could even last long enough to get the condom on. He plucked the wallet out of her hands as she threw the pants aside. Taking the package from inside, he tossed the wallet on the bedside table.

"Let me." She didn't offer him a chance to deny her request before taking the condom from his hand.

Pressing kisses over his chest, she continued to move lower. Gage knew this exquisite torture was too much but when she pressed a kiss to his hipbone, electricity shot through him and he gripped her upper arms.

He let out a growl. "Not this time."

Leah's hand moved over his inner thigh, her finger-nails carefully raking the sensitive skin before moving to palm his length. "Okay," she whispered, her voice sweetly seductive, "next time."

Once she sheathed him, her lips pressed hot kisses over the planes of his stomach, over his chest and back to his mouth. This wasn't the slow, seductive lovemaking they'd shared the first time. She wanted to be in control, to prove something, both to him and to herself, but Gage was helpless to contemplate what it might be when she straddled him.

His fingers dug unto the soft curve of her buttocks as Leah met his gaze. He could see desire in her eyes. Like warm bourbon through his veins, it spread, heating him as he basked in it for a moment, until she slid down the length of him.

Slowly, agonizingly slowly. Gage arched his back, a groan of pure ecstasy ripping from his throat. Bracing her hands against his stomach, she rode him, her hair falling forward to cover her face. Gage wanted to see her, to watch her let go of the control she held so tightly.

"Look at me, baby." Gage heard the plea in his own voice, but he didn't care. He wanted her to know how much he needed her. He moved his hand to the nape of her neck, pulling her down so that her forehead rested against his, looking deeply into her eyes.

Leah opened her eyes, focusing on him, and he felt her tremble in his arms as her release shook her to her core. Gage couldn't hold back any longer as he poured himself into her, heart and soul.

He wouldn't hide anything from her again. Tonight they had taken their relationship to the next level. She admitted she'd fallen for him, and he was going to be just as transparent, no matter what it cost him.

Chapter Twenty-Seven

Leah took a tentative sip of the hot coffee and set it on the railing of the porch as the three dogs played a game of tag in the yard between her house and the main house. Gage came out and circled his arms around her waist from behind. Pressing a quick kiss to the shell of her ear, he made her entire body heat in response before he rested his chin on her shoulder.

"What has you so deep in thought?"

"What happens next?"

"You mean with us?" She nodded. "This is where we're supposed to live happily ever after, Leah."

She turned in his arms to face him and gave him a dubious look. "You know me. I'm not exactly a fairy-tale kind of girl."

"We'll just take it one step at a time."

She arched a brow and shot him a doubtful look. "I'm not exactly the fly-by-the-seat-of-my-pants, wait-and-see type either. I've had enough unknowns and chaos in my life. I like having a plan."

"You didn't plan on me, and look how well that turned out."

She smiled back at him, brushing her lips over his, reveling in his quiet groan of pleasure. "That's true, but you have a company to run, and a new foundation to start up in the city. My work is here."

"I told you I wasn't going to leave you. Apotheo is going to be based out of Sacramento. My life is nothing without you in it, so wherever you are is where I'll be."

"I see the two of you patched things up."

Jessie smiled brightly as she came around the corner of the house. Alfalfa leaves dusted her clothing, and Leah knew she must have just finishing feeding the horses. She tried to slip from Gage's arms, but he held her tight, glaring at Jessie.

"We did."

Leah was surprised by the intensity of his tone, practically daring Jessie to say more.

"Relax, Gage. I'm happy for you both."

"What?" He loosened his hold on Leah, obviously surprised by Jessie's admission. "But you said—"

"I know." Her grin pulled to one side, and her eyes sparkled impishly. "But, you've also stepped up and proven that I was wrong. I'm big enough to admit it."

Leah looked from her boss to Gage, wondering what had actually transpired between them without her knowledge.

"Does this mean you're not cleaning your things out of the cabin? Because I have a big group coming next Thursday, and we could use the space."

The thought of Gage leaving, even to move to Julia's a few minutes through the pastures, made Leah's heart plummet.

He nodded to Jessie. "Dylan and Julia already made up the spare room for me, so I'll get the rest of my things out today."

Leah heard the broodiness in his tone, making her feel more confident in the fact that he didn't *want* to leave. With his hand resting on her waist, it felt right to be in his arms, to have him standing on her front porch sharing coffee with her first thing in the morning. It had felt right to see him in the kitchen this morning with the dogs. Almost as comforting as it had been to wake up in his arms.

"Jessie would probably let you stay here."

The words fell from her lips, but she realized she had no desire to take them back. There was no hesitation or fear. She ignored the knowing smile on Jessie's face.

His gaze fell on her face, searching. "Are you sure?"

She wound her arms around his waist. "Someone needs to help me with all these animals."

"Now that sounds like the best plan I've heard." Jessie laughed as she made her way through the dogs, now playing tug-of-war with a stick. She whistled and her shepherd, Moose, trotted beside her. "You and Nathan can get your plans in motion while Leah and I actually get some work done," she teased.

Gage peered into Leah's face. "I don't have to stay here if you don't want that, Leah. I don't want you to feel pressured."

"I don't. I also don't want you even a few miles away."

Gage dipped his head, his mouth meeting hers in a kiss that made her release another fingerhold on the pain of her past and reach toward the promise of a future with Gage. She might not believe in fairy tales, but Leah had just changed her mind about happily ever after.

Acknowledgments

THERE ARE SO many people to thank for helping me along this incredible journey. The first three people I want to thank are the ones who keep me sane on this roller coaster ride, my editor extraordinaire, Rebecca Lucash; my agent, Suzie Townsend; and Sara Strickler. The three of you keep me laughing and throwing my hands in the air to enjoy even the scary parts of the ride.

To my BFF, Codi. I can't thank you enough for the late nights and early mornings of brainstorming, mind-melding, and plot twisting. You "get" me like no one else, my sister-from-another-mister.

To my writing buddies and Country Crew members. I absolutely adore each and every one of you and know that my life is a party now because of you!

To my readers. My heart soars every time I hear how much you love these characters that rattle around in my brain, begging for release. Nothing makes me happier than to know they are as real to you as they are to me.

To my family. I could never continue to do what I do without your support. From nights when you've had to fend for yourself to listening to mom prattle on about people who don't really exist as if they do. And, for my husband, who is too often neglected in favor of fictional heroes, know that you are the one I base all of these heroes on. I love you guys to the moon and back again!

About the Author

T. J. KLINE was raised competing in rodeos and Rodeo Queen competitions since the age of fourteen and has thorough knowledge of the sport as well as the culture involved. She writes contemporary Western romance for Avon Impulse, including four books in the Rodeo series and the Healing Harts series. She has published a non-fiction health book and two inspirational fiction titles under the name Tina Klinesmith. In her very limited spare time, T. J. can be found laughing hysterically with her husband, children, and their menagerie of pets in Northern California.

Discover great authors, exclusive offers, and more at hc.com.

Give in to your Impulses . . .
Continue reading for excerpts from
our newest Avon Impulse books.
Available now wherever ebooks are sold.

YOU'RE STILL THE ONE
RIBBON RIDGE BOOK SIX
by Darcy Burke

THE DEBUTANTE IS MINE
A SEASON'S ORIGINAL NOVEL
by Vivienne Lorret

ONE DANGEROUS DESIRE
AN ACCIDENTAL HEIRS NOVEL
by Christy Carlyle

An Excerpt from

YOU'RE STILL THE ONE
Ribbon Ridge Book Six
By Darcy Burke

College sweethearts Bex and Hayden were
once the perfect couple but is five years
enough time to heal broken hearts . . . and
give them a second chance at first love?

Ribbon Ridge, July

Hayden Archer drove into the parking lot at The Alex. The *paved* parking lot. He hadn't been home since Christmas, and things looked vastly different, including the paved lot instead of the dirt he'd been used to. The project to renovate the old monastery into a hotel and restaurant was nearly complete, and his siblings had done an amazing job in his absence.

He stepped out of his car, which he'd rented at the airport when his flight had arrived that afternoon. Someone would've picked him up, of course. If they'd known he was coming.

He smiled to himself in the summer twilight, looking forward to seeing his brothers' surprise when he burst in on Dylan Westcott's bachelor party. Hayden glanced around but didn't see anyone. They'd all be at the underground pub that Dylan had conceived and designed. It was fitting that its inaugural use would be to celebrate his upcoming wedding to their sister Sara.

Hayden could hardly wait to see the place, along with the rest of the property. But he figured that tour would have to wait until tomorrow. Tonight was for celebrating. And shocking the hell out of his family.

He made his way to the pub and immediately fell in love with what they'd done. He'd seen pictures, but being here in person gave everything a scale that was impossible to feel from half a world away.

They'd dug out the earth around the entrance to the pub and installed a round door, making it look distinctly hobbit-like. He wondered how much of that design had come from his brother Evan, and was certain Kyle's fiancée, Maggie, the groundskeeper of the entire place, had tufted the grass just so and ensured the wildflowers surrounding the entry looked as if they'd been there forever. A weathered, wooden sign hung over the door, reading: Archetype.

As he moved closer, he heard the sounds of revelry and smiled again. Then he put his hand on the wrought-iron door handle and pushed.

The noise was even louder inside, and it was nearly as dim as it had been outside. There were recessed lights in the wooden beams across the ceiling and sconces set at intervals around the space, all set to a mellow, cozy mood.

Hayden recognized most of the twenty or so people here. A few tables had been pushed together, and a handful of guys were playing some obnoxiously terrible card game while others were gathered at the bar. Kyle, one of his three brothers—the chef with the surfer good looks—stood behind it pouring drinks.

Hayden made his way to the bar, amused that no one had noticed him enter. "Beer me."

Kyle grabbed a pint glass. "Sure. What were you drinking?" He looked up and blinked. "Shit. Hayden. Am I drunk?" He glanced around before settling back on Hayden.

"Probably. Longbow if you've got it."

Kyle came sprinting around the bar and clasped him in a tight hug. He pulled back, grinning. "Look what the cat dragged in," he bellowed.

The noise faded then stopped completely. Liam, his eldest brother, or at least the first of the sextuplets born, stood up from the table, his blue-gray gaze intense. "Hayden, what the hell?" Like Kyle, his expression was one of confusion followed by joy.

"Hayden?" Evan, his remaining brother—the quiet one—leaned back on his stool at the other end of the bar. Like the others, he registered surprise, though in a far more subdued way.

"Hayden!" This exclamation came from the table near Liam and was from Hayden's best friend, Cameron Westcott. He was also the groom's half-brother.

The groom himself stood up from where he sat next to Evan. "What an awesome surprise." Dylan grinned as he hugged Hayden, and for the next several minutes he was overwhelmed with hugs and claps on the back and so much smiling that his cheeks ached.

"Why didn't you tell us you were coming?" Liam asked, once things had settled down.

Kyle had gone back behind the bar and was now pulling Hayden's beer from the tap. "Do Mom and Dad know you're here?"

Hayden looked at Liam. "Because I wanted to surprise

everyone." Then he looked at Kyle. "And no, Mom and Dad don't know." Hayden took his glass from Kyle and immediately sipped the beer, closing his eyes as the distinct wheat flavor his father had crafted brought him fully and completely home.

Kyle leaned on the bar. "Mom is going to be beside herself." He slapped the bar top. "Now this is a party!"

An Excerpt from

THE DEBUTANTE IS MINE
A Season's Original Novel
By Vivienne Lorret

USA Today bestselling author Vivienne Lorret
launches a new historical romance series featuring
the Season's Original—a coveted title awarded
by the ton's elite to one lucky debutante . . .

The Season Standard—the Daily Chronicle of Consequence.

Lilah read no farther than the heading of the newspaper in her hand before she lost her nerve.

"I cannot look," she said, thrusting the *Standard* to her cousin. "After last night's ball, I shouldn't be surprised if the first headline read, 'Miss Lilah Appleton: Most Unmarriageable Maiden in England.' And beneath it, 'Last Bachelor in Known World Weds Septuagenarian Spinster as Better Alternative.'"

Lilah's exhale crystallized in the cold air, forming a cloud of disappointment. It drifted off the park path, dissipating much like the hopes and dreams she'd had for her first two Seasons.

Walking beside her, Juliet, Lady Granworth, laughed, her blue eyes shining with amusement. Even on this dull, gray morning, she emitted a certain brightness and luster from within. Beneath a lavender bonnet, her features and complexion were flawless, her hair a mass of golden silk. And if she weren't so incredibly kind, Lilah might be forced to hate her as a matter of principle, on behalf of plain women throughout London.

"You possess a rather peculiar talent for worry, Cousin," Juliet said, skimming the five-column page.

The notion pleased Lilah. "Do you think so?"

After twenty-three years of instruction, Mother often told her that she wasn't a very good worrier. Or perhaps it was more that her anxieties were misdirected. This, Lilah supposed, was where her *talent* emerged. She was able to imagine the most absurd disasters, the more unlikely the better. There was something of a relief in the ludicrous. After all, if she could imagine a truly terrible event, then she could deal with anything less dramatic. Or so she hoped.

Yet all the worrying in the world would not alter one irrefutable fact—Lilah needed to find a husband this Season or else her life would be over.

"Indeed, I do," Juliet said with a nod, folding the page before tucking it away. "However, there was nothing here worth your worry or even noteworthy at all."

Unfortunately, Lilah knew what that meant.

"Not a single mention?" At the shake of her cousin's head, Lilah felt a sense of déjà vu and disappointment wash over her. This third and final Season was beginning on the same foot as the first two had. She would almost prefer to have been named most unmarriageable. At least she would have known that someone had noticed her.

Abruptly, Juliet's expression softened, and she placed a gentle hand on Lilah's shoulder. "You needn't worry. Zinnia and I will come up with the perfect plan."

As of yet, none of their plans had yielded a result.

Over Christmas, they had attended a party at the Duke of Vale's castle. Most of those in attendance had been unmarried young women, which had given nearly everyone the hope of marrying the duke. Even Lilah had hoped as much—at first. Yet when the duke had been unable to remember her name, she'd abruptly abandoned that foolishness. And a good thing too, because he'd married her dearest friend, Ivy, instead.

The duke had developed a *Marriage Formula*—a mathematical equation that would pair one person with another according to the resulting answer. Then, using his own formula, the duke had found his match—Ivy. As luck would have it, both Ivy and Vale had fallen deeply in love as well. Now, if only Lilah could find her own match.

"I have been considering Vale's *Marriage Formula*. All I would need to do is fill out a card." At least, that was how Lilah thought it worked. "Yet with Vale and Ivy still on their honeymoon, I do not know if they will return in time."

Then again, there was always the possibility that the equation would produce no match for her either.

Juliet's steps slowed. "Even though I couldn't be more pleased for Ivy, I'm not certain that I want to put your future happiness in the hands of an equation."

Lilah didn't need *happiness*. In fact, her requirements for marriage and a husband had greatly diminished in the past two years. She'd gone from wanting a handsome husband in the prime of his life, to settling for a gentleman of any age who wasn't terribly disfigured. She would like him to be kind to her as well, but she would accept any man who didn't bellow and rant about perfection, as her father had done.

"A pleasant conversation with someone who shares my interests would be nice, not necessarily happiness, or even love, for that matter," Lilah said, thinking of the alternative. "All I truly need is not to be forced into marriage with Cousin Winthrop."

An Excerpt from

ONE DANGEROUS DESIRE
An Accidental Heirs Novel
By Christy Carlyle

Rex Leighton dominates the boardroom by day and prowls the ballroom at night. Searching for the perfect bride to usher him into the aristocracy, he abandoned the idea of love the last time he saw the delicious May Sedgwick. But when he's roped into a marriage bet, Rex is willing to go all in. There's just one problem—he's competing against the only woman he's ever loved.

The duke strode into the sitting room first, stopping and gesturing toward the American.

"My dear, you must help me convince Mr. Leighton to join us next week. And see here, sir, we can even supply a fellow countrywoman to encourage you. Miss Sedgwick, may I present Mr. Rex Leighton."

The duke was speaking, making introductions. The minuscule part of May's mind still capable of processing words and considering polite etiquette told her to curtsy or extend her hand, but she couldn't manage any of it.

A man she'd relegated to her dreams had crashed in and collided with her Thursday afternoon. Impossibly, *he* stood before her. The man she kept confined in her heart and mind. The same man, and yet so changed. He looked nothing like the poor shop clerk she'd pined for, impossibly yearned for year after year until she'd almost forgotten how to yearn for anything else. The eyes were the same mercurial brew of gold and azure, and all the angles of his face still aligned with irritating perfection, set off by a divot in the center of his chin.

That gleaming dark hair she'd once sifted through her fingers shone like rich mahogany in the afternoon light.

But his gaze was remote, impassive, as if a pane of murky glass separated them. She was the one stuck on a curio cabinet shelf, and he was coolly examining her from the other side. His clothes were those of a prosperous gentleman, not the outdated and oft-mended single suit owned by Reginald Cross. Worst was the arrogant tilt of his chin. The Reg of her memories had only ever looked at her with admiration and pleasure, what she imagined in her silly youthful way was love. No one had ever made her feel as important with a single glance.

He wasn't the same man. Couldn't be. The duke called him Leighton, not Cross. A striking resemblance. Nothing more.

May reminded herself to breathe and stepped forward to be introduced to the polished gentleman who could not be the shop boy who'd broken her heart in New York City.

Mr. Leighton took two steps forward, and her momentary grasp on composure faltered. *Reg.* His scent, the firm line of his mouth, the large, elegant hand extended toward her—they belonged to Reginald Cross. Smarter, wealthier, older, and with an abundance of confidence his younger self lacked, but still a man she'd once known. The only man she'd ever loved.

Emily touched her arm, urging May to accept his offered hand. She obeyed and moved toward him, sliding her fingers against his until their palms met. Warm. How could a memory be so warm? But he wasn't a memory. He was real. Alive. He was in London, had been for goodness knew how long, and she was meeting him in her dearest friend's sitting room. By complete and utter chance.

"A pleasure to meet you, Miss Sedgwick."

Same deep-toned voice. Same ability to raise shivers across her skin. Even when there was something silvery and practiced in his timbre, even while he still wore that placid mask.

"How do you . . ." The rest wouldn't come. May knew the words she was expected to say. Felt the gazes of Emily and her father. Sensed their discomfort at her odd behavior.

His hand tightened around hers and the glass between them shattered. He blinked, a quick fan of sable lashes, and then those unique eyes of his saw her. Not as a stranger to whom he was being introduced, but as the woman he'd held and kissed. The woman to whom he'd broken every promise he'd ever made. She detected his recognition in the tremor of his lush lower lip, felt it through the heat of his skin, read it in his blue-gold gaze that flitted from her mouth to her eyes and over each aspect of her face.

"May." He breathed the word quietly, intimately, just for her to hear, as if a duke and his daughter weren't standing nearby.

Grief, too long repressed, welled up like floodwaters, fierce and fast and just as unstoppable.

May wrenched her hand from his with a burning friction of skin against skin. When she spun around, Emily's face whirled past, a blur of confusion and concern. Moving, walking away from him, felt good. Like victory. Like strength. Like she would finally get to choose the conclusion to their tale. She needed it to end and had never gotten the satisfaction of a proper parting. She would explain her rudeness to Emily later, but for now she needed to find the mettle to keep going, to leave him as he'd left her.

www.ingramcontent.com/pod-product-compliance
Lightning Source LLC
Chambersburg PA
CBHW010133150626
46552CB00023B/3242